Alys, Always

A Novel

Harriet Lane

Scribner

New York   London   Toronto   Sydney   New Delhi

SCRIBNER
A Division of Simon & Schuster, Inc.
1230 Avenue of the Americas
New York, NY 10020

Copyright © 2012 by Harriet Lane

First Scribner hardcover edition June 2012

SCRIBNER and design are registered trademarks of The Gale Group, Inc., used under license by Simon & Schuster, Inc., the publisher of this work.

For information about special discounts for bulk purchases, please contact Simon & Schuster Special Sales at 1-866-506-1949 or business@simonandschuster.com.

The Simon & Schuster Speakers Bureau can bring authors to your live event. For more information or to book an event, contact the Simon & Schuster Speakers Bureau at 1-866-248-3049 or visit our website at www.simonspeakers.com.

Designed by Carla Jayne Jones

Manufactured in the United States of America

1 3 5 7 9 10 8 6 4 2

Library of Congress Control Number: 2011040905

ISBN 978-1-4516-7316-6
ISBN 978-1-4516-7318-0 (ebook)

For G.S.C.

A violet bed is budding near,
Wherein a lark has made her nest:
And good they are, but not the best;
And dear they are, but not so dear.
—Christina Rossetti

Alys, Always

It's shortly after six o'clock on a Sunday evening. I'm sure of the time because I've just listened to the headlines on the radio.

Sleet spatters the windscreen. I'm driving through low country-side, following the occasional fingerpost toward the A road and London. My headlights rake the drizzle, passing their silver glow over gates and barns and hedgerows, the CLOSED signs hung in village shop windows, the blank, muffled look of houses cloistered against the winter evening. Few cars are out. Everyone is at home, watching TV, making supper, doing the last bits of homework before school tomorrow.

I've taken the right fork out of Imberly, past the white rectory with the stile. The road opens up briefly between wide, exposed fields before it enters the forest. In summer, I always like this part of the drive: the sudden, almost aquatic chill of the green tunnel, the sense of shade and stillness. It makes me think of Milton's water nymph, combing her hair beneath the glassy, cool, translucent wave. But at this time of year, at this time of day, it's just another sort of darkness. Tree trunks flash by monotonously.

The road slides a little under my tyres so I cut my speed right back, glancing down to check on the instrument panel, the bright red and green and gold dials that tell me everything's fine; and then I look back up and I see it, just for a second, caught in the moving cone of light.

It's nothing, but it's something. A shape through the trees, a sort of strange illumination up ahead on the left, a little way off the road.

I understand immediately that it's not right. It's pure instinct: like the certainty that someone, somewhere out of immediate eyeshot, is watching you.

The impulse is so strong that before I've even really felt a prickle of anxiety, I've braked. I run the car into the muddy, rutted margin of the road, up against a verge, trying to angle the headlights in the appropriate direction. Opening the car door, I pause and lean back in to switch off the radio. The music stops. All I can hear is the wind soughing in the trees, the irregular drip of water onto the bonnet, the steady metronome of the hazard flashers. I shut the door behind me and start to walk, quite quickly, along the track of my headlights, through the damp snag of undergrowth, into the wood. My shadow dances up ahead through the trees, growing bigger, wilder, with every step. My breath blooms in front of me, a hot, white cloud. I'm not really thinking of anything at this moment. I'm not even really scared.

It's a car, a big, dark car, and it's on its side, at an angle, as if it is nudging its way into the cold earth, burrowing into it. The funny shape I saw from the road was the light from its one working headlamp projecting over a rearing wall of brown bracken and broken saplings. In the next few seconds, as I come close to the car, I notice various things: the gloss of the paintwork bubbled with raindrops, the pale leather interior, the windscreen that hasn't fallen out but is so fractured that it has misted over, become opaque. Am I thinking about the person, or people, inside? At this moment, I'm not sure I am. The spectacle is so alien and so compelling that there's not really any space to think about anything else.

And then I hear a voice, coming from within the car. It's someone talking, quite a low, conversational tone. A sort of muttering. I can't hear what is being said, but I know it's a woman.

"Hey—are you all right?" I call, moving around the car, passing from the glare of the headlight into blackness, trying to find her. "Are you okay?" I bend to look down into windows, but the dark is too thick for me to see in. As well as her voice—which murmurs and pauses and then starts again, without acknowledging my question—I can hear the engine ticking down, as if it's relaxing. For a moment I wonder whether the car is about to burst into flames, as happens in films, but I can't smell any petrol. God, of course: I have to call for an ambulance, the police.

I pat my pockets in a panic, find my mobile, and make the call, stabbing at the buttons so clumsily that I have to redial. The operator's answer comes as an overwhelming, almost physical relief. I give her my name and telephone number and then, as she leads me through the protocol of questions, I tell her everything I know, trying hard to sound calm and steady, a useful person in a crisis. "There's been an accident. One car. It looks like it came off the road and turned over. There's a woman in there, she's conscious; there might be other people, I don't know, I can't see inside. Wistleborough Wood, just outside Imberly, about half a mile past the Forestry Commission sign—up on the left, you'll see my car on the road, it's a red Fiat."

She tells me help is on its way and I hang up. There's quiet again: the trees creaking, the wind, the engine cooling. I crouch down. Now my eyes have adjusted, I can just make out an arm, thrown up against the side window, but the light is so dim that I can't see any texture on the sleeve. Then she starts to speak to me, as if she has woken up, processed my presence.

"Are you there?" she's asking. She sounds quite different now. There's fear in her voice. "I don't want to be on my own. Who's there? Don't go."

I kneel down hurriedly and say, "Yes. I'm here."

"I thought so," she says. "You won't leave me, will you?"

"No," I say. "I won't leave you. There's an ambulance on its way. Just stay calm. Try not to move."

"You're very kind," she says. The expensive, cultured voice goes with the Audi, and I know—hearing that voice making that remark—that she makes that comment dozens of times a day, without even thinking about it, when people have shown her courtesy or deference at the farm shop or the butcher's.

"I've got myself into a bit of a mess," she says, trying to laugh. The arm moves, fractionally, as if she is testing it out, then lies still again. "My husband is going to be so cross. He had the car cleaned on Friday."

"I'm sure he'll understand," I say. "He'll just want to know you're okay. Are you hurt?"

"I don't really know. I don't think so. I think I knocked my head, and I don't think my legs are too good," she says. "It's a nuisance. I suppose I was going too fast, and I must have hit some ice. . . . I thought I saw a fox on the road. Oh, well."

We wait in silence for a moment. My thighs are starting to ache and the knees of my jeans, pressed into damp bracken, are stiff with cold and water. I adjust my position and wonder how long it will take the ambulance to get here from Fulbury Norton. Ten minutes? Twenty? She doesn't sound terribly hurt. I know it's not a good idea to interfere in a car accident, but maybe I should try to help her out somehow. But then again, if she has a broken leg . . . and anyway, I have no way of opening the car door, which is crumpled and pleated between us, like a piece of cardboard.

I cup my hands and blow on them. I wonder how cold she is.

"What's your name?" she asks.

"Frances," I say. "What's yours?"

"Alice," she says. I might be imagining it, but I think her voice is sounding a little fainter. Then she asks, "Do you live around here?"

"Not anymore. I live in London. I've been visiting my parents. They live about twenty minutes away—near Frynborough."

"Lovely part of the world. We've got a place in Biddenbrooke. Oh, dear, he will be wondering where on earth I've got to. I said I'd call when I got in."

I'm not sure what she means and I'm suddenly frightened she's going to ask me to ring her husband. *Where's the ambulance? Where are the police? How long does it* take, *for God's sake?* "Are you cold?" I ask, shoving my hands into my jacket pockets. "I wish I could do more to help make you comfortable. But I don't think I should try to move you."

"No, let's wait," she agrees lightly, as if we're at a bus stop, only mildly inconvenienced, as if it's just one of those things. "I'm sure they're on their way." Then she makes a sound that frightens me, a sharp inhalation, a tiny gasp or cry, and then she stops talking, and when I say, "Alice? Alice?" she doesn't answer, but makes the noise again, and it's such a small sort of noise, so hopeless somehow; and I know when I hear it that this is serious after all.

I feel terribly alone then, and redundant: alone in the dark wood with the rain and the crying. And I look back over my shoulder, towards my car, the dazzle of its headlamps, and behind it I can see only darkness, and I keep looking and looking, and talking—though she's no longer responding—and eventually I see lights, blue and white flashing lights, and I say, "Alice, they're here, they're coming, I can see them, it's going to be fine, just hold on. They're coming."

I sit in the front seat of a police car and give a statement to someone called PC Wren. The windscreen is coursing with rain, and the noise of it drumming relentlessly on the roof means she often has to ask me to repeat what I've just said. All the time I'm wondering what's going on out there, with the arc lights and the heavy cutting gear and the hoists. I can't see much through the misted-up window. Rubbing a patch clear with my cuff, I see a paramedic framed in the open door of the ambulance, looking at his watch and pouring something out of a thermos. Some of his colleagues must be out there in the woods, I suppose. Maybe they tossed a coin for it, and he got lucky. *No point us all catching pneumonia.*

Wren closes her notebook. "That's all for now," she says. "Thank you for your help. Someone will be in touch with you in the next day or so, just to tie up the loose ends."

"Is she going to be okay?" I ask. I know it's a stupid question, but it's the only thing I can think of to say.

"We're doing our best. My colleagues will be able to update you in the next few days. You're free to go now. Will you be all right to drive yourself to London? It might be sensible to go back to your parents', spend the night there instead."

"I've got work tomorrow. I'll be fine," I say. I reach for the door handle, but PC Wren puts a hand on my sleeve and squeezes it. "It's hard," she says, a real concern in her voice, and the unexpected kindness makes my eyes swim. "You did all that you could. Don't forget that."

"I didn't do anything. I couldn't do anything. I hope she's okay," I say. Then I open the door and step out. The rain and the wind come at me like a train. The woods, which had been so quiet, are now roaring: machinery pitched against the ferocity of a sudden winter storm. Caught in a huge artificial glow, a group of people are huddled close together, their fluorescent jackets shining with water, forming a screen around the car.

I run along the road, back to the Fiat, and get in, and in the abrupt silence of the interior I listen to my breathing. Then I start the engine and drive off. The wood falls away behind the car, like something letting go, and then there's not much to see: the flash of cat's-eyes and chevrons and triangles, the gradual buildup of the suburbs strung between darkened retail parks and round-abouts.

At home in the flat, once I've taken off my wet clothes and had a warm shower, I don't quite know what to do with myself. It's late, nearly eleven, and I don't feel tired, and I don't feel hungry, but I make some toast anyway, and a cup of tea, and grab the blanket from my bed and wrap myself in it. Then I sit in front of the television for a while, thinking about Alice, the voice in the dark; and, more distantly, about her husband. He'll know by now. Perhaps he'll be with her, in the hospital. Their lives thrown around like a handful of jacks, coming to settle in a new, dangerous configuration, all because of an icy patch on the road and a half glimpse of a fox. The thought of this, the random luck and lucklessness of an ordinary life, frightens me as much as anything has tonight.

For once, I'm glad to be in the office. I get in early and sit at my desk, sipping the cappuccino I picked up at the sandwich bar on the corner. The cups are smaller than the ones you get at Starbucks, but the coffee is stronger, and today, after a bad night's sleep, that's what I need. I look at my emails and check the queue: a few people have filed copy over the weekend, but not as many as had promised they would.

You'd have thought working on the books pages of the *Questioner* would be a doddle, that the section would more or less run itself; but every week it falls to me to rescue some celebrity professor or literary wunderkind from hanging participles or apostrophe catastrophes. I'm a subeditor, an invisible production drone: always out in the slips, waiting to save people from their own mistakes. If I fumble the catch, I'll hear about it from Mary Pym, the literary editor. Mary is at her best on the phone, buttering up her famous contacts, or at J Sheekey, where she takes her pet contributors as compensation for the disappointing nature of the *Questioner's* word rate.

One day, it is assumed, Mary's expenses (the cabs, the first-class train tickets, the boutique hotels she checks into during the literary-festival season) will have to be curtailed, as those of the other section heads have been. But for now, she sails on regardless. Stars still want to write for Mary, despite our dwindling circulation and the mounting sense that it's all happening elsewhere, on the Net.

No sign of Mary yet, but Tom from Travel is in, and we exchange hellos. Monday is a quiet day at the office: the newsroom on the west side of the building remains peaceful and empty until well into Tuesday. At the point when my weekend begins, when I've sent the books pages to press on Thursday afternoon, the newsroom is just starting to come to life, limbering up for the final sweaty sprint to deadline in the early hours of Sunday morning. Once or twice I've done a Saturday shift on the news-desk, and it's not to my taste: the swearing and antler-locking, the stories that fall through at the last minute, the eleventh-hour calls from ministers attempting to reshape a page lead. I always associate deadlines with the sour smell of vinegar-soused chips eaten out of polystyrene shells, a smell that is circulated end-lessly by the air-conditioning so that it's still just perceptible this morning.

Mary arrives, her coat over one arm, her enormous handbag open to show off the gigantic, turquoise Smythson diary in which she keeps all her secrets. She's on her mobile, unctuously attending to someone's ego. "I'll get it biked round immediately," she says. "Unless you'd rather I had it couriered out?" She cocks her head to one side, manhandles the diary onto my desk, and makes a note in her exquisite copperplate. "Absolutely!" she says, nodding and writing. "So thrilled you can do this. There is the *worry* that he's going off the boil rather. I'm sure you can make sense of it for us."

She ends the call and moves on to her desk without acknowledging me. "Ambrose Pritchett is doing the new Paul Crewe," she murmurs a few moments later, not looking around, as her terminal bongs into life. "Filing a week on Thursday. Can you get the book to him before he leaves for the airport at ten forty-five? He wants to start it on the flight."

I look at the clock. It's nearly ten already. I don't know where the preview copy is, and I know I can't ask Mary. That sort of thing drives her up the wall. ("Do I look like a fucking librarian, darling?") So I ring the courier desk and book an urgent bike, and then I start to search through the shelves where we store advance copies. I try to file books by genre and alphabetically, but as neither Mary nor her twenty-three-year-old deputy Oliver Culpeper (every bit as bumptious as he is well connected) can be bothered with that approach, it's not exactly a foolproof system. Eventually I find it, nudged behind Helen Simpson and the confessions of a cokehead stand-up with whom Mary shared a platform at Hay last summer. By the time I've written a covering note and shoved the Crewe in a padded envelope and taken it down to the couriers' office, it's quarter past. I'm standing in the elevator lobby, looking at my reflection in the stainless steel doors, when my mobile rings. I don't recognise the number.

"Frances Thorpe?"

"Speaking," I say. Somehow I know it's the police. It all comes back, the feeling of last night: the dark, the rain, the uselessness. I swallow hard. My throat is dry. In the doors, I see a pinched, nervous-looking girl, with blue shadows under her eyes: a pale, insignificant sort of person.

"I'm Sergeant O'Driscoll from Brewster Street police station. My colleagues in Fulbury Norton have passed on your details. It's with regard to the road traffic accident last night."

"Oh," I say, as the lift doors open. *Road traffic accident.* Why do they say that? What other sort of accident could there be on a road? "I've been thinking about her. Alice, I mean. Is there any news? How is she doing?"

"We were hoping you could come down to the station, so we could go through your statement with you," he says. "Just to make sure you're happy with it. Just in case anything else has occurred to you in the meantime."

"Well, yes, I could do that. I don't have anything more to say. I've told you everything. But if it'll help . . . How is she?"

There's a little pause. "I'm sorry to have to tell you this, Miss Thorpe, but she was very badly injured in the incident. She died at the scene."

"Oh," I say. Then: "How awful."

The lift doors part on the fifth floor and I go back to my desk and write down the details on a Post-it.

At lunchtime, I leave the office, wrapping my red-and-purple scarf tightly around my throat and pulling it up over my mouth against the slicing cold, and start to walk, skirting the mainline station with its multiple retail opportunities, passing the old gasworks and the new library, cutting down several Georgian terraces and crossing the canal with its motionless skin of litter. Every so often, I walk by a café or a cheap restaurant with steamed-up windows, and the sound of coffee machines and cutlery comes out as someone arrives or leaves, and then the door swings shut and the sound dies away.

Once I get off the main roads, not many people are about. It's a bleak, white winter day: the trees are bare, the patches of municipal grass are scuffed and balding, patrolled by the more desperate sort of pigeon. Now and then the cloud thins enough for a suggestion of the sun to appear, a low, ghostly orb behind the council blocks.

At Brewster Street reception, an empty room without any natural light, no one is behind the security window. I wait for a few moments, then I knock on a door, and a cross-looking woman comes to the screen and says Sergeant O'Driscoll's on his break and should be back soon. Annoyed, I take a seat on a moulded-plastic chair and, by the fizzing, popping illumination of a strip bulb, work my way through the sticky pages of an old *Closer*.

After a while I hear doors opening and shutting, and the buzz of a security lock being released, and then O'Driscoll comes out to fetch me, still licking his fingers and chewing the last of his lunch. He's young, as Wren was last night, maybe in his mid or late twenties. Younger than me, with lots of product on his hair, a raw sort of complexion, and spots on his neck. He takes me into a side room and pushes some pages over the tabletop: Wren's notes from last night, typed up, fed through a spellchecker and emailed across the country in a fraction of a second. I read through them carefully while O'Driscoll taps his teeth with a Biro, and though of course she hasn't caught my tone of voice or my turn of phrase, the facts are all correct and unarguable. "I've got nothing to add," I say, putting my hand flat on the report.

"It all seems pretty straightforward," O'Driscoll says, passing me the pen, along with the whiff of falafel. "If you could just sign—there. The reports are only preliminary at this point, of course, but all the scene evidence confirms your account of what she told you. The driver tried to avoid something in the road, and the black ice, unfortunately, did the rest. And if she was travelling at speed, of course . . ."

He lets the words hang in the air while I scribble my name on the line.

"There'll be an inquest, but it's just a formality. I doubt you'll be needed," he says, pulling the papers back to his side of the table and rapping them officiously against the Formica so they stack up, then rising to his feet. "Well, thank you for your assistance. Get in touch if anything else comes to mind." He stands back, holding open the door for me. "Oh, there is one more thing I should mention," he adds, as I wind the scarf around my neck and shrug myself into my backpack. "There's a chance the family will want to make contact with you. It can be useful for—you know—closure." I can tell that he'd like to be making ironic speech marks with his fingers, but knows this would be inappropriate. "Part of the grieving process. After all, as I understand it, you were the last person to have a, um, conversation with her. Would you have a problem with that?"

"No, I . . . I don't think so," I say, not at all sure how I really feel about this.

"Great stuff. Well, if the family wants to be in touch, they'll do so through the FLO."

"Who?"

"Oh, sorry—the family liaison officer. Anyway, they may not feel the need. We'll play it by ear," he says, slotting the Biro back into his pocket. "This may well be the end of the matter."

I stop in the doorway. "Who was she?" I ask, reminded how little I know about her, this person who spoke her last words with only me to hear them. "What can you tell me about her?"

He sighs briefly, probably thinking of the cup of coffee cooling on his desk, and flips back through the report. "So, Alice Kite," he says, running a finger down the text. "Midfifties. House in London and a weekend place, looks like, near Biddenbrooke. Married with two adult children." Then he's shaking hands, and saying good-bye, and I'm back out in the cold, retracing my steps to the office.

As I walk, I hear her saying again, "You're very kind": an easy remark it had sounded at the time, but now I know how much it must have cost her. It seems strange that I know little more about her than the automatic associations that come with a certain sort of voice, and turn of phrase, and make of car.

Maybe this will be the end of the matter, as O'Driscoll said.

"O*h, no, you poor thing!" says Hester. She's the first person I've* told. I have no particular confidantes at work, and I didn't want to call up anyone else simply so I could drop it into the conversation; but I do feel a relief, a lessening of tension, now I've finally put it into words.

"So you were coming back from Mum and Dad's, and you just saw the wreck on the road?"

"Well, sort of."

"Jesus," she says. "Was it, you know, traumatic? Could you see everything? Was she in distress?"

I know Hester's really asking: Was she covered in blood? Was she *screaming*? She sounds almost disappointed when I describe the scene, the oddly formal nature of my conversation with Alice, which in any other circumstance might be comical. "How are you doing, really?" Hester asks, dropping her voice, inviting a greater intimacy.

"Oh, not too bad," I say. I adjust my position on the sofa and switch the phone to my other ear. I'm wondering whether to tell her about the times over the last few days when I've found myself back kneeling in the wet bracken, searching for the emergency lights in the distance, desperately willing them to appear. These memories feel every bit as sharp and shocking—as full of panic and uselessness—as the reality was. I have the sense the remembered experience is becoming more clearly delineated as the days go on, and I wasn't expecting that.

The sound of the crying, too, has begun to assail me at unwelcome moments, moments when my mind should be empty, when I'm at my most vulnerable. Late at night as I lie in bed, buried under a comforting weight of blankets, sliding towards sleep. Or early in the morning, long before the grey dawn. I've started to wake up early, and sometimes I can't be sure whether I'm hearing Alice or the sound of foxes out in the gardens.

"Will you just put that back, darling. No: I said, put it back," Hester is saying, and the moment passes. She comes back on the line. "I must go and start their bath. How were Mum and Dad, anyway?"

"Oh, you know," I say. "Same old."

We laugh together, back on more stable territory, and she invites me over for lunch on Saturday. I know I'll be expected to offer to babysit that evening, as long as I haven't made other plans; but to be honest a few hours of Playmobil and an M&S curry in front of Charlie's extravagance of TV channels sounds pretty good right now. There are worse ways to spend a Saturday night. I should know.

Once the call is over, I put a pan of water on the hob. I'm chopping tomatoes for the sauce while the onions and garlic soften, and the radio is on, and I have a glass of wine, and the flat's looking nice, everything in its place, and the pendant above the kitchen table is casting a cosy pool of light over the daffodils in the blue jug. Because of the warmth of the kitchen, they're just starting to shoulder their way out of their frowsty papery cases.

It's not bad, I think. *You're not so badly off, are you?*

A tiny movement outside the kitchen window catches my

eye, and I stop and lean over the sink and look out, down on to the street, and I can see—in the illuminated triangles beneath the streetlamps—that snow has started to fall, slowly and steadily.

*I*t *falls and falls, for days and days. It seems, for a while, that the snow* is the only thing happening in the world. It catches London off guard. Buses are left abandoned on roads. Schools are closed. Councils run out of salt. And when I wake up in the morning, my first thoughts are not of Alice, but of hope that the snow is still out there, still working its disruptive, glamorous magic.

On my day off, I walk across the Heath, through a sort of blizzard. All the usual landmarks—the paths, the ponds, the play areas, the running track—are sinking deep beneath lavish drifts. Under a pewter sky, Parliament Hill is glazed with ice. Blinded by flurries, people are tobogganing down it on dustbin lids, carrier bags, tea trays stolen from the cafeteria near the bandstand. The shrieks and shouts fade quickly into insulated silence as I walk on towards the trees, their branches indistinctly freighted with white. Soon the only sounds are the powdery crunch of the snow beneath my boots, the catch of my breath.

When I reach Hampstead, the flakes are falling less furiously; now they're twinkling down, decorous and decorative. I trudge up Christchurch Hill and Flask Walk, looking in the windows, which are always cleaner—more reflective, more transparent—than the windows in my part of town. I see earthenware bowls of clementines, books left facedown on green velvet sofas, a dappled rocking horse in a bay window. A tortoiseshell cat sits beside a vase of pussy willow, its cold yellow eyes tracking me without real interest. I pass on a little farther and am peering down into a basement kitchen when the person who is moving around in front of the cooker notices me and comes to the window and tweaks the angle of the plantation shutters, denying me my view.

In the high street I go into an expensive tea shop, grab an empty table in the window, and order a cup of hot chocolate and a pistachio macaroon. An elderly man in a dashing scarf sits at the next table, working his way through a newspaper full of weather stories: cancelled flights, ice-skating in the Fens, the plight of Welsh hill farmers. Outside, strangers are sliding around, clutching at each other for stability, laughing. There is a strange festive atmosphere: the usual rules do not apply.

I drink my hot chocolate and get my book out of my pocket and start to read, shutting everything out, enjoying the sense of being part of something and yet at arm's length from it. I do my best reading in cafés. I find it hard to read at home, in absolute silence.

"Is this seat taken?" someone asks. I look up reluctantly. It's a young woman with a toddler in a snowsuit, his round cheeks scalded with the cold.

"I'm just going," I say, knocking back the dark, syrupy dregs of my drink. Then I leave her to it.

I'm nearly home when my phone rings. Someone introduces herself as Sergeant Kate Wiggins. She says she has been assigned to the family of Alice Kite, to help them through "this very painful time." As I listen, the unwelcome sensations begin again: the prickle of panic, of helplessness. Feelings which, over the last few days, have started to recede a little.

I know what she's going to say before she says it.

"I don't think I can," I say quickly, without having to reflect. And saying the words, I feel the fear losing purchase, just slightly.

Kate Wiggins pauses. "I know it must be difficult for you," she says, in an understanding voice. "You've had a very traumatic experience. Sometimes, witnesses find that meeting the family can actually be cathartic, on a personal level."

"I don't want to. I've told the police everything that happened. I don't see what a meeting would achieve. It would just stir things up again."

"Of course, it's not helpful to generalise but quite often, in circumstances like this, the family isn't looking for answers. They just want to meet the person who was there. To say thank-you, really. I know, for example, that Mrs. Kite's family, her husband, her son and daughter, are relieved she wasn't alone at the end. I think they are grateful to you and it would mean a lot if they could meet you and tell you that themselves."

"Well—I have stuff of my own going on," I say, desperate to get her off the phone. "It's not really something I feel up to right now."

"Absolutely. Take your time," Kate Wiggins says generously, seizing on the tiny opportunity I've clumsily afforded her. "There's no hurry. Let me know when you feel ready."

"Fine," I say, pretending to take down her number. "Yes, of course." Then I go home and do my best to forget all about it.

O*liver is doing the post, tearing apart corrugated cardboard parcels* to reveal novelty golf guides and pink paperbacks with line drawings of high heels and cupcakes on the covers, chucking most of them into a large carton bound for Oxfam or (if he can be bothered, which he usually can't) eBay. There's an idiotic tyranny to the post delivered to the books desk: wave after wave of ghosted memoirs and coffee-table photography retrospectives and eco-lifestyle manuals, none of which even vaguely fit the *Questioner*'s remit. Maybe one book in ten is put aside, waiting to be assigned to a reviewer.

I do my best to have nothing to do with Oliver, the son of one of our more famous theatrical knights, but his voice—as fruity and far-reaching as his father's—makes this difficult.

"Oh, here's something interesting," he's saying to Mary, waving a hardback in her direction. "We should do something big, shouldn't we?"

Mary pulls her spectacles low on her nose and inspects the cover. "Oh, absolutely—ask for an interview, if he's doing any. I'm surprised they didn't push back publication. Maybe it was too late."

Oliver finds the press release tucked inside the flyleaf and picks up the phone. I hear him flirting in a bread-and-butter fashion with the PR. There's a little shop gossip about a book launch they both attended earlier in the week, and then he says, "The new Laurence Kyte . . . we'd love to have an interview." He listens, putting his head on one side and pulling a comedy sad face—furrowed brow, fat lower lip—for Mary's benefit, though as she is scrolling through a layout on-screen his efforts are wasted. "Oh, that's a shame," he says finally. "But of course, in the circumstances . . . Such a terrible thing to happen. Well, if he changes his mind . . . Or maybe we can do something when the paperback comes out? . . . Yeah—you, too. Take care, babe.

"He's not doing any publicity. She sounds sick as a pike," he adds, swinging his feet off the bin. "Should we get Berenice to review it? Or Simon?"

"Simon," says Mary without looking up.

Oliver puts the book on the shelves, awaiting dispatch.

Later, when they've both gone to morning conference, I go over and pick it up. It's a novel called *Affliction*. A fairly plain cover, a drawing of a man's shadow falling over a patch of city pavement: puddles, a cigarette butt, scraps of litter. I turn it over. A small photograph of the author is on the back of the dust jacket, nothing too flash, though it's nicely composed. He's standing in front of a tall, dark hedge, resting his hand on a sundial speckled with lichen. His face is, naturally, familiar. Laurence Kyte. Of course. I wonder why I hadn't made the connection. I didn't know he had a place near Biddenbrooke. Beneath the picture is printed in small italic font, *Author photograph by Alys Kyte.*

The biographical note is only two short sentences, as is usually the way with the big hitters: *Laurence Kyte was born in Stepney in 1951. He lives in London.* No mention of the Booker, then, though he won it five years ago, or was it six? No mention of the ghastly movie Hollywood squeezed out of *Ampersand*; no mention, either, of the rather more successful adaptation—he did the screenplay, I seem to remember—of *The Ha-Ha*, which earned Daniel Day-Lewis an Oscar.

I flick through the pages. I've not read any Kyte but I know the spectrum of his interests: politics, sex, death, the terminal malaise of Western civilisation. In Kyte's books, middle-aged, middle-class men—architects and anthropologists, engineers and haematologists—struggle with the decline in their physical powers, a decline which mirrors the state of the culture around them. Kyte's prose style is famously "challenging," "inventive," and "muscular"; usually it's "uncompromising," too. Not words that do it for me, particularly. I read the first few pages. It's all very clever. Then I read the dedication. *For Alys. Always.*

I didn't save Kate Wiggins's number, but it's stored on my phone anyway, under "Calls Received."

"Hello, it's Frances Thorpe," I say when she answers. "You called me the other day, about the accident involving Alys Kyte? I've had the chance to get myself together a bit. If you really think it would help them, I guess I feel up to meeting the family now."

The *Highgate house is set back rather grandly from the street:* gravel, gateposts, the humped suggestion of a shrubbery. A dingy pile of old snow is lying in the lee of the garden wall, evidently out of reach of the winter sun on the rare occasions when it might appear; otherwise little sign of it is left in the front garden, and the wide front steps have been scraped clear of ice. Apart from the glow of the stained-glass fanlight—smoky-purple grapes spilling forth from a golden horn—the house is dark. It's five o'clock, teatime, but could just as well be midnight.

A security light clicks on as I walk up the steps and press the bell, but I hear nothing: no chime, no footfall. I was nervous enough about this meeting to start with, and now, before I've even gone inside, I'm feeling caught out, on the hop.

Perhaps I didn't press the bell hard enough? Perhaps it's broken?

I wait another few seconds, just to see whether anyone's coming, then press it again, firmly this time, though with a similar result. A moment passes, then I hear the sound of light footsteps, followed by the snap of the lock. A trim-looking, young woman in a zippered fleece and knee-length corduroy skirt opens the door.

"Frances," she says, clasping my hand and looking me squarely in the face, an onslaught of sincerity. "I'm Kate Wiggins. The family's downstairs."

In the hall, I take off my scarf and jacket. There's a worn scarlet rug underfoot, Turkish, by the look of it. A tall pot of umbrellas and cricket bats. A rack of Wellingtons and shoes and hiking boots. A wall of coats, slumped there like so many turned backs.

The air is full of scent: flowers, the creamy sweetness of their fragrance. A bowl of hyacinths is on the hall table, next to the spill of unopened post, and as we walk down the corridor, I look off into the shadowy reception rooms on either side and see containers filled with roses, lilies, irises, freesias, mostly white and still bound in luxurious cellophane ruffs and curls of ribbon.

The staircase at the end of the hall curves down into the open-plan kitchen: a judicious combination of heritage (flagstones, butler's sink, Aga, a dresser stacked with Cornishware) and contemporary (forensic lighting, a stainless-steel fridge the size of a Victorian wardrobe). More flowers are crammed into jars and jugs along the bookshelves and the windowsills and the oak refectory table, around which three people are sitting. A fourth figure, a girl, stands at the French windows, a cat angling around her ankles. As I descend, the girl glances away from the back garden, the golden rectangles of light falling on the preserved fragments of snow, and fastens her pale eyes on me. It's a desperate sort of scrutiny. It makes me feel even more self-conscious. Carefully, I look down and watch my feet moving over the last few stairs.

"Laurence Kyte," he says, rising from the table and coming towards me. "Thanks for agreeing to see us. Can I call you Frances?"

I take his hand. "I'm so sorry for your loss," I say.

He swallows. The cheap remark is fresh, still a shock, for him. Seeing his vulnerability, I feel a strange tremor of excitement. This man I know from the half-page reviews and the diary pages and the guest slots on *Newsnight,* with his authority and remorseless judgments, is standing here before me, shouldering his grief, bowed down by it. *I have something he wants,* I think, with a prickle of possibility. *I wonder if I can give it to him.* "Thank you," he says. "These are my children, Edward and Polly."

Edward is midtwenties, tall, fair, slight-looking, and his greeting is noncommittal, courteous but impersonal. Polly, a few years younger, comes away from the French windows towards me, and as we shake hands, she twists her mouth to stop herself from crying. Her narrow, white face is blotchy with old tears.

She looks like a little mouse, I think. I squeeze her hand. "I'm Frances," I say.

"And this is Charlotte Black," Laurence Kyte says, indicating the third person at the table, a woman in her fifties. Plain, dark clothes, the sort that cost serious money, a heavy silver cuff on her wrist. "A friend of the family."

Of course I know of Charlotte Black, Kyte's agent. She has quite a reputation.

Kate Wiggins has been standing back, letting us get on with it. Now, in her supportive administrative role, she offers me a cup of tea or coffee. I feel too nervous to have a preference. "Water's fine," I say.

"Well, I'm having a glass of wine," says Laurence. "I think we can probably all agree this situation calls for a drink."

He locates a particular bottle of red in the rack under the counter and brings the glasses to the table. While he's doing this, his children are taking their seats at it, side by side, not looking at each other. *They are dreading this,* I think. *They want to know, but they're scared of what I might tell them.*

Charlotte, at the end of the table, smiles reassuringly at me. "Kate was saying you don't live far away?"

"Down the hill," I say. "No, not far at all." Of course, my part of north London, maybe a mile off, is quite a contrast to this one, as it's dominated by arterial roads, betting shops, and the empty midrise office blocks which no tenants can be persuaded to occupy. The Kytes live in a very different London. Their neighbourhood is a sequence of broad, moneyed avenues running between green spaces—various woods and parks, the Heath—and what the locals call "the village," a high street full of coffee shops, estate agents, and boutiques selling organic face creams and French children's wear.

Laurence uncorks the bottle and starts to pour. Kate Wiggins shakes her head when he looks at her, but everyone else accepts a glass. Finally, we're all sitting at the table, ready. I hold the glass in my hand. It's a solid, simple goblet. Danish, I expect. When I taste the wine, I try to concentrate on it, but I'm really a bit too on edge, waiting to see how the Kytes want to play this.

Let them set the pace, Wiggins had suggested. *They'll let you know what they need to know. And if you can't answer their questions, just say so.* I put my glass down and fold my hands in my lap. The table vibrates slightly: Edward, jiggling his foot, betraying his nerves. To my surprise, he speaks first.

"We wanted to meet you to tell you how grateful we are," he begins, as if he's finally delivering a speech which he has privately rehearsed many times. "We've been taken through your statement, and it has been a real comfort to know that Mum wasn't on her own at the end. That she had someone to talk to . . . someone who could talk to her."

Polly looks up, her eyes blurring, and asks in a burst, "Can you tell us what she said? We know what you told the police, but . . . did she sound like herself?"

Kate Wiggins says, "Polly, I'm not sure whether Frances can—" and then I interrupt her, with a firmness I don't feel, and I say, "We talked. She was quite . . . together. She wasn't in distress, or at least if she was, she controlled it. You know I couldn't see her?"

For some reason, I want them all to be reminded of this. Polly nods, her pale eyes fixed on me.

I glance around the table. Everyone seems to be waiting for something—for me to continue, I realise. I have everyone's absolute attention. It's an alarming feeling, but not altogether disagreeable.

"It was very dark," I say, my voice sounding small in that huge white space. "And because of that and the position of the car, I couldn't see how injured she was. I didn't know. She told me she might have hurt her legs, but otherwise she seemed okay. She didn't seem to be in pain. She said she'd come off the road avoiding a fox. She talked about living nearby, she mentioned the car had recently been cleaned."

At the edge of my vision, I see Laurence suddenly drop his head, staring down at his hands, processing this reminder of a previous life.

"Yes," I say, as if it's all coming back to me, "She cracked a sort of joke about how her husband—you—had just had the car cleaned."

Polly makes a noise at this point: part laugh, part sob. Her cuff winking in the light, Charlotte Black pushes the box of tissues across the table and reaches out to catch hold of Polly's fingers.

"She thanked me for keeping her company. I remember thinking what a dignified sort of person she seemed." As a matter of fact, this thought had crossed my mind only subsequently, reading over my statement with O'Driscoll, but it's the sort of thing I imagine they'd like to hear—*need* to hear, really.

Polly's really crying now, into a handful of Kleenex. Edward is very still. I leave a little pause, just a tiny beat, and then, because it's irresistible, I say, "And of course, when I told her I could see the ambulance coming, she said, 'Tell them I love them.'"

As I speak, I feel Wiggins shifting slightly beside me. *This wasn't in the statement.*

"Just that," I say. "'Tell them I love them.' It was the last thing she said to me."

I look up, into Laurence's face, the eye of the storm, and I see him exhale, and as that breath leaves him, his energy seems to leach away with it. He looks more like an old man now, weak and tired, hollow with exhaustion. When he lifts his glass to his lips, his hand is trembling. Charlotte Black presses knuckles to her eyes. I get the feeling she's startled and embarrassed by her reaction. Edward is staring at the table. The only sound is Polly weeping.

"There's really nothing else I can tell you," I say. "I'm sorry, it doesn't seem very much."

"Well," says Laurence finally, "I have no questions. You've been very kind, Frances. Very sensitive. Thank you for that, as well as . . ." His voice trails off. Then he looks around, remembering himself, consulting his children, clearing his throat. "Does anyone else want to ask anything?"

The room stays quiet.

"I really wish I could have done more," I say. Then I have another sip of wine. It's an intensely dark red which briefly stains the glass when you tilt it. Were I more knowledgeable, perhaps it would taste like the wines I read about in novels and restaurant reviews, which always seem to taste of plums and cherries and cinnamon. I'd quite like to finish it, but this might seem inappropriate, greedy, so I push the glass away with a tiny sigh. Kate Wiggins gives me a discreet nod and starts to ease her chair back from the table. I am being dismissed.

"I should be on my way," I say. "But if you have any more questions, if I can do anything . . ."

"Won't you finish your glass? Stay for some supper?" says Polly, her fists full of damp tissues—she has managed to collect herself at last—but I can tell the rest of the family is surprised and slightly disconcerted by her offer. I shake my head and stand up. Charlotte Black says she will see me out, and after a pause, Kate Wiggins gives me a smile of thanks, and then I'm saying good-bye to them all, one by one. When I come to Polly, I put my hand on her sleeve and apply just a little pressure and I make sure our eyes meet while I say, "Take care, won't you?" and then I follow Charlotte back up the stairs.

"What wonderful flowers," I say, as we walk down the corridor, back towards the front door.

"They keep coming—even this long after the funeral," Charlotte says. "People are so incredibly kind, but it's almost too much, there are no more vases, we've had to put them in ice buckets, and all the sinks are full of them. Alys loved flowers. You know about her garden at Biddenbrooke? Oh, it's quite famous. You should see it in June. All white flowers, of course."

She watches me while I put on my jacket and scarf. "Wait a minute," she says. Then she goes into one of the rooms, and when she comes back out, she has a big hand-tied bouquet in her arms: creamy roses and ranunculus trussed up in thick, rustling layers of tissue paper, purple and sober dove-grey.

"They won't miss them," she says. "Take them, for heaven's sake. Alys would have hated those flowers to just sit there in a dark room, not being looked at. Honestly, it's fine, no one minds. Take them."

I walk back through the slippery streets holding the flowers, the white petals cool and firm when they brush against my cheek; and although my hands are soon numb with cold from the wet stems, I find myself enjoying the conspicuous beauty of my trophy, the glances it attracts and the alternative life it seems to suggest.

In the flat, I remove the tissue paper and cellophane and discover the little note tucked inside, which I realise is from the controller of Radio 4 and her husband (*To Laurence, Teddy, and Pol. All our sympathy and best love*), and then I trim the stems and put the arrangement in my bedroom, so I can drift in and out of the scent as I sleep.

A week or so later, as the petals begin to tumble off in milky clusters, I find an envelope waiting in my pigeonhole when I get home from work. A stiff white card inside, the scratch of a fountain pen, the pulse of blue-black ink. It's from Polly, inviting me to the memorial service in a month's time. *We would be so glad to see you if you felt like coming,* she writes. Beneath her name, three quick, automatic kisses: *XXX.* I put the note on the mantelpiece, and when I mention it to Hester, I say I haven't decided whether to go or not. Of course, this isn't strictly true.

I sit at the back of the church, which is spectacularly full. It's an expensive crowd: plenty of familiar faces behind the outsize shades. I see Mary Pym several pews in front, leaning over to greet a playwright; one entire row is occupied by senior representatives from McCaskill, Laurence Kyte's publisher. As well as some distinguished actors and academics and a few cabinet ministers, there's a healthy showing from his old Soho cohort, the poets and raffish literary hacks he ran with after Oxford (he still plays tennis with Malcolm Azaria and Nikolai Titov at weekends, according to the cuts I've been browsing online).

Kate Wiggins, in a tidy jacket and shiny heels, comes over to say a quiet hello before the service starts. "I wondered if you'd be here," she says. "Polly asked for your details, I hope it was okay to give them to her."

Of course, I say. She's on the point of saying something else—possibly a reference to the little extra that I dropped into the discussion in the Kytes' kitchen? Most likely she's forgotten all about it—when there's a general fluttering as people reach in unison for their orders of service. She murmurs, "I'll see you later," and returns to her seat.

Yes, Laurence and his children are entering the church, coming down the aisle. Edward—Teddy—is erect and inscrutable, wearing a defensive social polish which allows him to smile at people in the congregation, but Polly, drooping in black, reminds me of a bird in the rain. A fragile-looking elderly lady whom I take to be Alys's mother walks with them, clasping Laurence's arm. He has lost some weight, I think.

We stand to sing "Eternal Father, Strong to Save." Initially this trawlerman's hymn strikes me as a strange choice, but as we work through the verses, its vision of the tin-pot vulnerability of human existence seems increasingly fitting.

All around me, people are fumbling in pockets and bags for tissues.

Teddy, composed, reads a poem by Christina Rossetti. A middle-aged woman—an old schoolfriend? A neighbour from Biddenbrooke?—rushes through a passage from one of Vita Sackville-West's gardening columns and then sits down, blowing her nose. A tenor sings a song by Peter Warlock.

Then Malcolm Azaria, bearish and grizzled in a black mole-skin suit going grey at the knees, delivers the eulogy.

He speaks with tremendous warmth and affection, but without attempting to disguise Alys's quirks and flaws. If anything, he draws our attention to them. In doing so he conjures up Alys as a vivid presence where previously I've found only an absence.

I listen, holding my breath, as he talks about first hearing about her one evening at the French House, shortly after she'd arrived at art school from Salisbury. "We were all very down on Alys," he says, with a dry, little cough of amusement. "We thought she must be some ghastly Lorelei, come to steal Laurence away from us. And that belief flourished until we actually met her. And then we all, without exception, fell in love with her."

As Azaria speaks, she's coming into view: her enthusiasms, her eccentricities, her weaknesses. Someone with an eye for beauty and for the absurd; a dreamy sort of person, given to absentmind-edness, always generating ("along with damson jam and those famous mountains of meringues we enjoyed beneath the apple trees at Biddenbrooke") a certain carnival atmosphere of chaos.

There's an amused, affectionate rumble of recognition as he talks about the lost passports, the missed trains, the Sunday lunches eaten in the very late afternoon.

"And yet she never forgot the truly important things," he says, raising a finger. "When you got a terrible review, Alys was always the first person on the phone—the only person you could face speaking to—to suggest a long walk, a bottle of claret, or a light spot of firebombing."

Briefly, he describes her occasional fits of melancholy: "Her extraordinary talent for happiness was not always best served by the world around her." He talks at more length about the most reliable sources of that happiness: the pleasure she took in her garden, her children, and her partnership with her husband. "Other people's marriages are invariably a mystery to outsiders," he says. "But this one, you always felt, was the best sort of mystery, with secret caves and smugglers and Gypsy caravans and a proper high tea at the end of it." He stops to let the muted, grateful laughter subside, gestures clumsily towards the front row, and says, "Truly, Laurence, Teddy, Polly—our hearts go out to you." Then, quickly, he steps down and returns to his seat.

I see Laurence leaning over to thank him, putting a hand out to touch his.

After the service, the crowd ebbs gradually out of the church, small groups forming and breaking off during the procession towards the Kytes' house: middle-aged couples, gangs of tall, tearful-looking girls, an elderly lady with a guide dog. It's a blustery early-spring day: the wind whipping through the trees in the Grove, patches of blue coming and going like little shocks in the sky. The tension is easing. People are kissing each other in greeting, and smiling. There's the relieved sense that everyone has been through an ordeal, and that a stiff drink is not too far off.

I see Azaria and Paul Crewe pausing by the small stone cross to light their cigarettes, deep in discussion with Charlotte Black and a younger woman whose black tangle of hair is streaked with a badger flash of white at the temple. Then a sudden squall of rain hits, and the group moves off in a hurry, pulling jackets and scarves over heads, hastening along in the usual inelegant manner.

I've stopped under some trees and am waiting there, warily looking up at the sky, when I hear someone calling my name.

"Frances," says Polly, bringing her umbrella over my head. "I hoped I'd see you. You are coming back to the house, aren't you?" I get the feeling that she hasn't any tears left for today, and free of the blotches and the red-rimmed eyes, she is really rather pretty, in a silvery, insubstantial fashion.

We walk on together, in the dark intimacy of the umbrella's shelter. At first, we keep bumping into each other, falling out of step, until she nudges my arm with hers and says, "Hook in, will you?" After that, it's much easier.

I say how good the service was, how affecting I found Malcolm Azaria's address.

"Oh, yes," says Polly. "Malcolm always knows what to say. He's one of Dad's oldest friends, you know. He and his wife, Jo—she's the one in the turquoise coat—have been very good to us since Mum died. Keeping an eye on Dad, popping round, taking him out to lunch, that sort of thing. Making sure he's okay."

"And . . . how is he?"

"Mmm," says Polly with a shrug, a little gesture of grief and bafflement. "It's hard to say, really. He gets up, goes for walks, picks up books from the bookshop, goes into his study, comes out for meals. I don't think he's writing anything yet, and I think that's worrying him. Personally, I think it's far too soon for anything like that. But what do I know."

"And what about you?" I ask, as we turn into the Kytes' street.

"Me? Oh, okay. You know."

"No, I don't," I say. "I don't know anything about you."

This isn't true, of course. From my online research (from various profiles of her father, from her slack Facebook privacy settings, and her Twitter feed) I know that she's nineteen and at drama college, not a topflight one, but a decent one nonetheless. I know that she went to a London girls' school until sixteen, and then to an arty liberal boarding school where she fell in with people called things like Tabitha and Inigo. I know she spent her year off teaching in South Africa and interning in an administrative capacity at the National Theatre. I know she has just split up with a BBC trainee called Sandeev.

Polly stops and stares at me. "No. No, of course you don't. It's ridiculous, but somehow I feel as if you know everything already."

She tucks my arm back into hers and starts to walk again. The shoes I bought for the occasion are soaking up the rain; it's hard to navigate puddles when you're being marched along like this. I feel as if I'm being swept up by the sheer force of her personality.

"It's pretty shit, I guess," she says, as lightly as she can manage. "People tell me it takes a long time to get used to something like this, let alone get over it. . . . As if that will *ever* happen. Some mornings I wake up feeling okay about stuff, and then there's this horrible moment when I remember. It's like falling." Her voice trails off.

"I think about her all the time," she says bleakly, eventually. "Wish I could tell her stuff. Ask her things."

We're going up the drive now. The gravel skitters away under our feet. As we come up the steps into the warmth, we're met by a man in a white jacket who takes our coats and the umbrella and retreats with them into one of the rooms off the corridor. A tray of glasses is set out on the hall table. Polly takes a flute of champagne. "Really?" she says disbelievingly when I choose orange juice.

A group of people comes into the hall behind us in a burst of wind and raindrops. Mary Pym is among them, her hair slightly coarsened by the weather. She starts to prink in the hall mirror, then catches sight of me over her shoulder.

"Oh!" she says, turning around. "Frances! What a surprise to see you here."

I smile at her politely as Polly pulls at my sleeve. "Come on," she urges, bored by the new arrivals. "I've got to get something from my room, it won't take a minute."

"See you later," I say to Mary as I follow Polly's slender, little figure up the oatmeal-coloured stairs.

We ascend, passing on the half landing a door, just ajar, permitting a glimpse of Laurence's study: a bright, barely furnished room, a dinosaur of an old Mac on a trestle table, an ugly office chair, white blinds at the window, walls lined with books, with more piled along the skirting.

Up again, past the jumbled tilting frames of old *Private Eye* cartoons and Ravilious prints and artwork for various novels in French and German translations, past a bathroom with a rolltop bath, a snatched impression of an airing cupboard luxuriously stashed with fat, white towels, past a shut door—the master bedroom?—and on, as the staircase narrows, up to the top floor, illuminated by an enormous rooflight smeared with drizzle.

Polly's room is painted robin's-egg blue. A string of chilli-pepper fairy lights is looped around the barley-sugar twists of her white bed. There's a poster for a Théâtre de Complicité show tacked to a pinboard, along with some curling strips of Photo-Mes, old Glastonbury and Latitude passes, and a handful of postcards: Botticellis, a Tracey Emin sketch of a shoe, one of Sargent's self-possessed socialites, leaning back complacently against some upholstery.

She closes the door and takes a packet of Camels out of the

chest of drawers. Then she pushes open the window, letting in the cold, drags a knitted throw off her bed and over her shoulders, and sits down on the ledge. "Want one?" she asks, waving the packet towards me. I shake my head.

"Do you still live here?" I say, idly moving to her dressing table, my eyes quickly going to the framed photograph standing there among the little tubs and bottles, the dishes of hair clips and scented erasers and novelty lip balms, the detritus of a childhood which she is evidently not ready to leave behind quite yet.

So she says no, she's living in Fulham with a friend from school. She tells me about drama college, how she wanted nothing more than to get in, and now she's actually there, it's a bit of a disappointment, frankly. Since Alys died, it seems, she hasn't really been turning up much. Her course tutor phoned her last week, and she had to agree to go in and see him next Tuesday. "Fucker better cut me some slack," she says, breathing a steady plume of smoke into the wet trees.

All the time, while I'm making little sounds of agreement and sympathy, I'm examining the photograph on the dresser. Alys is sitting on a shingly beach, wearing flip-flops and a sunshine-yellow sundress, her hair blowing over her face. Strong, square shoulders, swimmer's shoulders. Her mouth is opening as if she's about to say something funny to the photographer.

Where Laurence is dark, she is fair: the silvery sort of fairness that Polly has inherited. The sort of fairness that makes me think of birch woods.

So there you are, I think, meeting Alys's gaze. *There you are.*

Polly taps her ash into the window box and sips her drink. Now she's telling me about Sandeev. She dumped him before Christmas, she explains, and of course I sit tight and nod, even though I know, from the commiserating comments on Facebook, that it didn't happen quite like that.

It was the right thing to do, she says, sighing, it wasn't going anywhere, and they haven't seen each other since the split, but he rang when he heard the news—he was incredibly upset, he and Alys always got on like a house on fire—and he might be coming today. He couldn't make the memorial because he was on shift, but he said he'd come afterwards if he could.

Polly's young, of course; and on top of that she has the performer's transparent and somehow rather tawdry desire for attention. She is entirely at ease talking about herself, as if it's her birthright to be heard. That's good. She has hardly noticed how uneven the conversation is. That's good, too.

Her cheeks hollowing effortfully, she takes a final drag, pings the butt out into the street, and pulls the sash window down with a clatter. "I like being with you," she says slowly, as if the thought is just occurring to her. "Everyone else seems to want to tell me how I should be feeling—'You're feeling guilty because you always gave her the runaround,' 'You're feeling lost because she kept you on the straight and narrow,' blah blah fucking blah—but you don't do that."

"Anytime," I say. "Really, Polly, I'm always here if you want to talk. I hope you'll remember that."

"Mmm," she says. She's at the dressing table, rooting around for a tube of mascara. "Didn't bother before the church," she says, holding still, raptly intent on her reflection. "Didn't want panda eyes. I think I'll be all right now." She pokes the wand back into the tube, sprays some scent into the air, steps into the cloud of vapour, then moves to the door. The room is full of cigarette smoke and tuberose. "Shall we?" she says.

Jolly knots of people are exchanging gossip in the hall; they break off respectfully when they see Polly coming down the stairs. Murmuring apologies, a woman edges past us, shouldering her way into her coat, and as she goes, I notice the pallor of her face, the white flash at her temple.

In the kitchen, waiters are manoeuvring themselves through the crowd with polite difficulty, offering top-ups and hot, little snacks: angels on horseback, sausages jumbled around bowls of English mustard.

Polly sails off without a farewell, claimed by the Azarias. *Fair-weather friend*, I think, not at all surprised.

I move through the room without any sense of destination, listening to people talking in low tones about the family, how they're bearing up, the terrible hole in everyone's life. "It's such an appalling *shock*," people say, over and over. And, "You never know what's around the corner." This may be a literary crowd, but at times like these everyone resorts to the commonplace, I suppose.

Alys's mother is sitting in a chair by the French windows, with the cat on her lap, talking to Charlotte Black and someone from McCaskill. The garden beyond her, invisible on my first visit, is still in its winter disarray, but is charming nonetheless. A robin, a sequence of tiny clockwork movements, is pecking at something on the brick path which winds down, between the bony-looking fruit trees and the curves of hedges, to a summer-house.

I can imagine the two of them out there in the summer evenings, sitting on the wooden bench, bare feet in the warm grass, faces tilted blindly to the last of the day's sun.

"Twice a week, rain or shine," an elderly woman is saying, and I notice the golden Labrador sitting patiently at her feet, the reflective band of the harness. "She had such a lovely voice. So expressive. She did marvellous things with Edith Wharton."

"Hello," says Teddy, in passing. "How are you?" But he doesn't wait for an answer. A pretty girl with a serious expression is waiting for him at the bottom of the stairs. When they kiss hello, she puts her hand on his forearm and leaves it there for an extra beat while she comes out with one of those useful sympathetic clichés. I can see that kiss might just be the beginning of something.

She is, I'm fairly sure, someone's daughter, the child of one of the playwrights or critics around me, mindlessly refuelling on wine and oysters. A family friend.

I watch her—the messy ponytail, the lankiness, the string of plastic beads, the expression on her face—and something's bugging me. She reminds me of someone. Who is it? It's almost there, just coming within reach, when Laurence steps backwards, holding an empty glass, and knocks me lightly with an elbow. He swings around, apologising. For a moment he is, I can tell, unable to put a name to my face. I see myself through his eyes: pale, nondescript, as dull as my clothes. No one in particular.

"Frances," I say helpfully.

"Of course, of course," he says. Clearly, he didn't know I was invited. "Good of you to come."

"I found the service terribly moving," I say, looking up at him, noting the grey planes under his eyes, the looseness around his collar. "And it was lovely to be able to spend some time with Polly." Some distance behind him, Mary Pym is cosying up to the host of a radio books show, but I can see her attention has now shifted to Laurence, and to me. I lean forward and say, "Let me get that for you," and then I dab something—possibly some mustard, possibly a bit of lint—off his sleeve.

"Ah," he says. "Thanks."

"I'm afraid I'm due somewhere else," I say. "I'm late already. I just wanted to make sure I spoke to you, to say how touched I was to be asked. It really means a great deal to me."

"Well, it's good that you could make it," he says, directing his gaze over my shoulder, processing, assessing, wondering—with a certain weariness—how much longer this thing will go on. I step towards him and reach up and kiss him on the cheek and see, from his expression, that this was rather unwelcome, and then I give him a little smile and push away through the crowd towards the stairs.

"Take care, Teddy," I call, my hand on the newel. He waves vaguely at me, polite in only the baldest sense of the word. The girl doesn't even look over. He turns back to her. "Oh, Honor, give me a break," he's saying. As I start to climb the oatmeal stairs, she says (in the sort of deep, husky, modulated voice that requires, in my experience, some cultivation), "For Christ's sake, you've got to let yourself get *used* to what's happened. You should take some time off. Fuck's sake! They owe you. Plus, in any case, they *love* you."

As I wait in the hall for the helpful young man in the white jacket to find my coat, I remember the Sargent postcard, the air of entitlement, the absolutely impermeable confidence, and I think, *Ah, yes. That's it. You remind me of her.*

As well as my coat, the helpful young man brings me Polly's umbrella. It has stopped raining, but I take it anyway.

Most mornings, you hear Mary before you see her. She's one of those relentlessly, conspicuously busy people. Even the longueurs spent waiting for or in the lift are put to use. When the doors open, releasing her onto the fifth floor, she's midconversation, talking about her weekend, the weather, the dogs. Her voice carries down the quiet expanse of office carpet, over the banks of angled screens. It's the sound of long, wet walks on the beaches of north Norfolk, the sound of children boarding at Winchester and Wycombe Abbey, the sound of a holiday home in the Auvergne. I never feel good listening to Mary's riffs.

Still, this is a work call; she's speaking to one of her grander contributors. This becomes apparent when she says, "Oh, file when you're ready, darling. Anytime on Thursday will be fine." This means copy will arrive late afternoon, just when the pages are due to be sent to the printers. Mary will read it, scribble little queries all over it, and pass it over to me. Then she will depart, smartly, to meet her husband, the corporate lawyer, at a drinks party in Primrose Hill, and I'll be stuck here for an extra hour or two dealing with the fallout.

My desk is quite near the window, and though I'm meant to be giving Ambrose Pritchett's latest review a quick read-through, I find my attention keeps wandering from the screen. A pan-lid sky hangs over London. The forecast is for rain. Half-listening to Mary as she emerges from the elevator lobby, I watch the dull silver ribbons of trains flowing in and out of the station, the slow rotation of cranes over distant building sites. Beyond the cloud, beyond the city, a margin of green—the Surrey hills—is startlingly bathed in sunshine.

Turning back to the monitor, I wonder why so few people understand the difference between *practise* and *practice*.

Mary arrives at her desk, drops her bag on her chair, and turns to me. She has two cups of coffee in a cardboard holder. "Got one for you," she says, shouldering off her aubergine wool coat. "Do you want cappuccino or latte?"

"Either's fine," I say. In the seven years I've worked with Mary, she has never once bought me coffee.

"Good, I'll have the cappuccino. Croissant?" she adds, passing me a white paper bag. "No, go on, it's for you."

"Thanks very much," I say. From the lettering on the bag, I can see that she stopped by the high-end deli, the one I visit only when I feel I deserve a treat, the one with salami slung festively from overhead beams and big glass jars of amaretti on the counter. I take the lid off my latte and break a horn from the croissant.

Buttery flakes shower down on my mouse mat. "I've just started working on Ambrose's review," I say.

"How is it?"

"Not too bad," I say, dipping the croissant into my cup. "Oh, Alison Freiberg rang. Can you call her back?"

"Will do." Mary is unpacking her bag, locating her turquoise diary. She flicks through it, the gold-edged pages rippling luxuriously, and pauses, a pensive look on her face, tapping her teeth with her Montblanc. Then she comes over to my desk and stands at my shoulder. It's disconcerting. *Perhaps she's going to sack me. Perhaps the croissant was a sop to her conscience.* I ignore her and concentrate on the screen, the comfort of the two neat columns of words.

"So, I saw you at Alys Kyte's memorial service," she says, as if the memory has only just occurred to her. "You're a friend of the family's, are you?"

"Well, I guess you could say that," I say. I run the cursor over a sentence, highlighting a repetition and then cutting it, so the overmatter shrinks back into the layout. Then I turn my chair around to face her. "It's really so sad," I say, picking up my cup, as if we're going to have a little heart-to-heart. "I don't think Laurence is dealing with it terribly well, do you? Lost lots of weight. I suppose it's only to be expected. Polly, though . . . we had a proper chat, I think she's doing okay, all things considered."

Mary is looking at me with a strange expression on her face. *My God, you're avid for it, aren't you?* I think. *You were only invited to the memorial service in your professional capacity—and there I was, on the other side of the velvet rope. You're dying to know why and when and how, aren't you? All those questions—but you can't quite bring yourself to ask them. Not yet, at any rate. I'll give you a few days, a few more posh coffees, and maybe I'll let some more details slip. But you'll have to work for them.*

"Do you know the Kytes well?" I ask innocently, blowing on my coffee and then taking a sip.

Mary widens her eyes behind her expensive narrow spectacles and steps back. "God, no. Hardly at all. No, the invitation came in via Paula at McCaskill, and I thought it was important to represent the paper. Well, of course, I've met Laurence on numerous occasions—parties, launches . . . a few years back we judged the Sunderland prize together—but I never met Alys."

"No . . . she wasn't keen on parties. She was always better in small groups," I say, smiling, as if Mary has reminded me of some little memory—something almost painfully intimate. "She was wonderful with the Azarias and the Titovs, and she could keep her end up, but she was never particularly at home with all that. She always seemed happiest pottering around the garden at Biddenbrooke."

Mary listens, head cocked. I can see her hoovering up the insights—details from an old diary item in the *Telegraph* which I'd stumbled on during my Internet trawling. *That's enough,* I think. *Just stop there.* I give Mary a sad, little smile, and then I say, "Well, thanks for the coffee. I'd better get on," and turn back to the screen.

She leaves me alone for the rest of the morning, which is punctuated by the usual landmarks: the arrival of the post, the tea trolley, and Oliver, who sidles in just before eleven, unshaven and wearing what I'd lay money on are yesterday's clothes. Mary pulls her spectacles low on her nose and gives him a cool look, but says nothing. He has been at his desk for only twenty minutes, talking on the phone in a low, urgent voice and occasionally sniggering, when Sasha from Fashion comes over and they head off for a smoke. At twelve thirty he leaves for a lunch in Covent Garden with some PRs.

I go out to the sandwich bar and buy a roll with some Parma

ham, and I'm eating it at my desk, out of a shiny packet of grease-proof paper, flicking through the *Guardian*, when Mary stops by my chair again. She puts down a proof copy. It's the new Sunil Ranjan. "Does this interest you?" she asks.

I say I've read one or two of his other novels.

"Oh, good, good," she says. "Six hundred words, a week on Thursday? I was going to get Oliver to do it, but—well, you know."

I make a discreet, understanding noise, and she pats my shoulder and moves off.

Interesting, I think, picking up my sandwich again. *Very interesting.*

"**S**o!" *says my mother brightly. She's sitting bolt upright on the* tightly upholstered button-back chair, holding a teacup and a petticoat tail, doing her best to look entirely at ease. I've been in the house for only ten minutes, and we have already exhausted the drive, the dreadful traffic around Ipswich, and the weather. "How is London? Busy, is it?"

Like so many of my mother's questions, this one anticipates a particular answer, in which she will take only the most limited interest. Conversation with my mother rarely goes anywhere unexpected. She has a horror of the unexpected and her entire life is structured to keep it at bay.

"Pretty busy, yes," I say, taking a sip of tea. We look together at the shrubs thrashing around beyond the patio doors. My mother considers herself green-fingered, which simply means she subscribes to a lot of gardening magazines and pays a man to mow the lawn in the summer. She calls him "the gardener." My dad does all the legwork—digging in the compost, pruning, planting bulbs—under her instruction.

It's a very tasteful garden. There's little colour or scent in it—my mother thinks most flowers are vulgar, and she has a deep-seated fear of vulgarity, as if it might suddenly overpower her in a dark alley—but plenty of texture and shapes. At this time of year, as the dusk consolidates, it looks drearier than usual.

"Your father should be back any minute," my mother says, taking another tiny bite of biscuit and dusting an invisible shower of crumbs off her skirt. At the far end of the house, the dog barks manically.

"How is the dog?" I say. The dog is called Margot, after the ballerina. She's a Jack Russell, enormously fat and badly behaved. My parents have always had dogs, but by the time they got Margot they'd run out of energy and never found the time to train her properly, so she has to be shut up in the sunroom, like the first Mrs. Rochester, whenever anyone visits.

"Getting on," says my mother, adjusting the knife-pleat in her skirt. "Poor old thing."

"Maybe I'll take her for a walk later," I suggest, as I always do, for my own amusement. "She could do with it, I expect. Take her over the common, down to the reservoir?"

"Oh, I'm not sure that's a good idea," says my mother, as I knew she would, as if I have suggested something terrifically reckless. "Poor old Margot, she gets ever so out of breath nowadays."

I know the reason why Margot never goes for walks, and it isn't because of her old age, or her inability to behave herself on the lead, or anything like that. My mother has always been most comfortable on her own territory. Nowadays even minor local expeditions (trips to the seafront with Hester's children, or the Pearsons' Boxing Day drinks) make her jittery. She'd never admit it, of course. So there's always a reason why she can't come or must leave early, and usually it's something to do with mass catering.

"I've got to put the potatoes in," she'll say with a tiny smile of martyrdom. "See you back at the house!"

I finish my tea, and as soon as I've put the cup back on its saucer, my mother has risen from her chair, whipping them (and the plate of biscuits and the little stack of napkins) off the coffee table, and bustling back to the kitchen, where I hear her carefully rinsing and then arranging the china in the dishwasher, in what is always a very particular formation.

"Why don't you go and put your things in your room, Frances?" she calls gaily, over the roar of tap water.

I take my bag and climb the stairs. My parents live on the edge of a pretty village, in a comfortable three-bedder built in the seventies: white-painted boards and Cambridge brick, pine panelling in the dining room, bubbled glass in the bathroom door. At the front, the view is of the village green, with its bus shelter and pink-washed pub and occasional uninspired games of cricket. At the back, you look out over the garden and fields of rape and cabbages, and the strange dwindling architecture of pylons processing off into the next county. It's a flat, uneventful landscape.

My mother has gussied up the room for me, as she always does, as if the gussying up will somehow distract me from the shot springs in the bed, which I've had since primary school. It's like a little stage set, every painstaking detail suggesting gracious living.

The pair of scatter cushions arranged against the pillow. The guest soap, still in its wrapper, laid upon the flannel. Three padded, satin coat hangers fanned out on top of the duvet. The stack of *Good Housekeeping*s and *House & Garden*s on the bedside table, next to the tray of tea things—minikettle, sugar sachets, UHT thimbles—as if I'm being accommodated in the East Wing, as if the kitchen were half a mile away.

I drop my bag and sit down on the bed, then I reach over and pick up a magazine and flick through it. It's full of candlemaking, beetroot recipes, charmingly mismatched blue-and-white crockery. There's a special offer on glass cloches and brooms made in Sweden by the partially sighted. I don't believe any of it. I put the magazine back with the others, taking care to line up the spines. I don't want my mother to think I actually looked at them.

All my personality has long since gone from this room. The rosettes and posters and framed class photographs, the joke books and sets of C. S. Lewis and Laura Ingalls Wilder, the cushion cover I cross-stitched when I was nine: so many dust traps, all got rid of. The bottom drawer in the little chest contains my A-level and degree certificates, my stamp collection, and a shoebox of old snapshots, and that's really all that is left of me in the house.

Here in my bedroom, the curtains in the little dormer windows were once yellow with a scarlet-and-orange rickrack trim; now they're toile de Jouy shepherds and ladies on swings, toes pointed and hat ribbons flying. When did one replace the other? I can't remember. Was my permission, or even my inclination, sought? I am sure it was not.

There is a rattle from downstairs as my father opens the glazed front door and closes it behind him.

I spread my hands on the duvet cover, feeling the heat trapped in my palms by the polycotton, the light, uneven give of the springs. Then I stand up and unzip my bag and take out my toothpaste and toothbrush, my hairbrush, and the Sunil Ranjan proof copy. Seeing it lying there on the bedside table makes me feel like a slightly different person; someone, possibly, whose opinions might just matter a little.

When I go downstairs, my mother is busy in the kitchen, and my father is circulating with a jug of water, charging the tumblers set out on the dining table. He puts down the jug to greet me and we kiss hello. I am filling him in on the highs and lows of my journey ("Did you see the new B&Q they've built outside Tewford?")

when my mother—mouthing a tiny *O* of anxiety as she bears a Pyrex dish of mince and potatoes before her—enters, obliging us to separate. We both step back to the edges of the room so she can get to the table.

"I hope you've worked up an appetite!" she says, settling the dish on the trivet, which is laid upon a cork mat, which is laid on top of a tablecloth, which is laid on top of an oilcloth, as if the table itself, somewhere deep beneath these protective strata, happened to be Georgian mahogany rather than an ugly Formica.

The meals at my parents' house always come thick and fast, and in between there's a constant opportunity to supplement. The food rolls out in marshalled surges, like Bomber Command. There is no letup. Someone is forever passing around foil-wrapped chocolates, cheese straws, yellow slices of Madeira, salted luxury nuts, little fruited scones anointed with scarlet jam, cubes of mild cheddar speared with cocktail sticks, decorative tins containing layers of scalloped Viennese biscuits. It's a relentless battery of snacks. The food and the constant preparation and clearing away of it quite often get in the way of other things we might profitably be doing, things normal families seem to do when they convene: going for walks, playing Scrabble, talking about subjects other than roadworks or the weather we've been having lately.

From time to time, the real world makes itself known to my mother: strikes, petrol shortages, heavy snow, a rise in the price of wheat. Such events prompt panicked phone calls, sometimes two a day, suggesting I stock up on basic provisions as the local supermarkets have had a run on bread and milk. The chest freezer out in the garage accommodates several weeks' worth of apocalyptic menus—chicken à la king, beef olives, gypsy tart—stashed in neatly labelled containers that once held soft-scoop ice cream.

Occasionally, when it's entirely unavoidable, my parents come to London, and though they usually stay with Hester (who has a proper spare room in the house in Maida Vale), once in a blue moon they have to stay on my sofa bed. Of course, these visits are always an ordeal for my mother, who applies herself strenuously to the task of appearing easy and relaxed in what is essentially enemy territory. "This looks smart," she'll murmur faintly, as I put a risotto on the table or scoop some avocado into a salad. "Just half for me." After one such meal, when I came unexpectedly into the room, she turned her back on me, unable to speak, her mouth full of biscuit.

The chocolate wrappers and apple cores I find in the bin when they've left are always exquisite little reproofs.

We sit and eat. It's constantly disconcerting, my mother's cooking. She models herself on the ideal hostess, but she cooks like a prison caterer, as if the activity is a punishment which she is obliged to pass on to others. This cottage pie is no exception.

"Frances was saying London is very busy," my mother informs my father.

My father picks up his fork and says Stewart Pearson was down in London last week, visiting Clare and the grandchildren.

"Clare lives not far from you, doesn't she?" says my mother. "Do you ever see her?"

Clare lives, I believe, in Acton. I barely even know where Acton is. I had nothing in common with Clare when we were at primary school together, and now she's a marketing manager at Unilever with a husband and two children we have even less to talk about when our paths cross at the Pearsons' Boxing Day drinks. "I thought I saw her going into Selfridges last week," I invent. "But she was quite far away, I couldn't be sure." I rake my fork through the pale, uncrisped mash so the gravy seeps down the channels, just as I used to as a child, before I knew that not all food tasted like this.

"Have you seen Hester and Charlie recently?" my father asks.

I say I babysat for them a few weeks ago, and we talk a little about Toby and Rufus. I quite enjoy my nephews, as long as I don't see them too often or for too long. Overexposure is never satisfactory, not least because I'm frequently rather dubious about some of Hester's parenting techniques. But I know from experience that my parents don't want to hear about that. My parents are always more enthusiastic about the idealised notion of the grandchildren than they are the noisy, messy reality. That much is clear when we all congregate here or at Hester's house at Christmas.

I sometimes suspect that, as far as my mother is concerned, the real purpose of family is to ensure she always has something to talk about if she bumps into Mrs. Tucker at Tesco.

As is customary, she only half-listens to what I am saying about Toby and Rufus. My mother has never been an engaged listener. Other people's speech is useful mainly as a prompt. So when I mention Toby's passion for Playmobil, she launches on an anecdote about a den Hester and I once built together using the clotheshorse and all the clean towels in the airing cupboard—a story I've heard countless times before (although I now have no memory of the actual incident). I wonder how much of a connection my mother makes between the child I once was and the adult I now am. Usually she talks of my childhood as if it were something that really happened only to her, as if I were only distantly involved.

We have crème caramel in stemmed glass dishes for dessert, and then I help to clear away. The evening stretches ahead of us: acres of it, as flat and featureless as the fields around the house. None of us can decently go to bed for hours.

We fill the time with coffee and mint chocolate thins in little slippery envelopes, and my mother lays the table for breakfast, and then we watch several finalists competing for a part in a London stage musical, and after that there's a film, an action movie set in ancient Rome. My mother fidgets uneasily during the fight sequences and the sex scenes. In the second commercial break, she collects the cups and chocolate wrappers and says, "Well, Frances, I hope you have everything you need. Sleep well, dear." Then it's just my father and me, sitting side by side in the darkened room, eyes fixed on the screen like astronauts preparing for countdown.

From time to time, I can hear the dog barking. It's a less angry sound now, as if she has started to adjust to her new status, as if she is now merely disconsolate.

We don't watch the end of the movie, but switch over for the ten o'clock news.

Later, as I move around my room, picking the plastic film off the soap (as tiny and pearly pink as prawn dim sum), brushing my teeth at the rinky-dink basin and running the flannel over my face, I hear my father escorting Margot through the house and ushering her, with a strange sort of chivalry, out the front door ("Come on, old girl, time for some fresh air"). I poke back the curtain an inch with a finger and watch the pair of them beginning a circuit of the village green, moving slowly between the benison of the lampposts, a stout, elderly man and a stouter, elderly dog, out in the wind and the dark.

Fifteen minutes later there's the slight reverberation as the front door clicks. Lying in bed with the novel propped open on my chest and a notebook and pen ready on the bedside table, I hear Margot's nails skittering down the corridor and my father's muttered good-night as he shuts her in the sunroom and then comes upstairs, wheezing faintly on every step.

The buzz of the bathroom extractor fan, the toilet flush, the fan switching off. Finally there's silence.

This is the house where I grew up, and it means nothing to me, just as I mean nothing to it. There's no sense when I'm here of being safe or understood. If anything, this is the place where I feel most alone, most unlike everyone else.

I learned to talk and walk here; I sat at the dining-room table painstakingly crayoning letters on sugar paper; I sowed mustard and cress upon thick, wet layers of kitchen roll; I came down on Christmas mornings and received dolls and roller skates and bikes and, as time went on, book tokens and jeans that I'd picked out myself; and I lay on my stomach on the lawn underneath the elder tree, reading and reading; and then I moved away, and it was as if I'd never lived here at all.

The radiator gurgles as the central heating shuts off for the night. I shift position in the narrow bed, looking at the shadow the pendant lampshade casts across the ceiling, trying to remember what it felt like, growing up in my parents' house. I don't remember being especially happy or unhappy here. Childhood just happened to me, as I suppose it happens to most people. At the time, it seemed an endless succession of fears and dreams and secrets, but from this distance it looks as dull as the life I've gone on to lead. Did I tell my mother when things went wrong or well at school? I'm fairly sure I did not. She was never at leisure to be interested in me. She had other things to worry about.

Hester was always kicking off, throwing down challenges, sneaking out to meet boys. I remember the general relief when she went off to university. But I wasn't like that. I was the good girl: biddable, compliant. I did what I was told, I kept my nose clean, I was no trouble to anyone. But the farther I travelled from the house where I'd grown up, the less I seemed to belong; the less it looked like home.

The Pearsons are coming for a quick drink before Sunday lunch. And Terry and Val Croft might look in, if they have time, although there's an antiques fair at Fulbury Norton that they're hoping to visit. Before retirement, Terry and my father were partners. Thorpe & Croft Solicitors. The office was on Beck Street, between the precinct and the leisure centre.

While I was at school, if I missed the 5:00 p.m. bus, I used to head up there and wait for my father to give me a lift home. There were two wing-backed chairs in reception, and I'd sit on one of them and do my French homework on the coffee table, clearing a space between the elderly Sunday supplements with the recipes ripped out of them. If she happened to be in a good mood, Penny, the secretary, used to make me a cup of tea and slip me the pink wafer from the tin she kept in the bottom drawer of the filing cabinet. I wonder what happened to Penny. There was always something funny about her, then one day I realised that she wore a hairpiece.

My mother is almost beside herself with anxiety.

"You'll have to find your own way around, I'm afraid, dear," she says, with an air of extravagant restraint, as I appear for breakfast. "You know where everything is. I'm a little tied up, as you can see. . . . Weetabix in the cupboard, muesli, cornflakes, so on and so forth. No, not that milk, dear, there's one open on the lower shelf. Bread in the breadbin. Jam's in the cupboard, or perhaps you'd like Bovril?"

The dishwasher is roaring away, pans are on the stove, and the counters are covered with trays of glasses and napkins. As I pour milk on my cereal, my mother drains the green beans and pops them into the top of the oven, ready for lunch in three hours' time.

My father has been out to buy the paper—they don't take the *Questioner,* it's too left-wing—and now sits on the sofa, systematically working his way through it. Every so often, he'll laugh or shake his head, and when I've come through to join him, he starts reading out random paragraphs to me: stories about a killer virus afflicting horse chestnuts, or the latest transgressions of a minor royal, a particularly withering passage in a restaurant review. "Listen to this one, love," he says, wrestling the paper into shape. "You'll like this."

"Don't bother to strip your bed," my mother calls through. "Just leave it. I'll do all the sheets on Tuesday."

"Right," I say, getting up.

I've just stepped out of the bath when I hear the doorbell. The Pearsons and the Crofts have arrived simultaneously, and when I get downstairs, I see my mother has her special social carapace on: glassy, panicked smile, apricot lipstick, and lots of Elnett.

I tour the room, kissing people and shaking hands. Stewart Pearson addresses me as Hester and then looks rather put out when he's corrected. "Of course—you're in journalism," he says. I always wonder how much spin my parents put on my career. Hester, who teaches history at a well-regarded London girls' school, does not require their help.

"If you can call it that," I say. My mother inserts a dish of crisps between us. Terry Croft switches his glass of beer from right hand to left and helps himself.

"Not a good time to be in newspapers, I imagine," he says compassionately.

"No, that's true," I say. "We've just been through one round of cuts, but we've been warned to expect more."

"Well, I'll bet you're a survivor," Stewart Pearson says, very jovial. "What's your technique? How do you make yourself indispensable?"

"Oh—just keep your head down, I suppose," I say. "Lie low. Dot the eyes and cross the tees. Hope for the best."

"Are you working on anything interesting at the moment?" asks little Val Croft, looking up over her schooner of sherry with shiny, impressionable eyes.

This sort of question always throws me. If I told her the truth—that I spend my days correcting spelling mistakes and moving commas around—she'd barely believe it. "Well, I'm reviewing a book at the moment," I say, rather liking the sound of the words, despite myself. "Just getting some thoughts together. Sunil Ranjan's new novel."

"Oh, the Indian chap?" says Stewart Pearson.

"Bangladeshi," I murmur into my glass of sweetish white wine.

"I hear he's a terrific wordsmith," he says encouragingly. "On my list. Definitely on my list. Just wish I had the time to read. I don't know when people fit it in."

And then they're off, talking about all the other claims on their time: golf, fishing, Rotary fund-raising, church committees, the evening lectures at the local institute. The implication being that reading is a frippery for dilettantes. *Salt of the earth,* I think, listening to them. *Pillars of the community. Jesus wept.* I find myself wishing we could talk about something—anything—else: the new vicar, the proposed bypass, Mrs. Tucker's teenaged granddaughter's pregnancy. As the competitive self-justification goes on, I think I'd even welcome the question I dread more than any other: *So, is there anyone special at the moment?*

"Well. With all that to keep you busy," I say eventually, to the room at large, "it's a wonder you find time to draw breath."

As I say it, I see my mother looking at me with her mouth slightly open, as if she's catching the sound of a distant detonation, and I know I'm on the cusp of going too far.

"To be fair, though," says Terry Croft, "Val's a reader. Always got her nose in a book. Isn't that right, Val?"

Val Croft flushes pink. "Well . . . I do love my Judy Arbuthnots," she admits, in a small embarrassed voice. "Not . . . literature. You couldn't call it that. Frances wouldn't, anyway."

I give her a big understanding smile and then I ask her whether she is still helping out with the local Brownie pack.

"How is that dog of yours?" asks Sonia Pearson, dusting pastry off her jersey, as the barking starts up again.

"Oh—Margot loves it when the children visit," my mother sighs, clasping her hands together in front of her, as if she's about to say a prayer or burst into song. "After they go, she always mopes about the house—doesn't she, Robert?—looking behind the sofa, trying to find them. She simply adores Frances."

I hear her saying these things, mouthing these lies, and I look at my father, who hasn't reacted but continues to sip his lager while staring out the window at the shrubs thrashing around; and then I feel a tremendous urge to laugh, to expose my mother's ludicrously conventional little fantasy. But I don't. And driving back to London that afternoon, passing first the sign to Biddenbrooke and then shortly afterwards the white rectory with the stile at Imberly, I think, *Maybe it's not really lying if you barely know you're doing it. It should be true. It's the way it should be, in an ideal world.*

I submit my review to Mary.

A few days pass before she gets around to reading it. Storm clouds are gathering over the *Questioner* again. Sitting at my desk, I hear people assembling in indignant knots by the printer, talking about pay freezes and voluntary redundancy schemes and the ridiculous amount Robin McAllfree, the tiny little bullet-headed editor, is splurging on Gemma Coke, his new star columnist. (The general assumption is that he must be screwing her. Her copy is certainly not worth the figures being bandied about.)

Emergency meetings are convened in the Albatross. Our in-boxes fill up with emails from the managing editor and the direc-tor of Human Resources and the company CEO and the mother and father of the NUJ chapel, and none of them are saying any-thing remotely reassuring.

Even Oliver is getting twitchy. Over the last few weeks, as well as making more of an effort to get in on time, he has been doing his best to stick around until the moment when Mary departs for the day. And he's diligently covering his arse, as people tend to when they feel vulnerable.

On the Monday morning, just after Mary has arrived on the fifth floor, he walks over to my desk holding Sunday's paper, which he has folded back to one of the books pages. He drops it down on my keyboard, his finger stabbing at his review of the latest Jane Coffey, specifically at a typo which has somehow sneaked past me. "This looks pretty shabby, doesn't it, Frances?" he says, in a voice loud enough to reach the desks on the other side of Books, which are occupied by TV and Travel. "It rather spoiled my Sunday. I mean, fuck's sake."

TV and Travel, I can tell, are sitting up straight and nudging each other, enjoying the prospect of someone else getting a bol-locking for a change.

I feel faintly nauseous, as I always do when I've made a mis-take. In these situations, it's best to hold up one's hand and accept responsibility, even though it wouldn't have happened if Oliver had filed on time, rather than at the last possible moment, and if he'd bothered to read his copy through before sticking it in the queue. But really, there is no excuse. So I pick up the paper and look at it and say, "God, I am sorry. That really shouldn't have hap-pened."

Oliver isn't placated. He's drawing breath, about to come in for round two, when Mary looks up from the letter she is reading

and says, in a just-between-ourselves murmur which is neverthe-
less precisely calibrated to reach the eavesdroppers, "Frances isn't
here to nanny you, Oliver. We have plenty of contributors who
already make that kind of demand on her time, and they tend
not to be on staff. So perhaps you could save us all some trouble
by making sure you check your copy once you've finished writing
it, and by filing when you are supposed to." Then she gives him a
little smile and returns to her paperwork.

Oliver stands by my desk for a moment, unsteady and dis-
oriented. A dark rash of humiliation is spreading over his neck
and up into his soft baby cheeks. "No, I take your point," he says,
gathering up the paper and moving away, back to his desk. "My
mistake, Frances. Won't happen again." I glance over at TV and
Travel and see Tom, one of the subs, giving me a thumbs-up and
mouthing, *Dickhead*.

"Oh, and, Frances," says Mary. "Nice copy. Thanks."

Oliver is terribly helpful after that, at least while Mary is
around. He makes eye contact and comments approvingly on my
piece and asks for my opinion on standfirsts and headlines.

Once or twice I look up from my screen and catch him watching me. He drops his eyes when this happens, and we carry on as
if nothing has taken place.

S ome weeks later, Polly sends me a text. *It's all shit, apparently, and*
she wants to meet for a coffee one morning. I text back
suggesting my day off, expecting her to nominate a Caffè Nero near
her flat. Instead she messages to say she has made a reservation for
11:00 a.m. at the Wolseley.

I get there too early and walk around Green Park for a bit, not
wanting to be on time. I'm sure Polly will be late. Pale new growth

bubbles through the trees; the sky is that faint, heart-stopping blue that would have you believe anything is possible. The deck-chair attendants are circulating, probably for the first time this year. I watch a woman in a little navy jacket and off-white pumps stop, put down her quilted leather shopper, and lift out a small Pekinese, which sniffs suspiciously at the grass as if it barely knows what it is. On the far side of the park, along the Mall, the cherry pickers are out, putting up flags for some state visit or other.

I leave the park and cross the road by the Ritz, borne along by the surge of tourists heading to the Royal Academy, and find the restaurant's entrance, which is rather anonymous and easy to miss: a discreet brass plaque, thick blackout curtains obscuring the windows. The doorman steps forwards and smiles as if he recognises me, and then the doors are opening and I'm passing through them, suddenly confused by the dim, even crepuscular light within. As my eyes adjust, the space takes shape around me. I didn't know what to expect. It's almost as glorious as a cathedral.

I give Polly's name to the girl at the lectern, and without looking down to consult her ledger she says, "Of course, Miss Thorpe. Miss Kyte has already arrived."

It may be late morning, but in here, partly because of the black lacquer and the glow of the little shaded lamps, it feels like the evening. The place is full, and even though most of the people present are conducting business, something sparkly and frivolous is in the air. The atmosphere crackles with gossip and speculation. And cash. The place is full of cash.

Little groups of women in proper jewellery, drinking Bloody Marys. A captain of industry joking with a newspaper proprietor. A film star in shorts and heavy stubble sitting alone, eating an omelette and pencilling his way through a pile of notes.

I'm conscious, as I follow the girl across the black-and-white marble, between little tables shining with silver cutlery and polished glass, that people are automatically glancing up to see whether they know me.

Polly, seated at a table in the central circle, reaches over to kiss me hello. She looks different again today, a little nouvelle vague in a beanie and tight striped jersey, with lots of eyeliner, but I'm realising this is part of her look: she can take it in any direction, at will.

"Hope this is okay," she says, gesturing around her, as I slide into the banquette opposite. "I couldn't think of anywhere else."

"It's perfect," I say, unwinding my red-and-purple scarf.

Without otherwise acknowledging the waitress, Polly orders a black coffee and Birchermüesli. I'd really prefer the eggs Benedict, but I say I'll have the same.

"Thank you," I add, carefully, to the waitress.

"You work at a newspaper, don't you? The *Questioner?*" Polly says, suddenly sharp, when we are alone.

I say that's right, I do.

"Well . . . I know it sounds silly, but this is all in confidence, right? All this family stuff?"

"Of course," I say, watching her fingertips running over the grain of the tablecloth, the curve of the knife. "I'm not that sort of journalist, anyway."

"Well, sure," she says, not really listening. "It's just that Daddy is—well, you know. He's Laurence Kyte, isn't he? The big man. Mr. Letters. People always want to know about Laurence sodding Kyte."

"Don't worry about me," I say. "I'm here for you. I'm not interested in Mr. Letters."

She looks at me and sees the expression on my face, and then she starts to giggle, and I smile back at her, relieved, and suddenly I'm laughing, too, really laughing.

"Mr. Letters!" I say, in bursts. "Mr. Letters! Where did that come from?"

Snorting, Polly presses her hand against her stomach. "Oh, God," she says eventually, when she's back in control. "Stop. Please. I'm out of practice. It hurts."

"Okay," I say, pulling a poker face. "That's fine. Cross my heart and hope to die, that's the last time I'll ever refer to Mr. Letters."

And then she's off again.

The waitress comes back with the order, and Polly composes herself.

"I'm sorry if I seemed kind of grumpy," she says, as our coffee is poured. "It's just that it's all a bit horrid at home at the moment. And I wanted to talk to someone about it, but someone who isn't part of it, if you know what I mean."

"Sure," I say neutrally, stirring some honey into the muesli.

"Sometimes I feel like they're all his spies," says Polly. "Yeah, I know. It's stupid. But it's how I feel. Teddy. My friends. My friends' parents. Charlotte. My tutors. They're all on his side."

"Have you fallen out with your dad?" I ask.

Polly wrinkles her nose. "Not exactly," she says. "But we are currently having a, um . . . a *disagreement*." She likes this word, I can tell. She thinks it sounds grown-up, as if it dignifies the thing it describes. "Thing is," she says, twiddling her spoon in her dish, "thing is, Daddy has never really understood me. That was always Mum's thing. Mum understood. He used to leave us—me and Teddy—to her."

She looks at me.

"Oh, Polly," I say, reaching out to touch her sleeve. "Oh, you poor thing. I am so sorry."

For a moment, we sit there, quite still. Then she looks down, sniffs, and moves her hand away so she can press her napkin under her eyes. I can see she's taking care not to smudge her makeup. When she raises her face again, all evidence of tears has disappeared.

"Anyway," she says, in quite a different sort of voice, "it's not going very well. I think I'm going to leave drama school."

"Drop out?" I say.

"I've got some mates, they're brilliant people, incredibly talented, and the plan is, we take a play—Shakespeare, maybe a couple of Shakespeares—on tour around the country. We'd just rock up and do *Love's Labours Lost* or whatever in scout huts and school gyms and stuff. Really taking it right into communities which ordinarily wouldn't be exposed to proper, you know, art."

They've got an old, decommissioned ambulance which they plan to drive from village to village, parking it outside church halls and sleeping in it overnight. But ten people are involved, maybe more, so they might have to take a tent or two. The weather will be getting better soon anyway so that side of things wouldn't be a problem. They'd cook on campfires or barbecues and wash in municipal toilets.

"It's going to be amazing," she says, licking her spoon. "Honestly, I know it sounds a bit ropy, but if you met them, you'd know it was a good idea."

"Has your dad met them all?" I ask.

She makes a face. "Well, he knows Sam and Gabe and Pandora from when I was at school. But I don't think he has given them a chance, really. He has just made up his mind, he thinks it's a rubbish idea, and that's that. Basically he just doesn't have any faith in me. He doesn't believe we can make it work! He's just so fucking negative."

"And what about drama school? Have you told your tutors? What do they think about it?"

"Oh, no, I haven't mentioned it to *them*," she says contemptuously. "And I'm hardly in their good books at the moment anyway. I had that meeting with my tutor, do you remember? Tony Bamber. He was all sympathetic at first, because of Mum, of course, and I thought he understood, and then he said that my card was marked, and I really had to make sure I worked on my attendance record otherwise I'd have to leave. And then Sam got in touch, and—well, it seemed like perfect timing."

"Mmm," I say noncommittally. "Because it's a great place to be studying. Lots of people would kill for that opportunity."

Polly rolls her eyes. "You know, that's exactly what these places want you to think. Then you get in, and you realise it's just the same tired old rubbish being churned out by this bunch of total losers—only everyone's too chicken to say so. It's like the emperor's new clothes.

"Anyway," she adds, "Dad is livid. But I suppose if it comes to it, if I've made up my mind to do this tour, he can't stop me. And neither can Charlotte, or any of them. They can't make me stay on the course."

"No," I agree. "But maybe you shouldn't rush into it."

"I'm not rushing into anything," she says hotly. "Sam got in touch, like, weeks ago! I've been really sensible about it. I've just been weighing it all up, and—well, anyway, now I've made up my mind."

I sit back against the upholstery, stretching my arm along the banquette, trying to look as if I'm considering the facts. The newspaper proprietor and the captain of industry are being helped into their coats. The actor is sipping his orange juice. The woman I saw in the park is being shown to a table, and as she passes, I glimpse the Pekinese gazing up placidly from the depths of the leather shopper, a princeling in a litter.

"I can understand why people aren't thrilled at the idea of you leaving college," I say, when the woman has been seated. "I guess this is a pretty difficult time for everyone."

"Of course that's true," Polly says irritably. "But in a way it has helped me make up my mind. I mean, I knew I hated the course from the start of the autumn term. But it wasn't until all this happened that I started to think, well, why waste all that time in a place that's making me really unhappy? You know—life is too short. I can't sit around, waiting for my future to happen to me. I've got to get out there and find it."

I think she has probably been reading some self-help books. "Polly, I don't know much about you. I don't really know what to say. I've never been in your situation. But I do know your dad loves you and I'm pretty sure the reason he's giving you such a hard time is because he wants the best for you."

"Oh, you're probably right." She sighs, suddenly deflated, as if all the fight has gone out of her. "I just wish I could make him see things from my point of view. What do you think I should do?"

"I wouldn't do anything right now. Just wait for a bit. Let him get used to the idea. How does that sound? What would your mother have said?" I ask. It feels like a risky question, maybe impertinent or dangerous. But Polly doesn't seem to mind. I'm starting to realise that she's so certain of herself, so assured of her charisma, that she accepts the curiosity of others as her natural due. I can't imagine what that feels like.

"Oh, Mum would have told me to give college another chance, I expect," she says. "And then she would have seen how miserable it was making me, and she would have given in."

"Was she a soft touch, your mother?" I ask. Again, I wonder whether I've gone too far.

But Polly doesn't notice. "Oh, a total pushover," she says. "Funny. Perceptive. Kind. The best, you know?" She touches the sleeve of her striped jersey, sliding the cuff out of the way so her watch flashes discreetly on her wrist. My heart sinks. *Just when we were getting somewhere.* The waitress is clearing the next table. Polly lifts a finger, signalling a request not for the bill, as I'd feared, but more coffee. I feel a burst of adrenaline. *Now you're talking.*

I take a sip of what's left in my cool cup, so I don't seem too eager. Then I ask one of the questions I really want answered. "So, how did it work, your family, when you were growing up?"

"You see—you *are* after a story, aren't you?" she says, but I can tell she's not serious. She trusts me. "You want all the dirt, don't you? The big scoop."

"I told you, I'm not that sort of journalist," I say mildly.

"What sort are you, then?"

"Oh, editing and stuff," I say. "Just behind-the-scenes. Nothing exciting."

"I wouldn't mind being a journalist," she says reflectively. "It must be fun. Screenings, private views, going to interesting places. I hear the freebies are pretty good. Long, boozy lunches."

"It's not really like that now," I say, as the waitress comes over with the fresh coffee, but Polly's tuning out, returning to a subject that interests her much more. "Do you really want to know?" she says. "What it was like, growing up with Mr. Letters? Hmm. Okay. Let me tell you." She leans back, arms behind her head, contemplating the ceiling, enjoying being looked at.

"I didn't really get it at first," she says. "At first, I thought we were an ordinary family. I mean, I knew we were a bit different to other people. Daddy didn't go out to work: he went upstairs, and sometimes he got into terrible moods and we had to keep out of his way, and sometimes he was wild, quite mad with happiness and excitement, and he'd turn up at school at lunchtime and charm the pants off the headmistress, and we'd jump in the car and head off to the seaside, or to that place in Oxford near where the dons used to bathe in the nude . . . what's that called? Parson's Pleasure. Big picnics. Games of French cricket. But most of the time it was pretty . . . regular. We didn't see that much of him. Mum held it all together. God knows, it can't have been easy for her when me and Teddy were little."

"Financially?" I ask.

"Financially, emotionally . . . you name it." Polly lifts her cup to her lips, blows on the surface, then drinks. "We were living in Kilburn at the time. My friend Louisa rents near there now, and it's quite a nice neighbourhood, but back then it seemed like we were on the absolute edge of civilisation. The Wiltshire grandparents got terribly jumpy when they came to see us. Dealers at the end of the street, fights and burglaries and stuff. And our house: well, the garden was the size of a hankie. It was all very *tiny*. And when Dad was in a temper, the whole street knew about it.

"But then he wrote the first really successful book, the Sidney Bark one, and everything took off. The Appleby prize, the residency at Princeton, and he started writing screenplays. That was very lucrative. We went out to LA for a while. Swimming pools. Lunch at the Coppolas'. Yada yada yada." She uses her fingers and thumb to mime a mouth, as if it's all incredibly boring, but I can tell she's in love with this story, she likes telling it, and has done so many times.

"We moved back when they bought the Highgate house, and then they found the place at Biddenbrooke, so Mum could have her garden. God, that garden! I wonder who will look after it now."

She puts her elbows on the table and rests her forehead on her hands. Then she straightens up. "You're a good listener, aren't you, Frances?" she says, examining me with her disconcertingly pale eyes. The dark rings around the irises, I notice, make them seem rather arresting. "Lots of people listen, but you really seem to hear what I'm saying."

I know this really means that I challenge her less than anyone else does; but still, there's a grain of truth to it. I am a good listener. It's a dying art. Most people seem to prefer to talk. They compete to be heard, filling the air with chatter; and for the most part it's worthless stuff: bad jokes, boasts, excuses. White noise. Hot air.

But just occasionally, if you pay attention, you'll hear something that might come in useful.

"Anytime," I say.

She finishes her coffee. The bowl in front of her is still half-full, but I get the feeling she's not much of a breakfaster. "I'd better get going," she says, picking up her phone and reaching for her bag, which she has slung over the back of her chair. It's a silver satchel, simple, undoubtedly expensive. "Sorry for all that . . . *venting*."

"I mean it, Polly," I say, winding the scarf back around my neck. "Anytime, just give me a shout. Not sure how much use I've been to you, though."

"Well," she says, getting to her feet and stretching a little, like a cat, so her jersey rides up, flashing a strip of skinny hip, "I do feel *slightly* calmer. I'm going to think about what you said. Think I'll leave things as they are for now. Won't rush into anything. Might go into college on Monday. Worth it just to see the look on Tony Bamber's face. Sam says we won't be starting rehearsals until the start of the summer anyway. He's got a job in New York next week, on a film set. Just as a runner," she adds, seeing my expression. "His dad knows the director of photography." She says that as if it makes things more palatable.

She bends to give me a kiss just as the waitress turns up with the slip of paper on a silver dish. "Let me know how it goes," I say, and she says she will, and she's turning on her heel and walking off, weaving precisely between the tables, adjusting her hat as she goes, while I sit there, my hand out for the bill.

After that nothing happens for a while.
    Hester and Charlie rent a cottage in a Cornish fishing village for a week in the Easter holidays and invite me to join them

for a few days. It's incredibly wet and windy; and the boys, who wake up at six thirty every morning, have streaming colds; and in return for the small, single bedroom overlooking the mossy court-yard garden, I'm expected to babysit most nights.

Mary asks me to do a few more reviews. I know she's asking me only because she doesn't have to pay me extra, but still.

One evening I've just stepped into an empty lift when I hear someone calling, "Hey, Frances, hold it," and though I quickly press the button marked GROUND for a second time, a foot is inserted between the doors before they close. It's Tom from Travel. "Thanks!" he says, easing in with a sigh of relief. I give him a stiff, little smile and get my phone out of my pocket, wanting to avoid conversation, but he's oblivious.

"I hear Culpeper outdid himself in conference today," he says chattily. "Crawling up Robin's arse over that China editorial. He never stops talking, does he? Is it a nervousness thing?"

I say I have no idea.

"Seriously, I hope it isn't," he says, as the lift door opens, "because I really don't want to start feeling sorry for him."

I can't help laughing at that, but as we are disgorged into the marble foyer, I hang back, getting busy with my coat buttons. Tom, though, is hovering by the revolving doors, waiting for me.

We step out onto the pavement together. "Well, night, then," I say, turning in the direction of the tube station.

"Are you doing anything?" he asks, falling into step with me. "It's just that a few of us are going to the Albatross. Fancy a quick half?"

It would be so easy to say no, as I always do. Or rather, as I always used to. Now I think about it, I realise that people have given up asking me to join them for drinks or the cheap set lunch at the Bay Leaf. Maybe it would be good to find out what's going on.

"Oh, why not?" I say, and Tom gives me a surprised grin. He has good teeth, I notice, and his eyelashes are long and sooty, like a pony's. "Attagirl," he says.

We go to the Albatross. Jerry Edgworth is there, and Sol from the picture desk, and Mike the deputy news editor, already glassy-eyed, tearing into the dry-roasted peanuts. Empty green bottles are lined up at his end of the table like skittles. Tom goes off to buy our drinks, and I sit down uneasily on one of the upholstered stools, not enjoying the attention as Jerry says, "Well, we don't often see you in here."

"Tom twisted my arm," I say. "Don't make me regret it."

Raising a glass to his lips, he snorts faintly, rather dismissively, not wanting to give me the credit for making a joke. Hacks are like that, I've noticed. They always want to be the funny ones.

He and Sol and Mike stop pretending to be interested in me and go back to pondering the fate of the business editor, whose drink problem is now common knowledge after he broke away from the press pack and created an unfortunate scene during the prime minister's trade mission to India. No one seems to know where he is now: possibly a clinic in Surrey, the one where the celebrities go. "He'll have some stories when he gets out," says Mike wistfully.

Tom comes back, sliding onto the stool next to mine, pushing my drink over the table towards me. "Has Mary let anything slip about the review?" he asks.

"Mary never lets anything slip, haven't you noticed?" I say, picking up my drink. "What are they saying at your end?"

"Oh, it's all speculation. No one actually knows anything. But they don't let that stop them."

"It's all mind games," says Jerry. "It's textbook. They're softening us up, preparing us for the worst, so we'll all be relieved if it's not actually that bad after all."

"It will be that bad," says Sol gloomily. "You wait and see."

Tom turns towards me, blocking the others off. "How long have you been on Books, anyway?"

I tell him, and he asks where I was before, and so I find myself explaining about the chain of unremarkable events that led me to Mary and her section. He listens attentively, although I can see he's dipping in and out of the office gossip at the other end of the table: Gemma Coke, Robin, Robin's wife.

"What about you?" I ask.

Tom says the job suits him pretty well, for now at least. It gives him some stability, a regular income, while he works on his screenplay. He has the grace to flush when he mentions it.

As I ask a few more questions, it emerges that he hasn't actually written it yet. He's working on an outline, some character sketches, doing a bit of initial research. "That's the challenge, isn't it?" he says, just a little shamefaced. "Actually knuckling down and getting the thing on paper. You heard about Parvaneh, didn't you?"

Parvaneh was in the subs' pool until she won a new writers' competition run by the Royal Court. Last I heard, the Weinstein Company had optioned her four-hander. Kate Winslet is interested, apparently.

"Really, it's great you've got a project you're working on," I say, though I suspect he'll never get further than talking about it. "You must keep going. You will, won't you? It's really very impressive."

I finish my drink and smile while he blusters a bit—bashfulness and hope fighting it out—and then I gather my things and call it a day, though I get the impression it's only just beginning, as far as they're concerned.

O ne Friday evening I'm just coming out of the tube, having had supper with Naomi, whom I've known since university—a dull evening, as she's newly married and pregnant, obsessed with nutrition and travel systems; I'm thinking about how I may have to let her go—when my phone beeps to say there's a voice mail.

I listen to the message as I head up the hill towards my street. It's Polly. She sounds a little bit drunk and upset. "Where are you?" she's wailing. "It's all going wrong. I really need to talk to you. It's all . . . well, just ring me when you get this."

It's nearly eleven, a mild evening at the beginning of summer, and at the top of my street some kids are milling around outside the takeaway, with cigarettes and bottles of beer; a handful of girls are biting their lips and twisting their heads from side to side, moving to the R & B playing tinnily on someone's phone. In the sodium glow, I notice a toddler in a buggy, a wrap of chips in her lap, looking around with wide, dazed eyes.

"It's me. Frances," I say, when Polly picks up.

"Where are you?" she asks, and her voice is tearful, a bit desperate, rather accusatory. "Where have you been?"

"On the tube," I say, stopping by the front door to find my keys, then letting myself into the communal hall. The lightbulb has gone again, so I have to fumble to fit my keys into the lock. The door gives, and I step into the flat and start to climb the stairs. "I've just got home. What's wrong?"

"Oh, I can't explain now," she says, as if I've said something moronic. "It's just a real mess." Then there's a stifled sound as she puts her hand over the phone. I can hear her voice, muffled, and then someone else is saying something—a man. Then the sound clarifies and sharpens again as she takes her hand away. "Yeah, what*ever*," she's saying, slurring slightly. "Fuck off, why don't you?"

"Where are you?" I ask, dropping my bag on the sofa and

switching on the table lamp. The usual dispiriting mess springs into view: drifts of old newspapers, the undercoated shelves I never got around to painting, the Rothko print in a clip-frame propped by the radiator. Wedging the phone between my chin and shoulder, I bend down and pick the TV remote and last night's pasta bowl off the rug.

"Camden," she says. "You're not far from Camden, are you? I'm locked out of the flat in Fulham, and my flatmate's away, and I don't want to go back to Dad's house . . . not like this."

So I say if she wants to crash somewhere, she could always come here.

The taxi ticks up the road about fifteen minutes later. I've hidden her father's books and done the washing up and put the papers into the recycling box, and because I've opened the windows quite wide—to freshen the place up a little—I hear her getting out, the weighted slam of the cab door followed by the unsteady percussion of her heels as she makes her way to the front step and leans on the bell.

She's flushed, feverish looking, with dark, artificial shadows under her eyes: evidence of tears or maybe just sweat from the heat of the place where she has spent the evening. She doesn't meet my gaze when I let her in, just slides past me, the smell of cigarettes in her hair, her ankles tiny above the brute wedge heel of her sandals as she climbs the stairs. "Thank God I got hold of you," she says as she comes into the sitting room, lifting the strap of her silver satchel over her head and letting it drop, and falling onto my sofa. The sprawl of her bare legs takes up half the room. She's wearing a little, waisted jacket over a sprigged dress which stops several inches short of her knees.

"Do you want a glass of water or a cup of tea or something?" I ask, standing in the doorway, looking down at her.

"I'd really like a cold glass of wine," she says, her arms outstretched beside her, palms to the ceiling: an attitude of dejection, or supplication. "Or a beer. I don't suppose you've got any beer, have you?"

"No, I don't. I don't have any wine either."

"Want another drink," she says. "Just one. Shit night. You know."

I don't say anything. I just stand there in the doorway with one hand on my hip. I'm feeling pretty tired, and I'm suddenly wondering what on earth I'm playing at, letting her in here.

My silence must have alerted her that she's pushing her luck, because she sits up straight and presses her fingertips to her face, then smoothes the hair off her forehead: it's a decisive little movement, and it suggests she's trying to pull herself together. "No, you're right. An herbal tea would be good, if you've got any. Thanks, Frances."

I go into the kitchen and fill the kettle.

When I carry the camomile tea through, I see Polly has taken off her shoes and paired them up against the skirting, as a child on best behaviour might. She's wandering around the room, examining things on the mantelpiece. Picking up the fossil I found at Golden Cap, then replacing it and absently moving on to the scented candle, which she lifts and sniffs automatically. As she runs a nail along the spines of my books, I know she's looking to see whether I have any of her father's novels.

"It's all old stuff," she says, half-pulling out a copy of *Rebecca*. "Don't you read anything contemporary?"

"Not much. If I do, it's mostly for work."

"Hmm," she says, slotting the book back in and coming over to take a mug. "Thanks. I am sorry for tipping up like this. I hope I didn't mess up your evening."

"It's fine." I sit down in the armchair.

Polly goes over to her bag. "Would you mind if I had a smoke?"

"Go ahead," I say, wondering whether my bedroom door

upstairs is open or closed. "And then perhaps you'll tell me what was going on when you rang me."

She lights her cigarette, blowing out the match and leaving it on her saucer. "Oh, it was just a misunderstanding. I don't really want to talk about it. Just some arsehole." The blue smoke hangs in the warm air, twisting a little.

"Right," I say, starting to get to my feet. It's too late for patience. "Look, I'll go and get some blankets and we can make up the sofa bed."

"Oh." I can see she's feeling hurt. "Of course, I don't want to keep you up."

I lean back into my chair. "I've been thinking about you," I say, relenting a little. "Wondering how you're getting on. What happened about the course?"

"Oh—that," she says savagely. "I'm still on it—just. I told you about Lord Strange's Men, didn't I? The travelling company? Sam came up with the name, it's a reference to something or other. I wasn't mad on it. Anyway, we're still planning to go—in fact, we should be starting rehearsals around now—but Dad has really started interfering. He rang up Sam's father and they've worked themselves up into a mutual *froth*, and now they've agreed to cut off our allowances if we drop out. Sam is absolutely livid. He thinks it's my fault somehow. If I hadn't got involved, his dad wouldn't have been dragged into it."

"That's a bit tough," I say, trying to stifle a yawn.

"Dad is being a total bastard," she says. "I can't make anyone see it from my point of view: not him, not Teddy, not even Charlotte. It's such a stupid mess." I can tell she's thinking about her mother, about how Alys would have sorted it all out somehow, made it all good.

I imagine all her friends are getting rather tired of this routine, which is why she has ended up here. The familiar avidity surges up inside me again. I take a sip of my drink and wait.

But Polly is looking around the room again. "Do you live here on your own?" she asks. I say I do. "It's nice," she says, not really meaning it, and as she says this, I see the room afresh, through her eyes: the racing-green sofa (a castoff from Maida Vale), its stains inadequately camouflaged by a patterned throw; the combination of lamps and cushions and rugs which, rather than looking charming and eclectic, simply seem ill assorted; and the view across the street of a little redbrick mansion block, metal-framed windows thick with nets and pulsing with blue light. There's a burst of laughter from the kids by the chippy, then the sound of a window being pulled open, and someone shouts, "It's nearly midnight, don't you have homes to go to?" and then another voice yells back, "Get over it, wanker."

Polly knocks her cigarette ash into her saucer and looks at me. "Keeping it real," she says.

"Of course, it's not Fulham," I say rather coldly.

"Do you have a boyfriend?" Polly asks. It's a retaliatory question.

"Not at the moment. Look," I say, moving again, "I think I'm going to go to bed."

"I'll tell you," she says, in a rush. "I've got to tell someone. And Teddy doesn't want to hear. And Dad is—well, it wouldn't get me anywhere. It might make things worse. But I need to talk about it. I have a right to."

"Tell me what?" I say.

"About what went on. On the day of the accident. I keep thinking about it, I can't get it out of my head. What she must have been feeling when she drove off. That's one reason why I was so keen to meet you when Kate Wiggins first mentioned you. I wanted to know if my mother talked to you about it, if things had been left unresolved. And then what you told us—you know, 'Tell them I love them' . . . I knew she'd made her peace with it. But I'm not sure if I have."

I'm feeling distinctly uneasy now, as if I'm losing my centre of gravity, as if a magnetic pole is gradually shifting position.

"Wait a minute," I say. "I've just remembered something." I go back into the kitchen and dig around at the back of the shelves for the dusty-shouldered bottle which I bought when Hester asked me to supply the brandy butter last Christmas. How do you drink brandy? With ice? I don't know, but a few cubes are in a tray in the freezer, so I pop them out into two glasses and pour us both a couple of fingers.

"Nice one," she says, tucking her legs up on the sofa.

"Why don't you start at the beginning?" I say.

So she does.

*I*t was a miserable January weekend, sleety and dour, in the post-Christmas doldrums. Polly hadn't planned to visit her parents at Biddenbrooke but she'd had an argument with her flatmate, Serena ("something pathetic—I'd finished her milk or not taken the rubbish out"); and though she had a party to go to that evening, she suspected Sandeev, the ex, might be invited, too, and she couldn't quite face him yet. So she rang her parents on the Saturday morning, trying Alys's mobile when the Highgate phone went unanswered.

Laurence took the call; Alys was driving. They were en route.

Alys intended to stay in Biddenbrooke till late on Sunday, and Laurence would catch the train back on Tuesday, or maybe Wednesday. He had the page proofs of his new book to go through before it went off to the printers.

"Why don't you come?" her father asked.

So Polly caught the train from Liverpool Street, and Laurence picked her up from the station and took her back to the house.

They were too late to go for a walk that afternoon, as it was already getting dark. Instead, Laurence lit a fire in the sitting room and Polly lay on the rug in front of it and they all read the papers and ate Alys's walnut cake and drank tea. They talked quite a lot about Teddy, recently promoted at the Sackler Gallery, where his days seemed to be spent appeasing and cutting deals with often unreliable artists and the Russians who could afford to invest in them; and they talked a little about Polly's course, though she tried to get them off the subject. The rain and wind lashed the windows. It was nice being there, in the warmth.

At six thirty Laurence opened some wine.

Then he went out to collect fish and chips from Biddenbrooke, and they ate their supper out of the paper wrappers, sitting around the kitchen table.

When her parents went to bed around eleven, Polly stayed downstairs, watching a movie. It finished around one. As she went upstairs and along the corridor to her room, she heard her mother talking in a low voice—though not what she was saying—and noticed the thin spill of light beneath her parents' bedroom door. She was surprised they were still awake.

When she woke up on Sunday morning and appeared at breakfast, an atmosphere was in the air, as insistent as the smell of burning. Something had happened. Yet you couldn't cite anyone's actions or remarks as evidence of it. If anything, Alys and Laurence behaved quite normally. Too normally. Laurence was as attentive to Alys as he usually was, but he was watchful, too, as if he was waiting for something. And Alys, always distracted and dreamy, seemed preoccupied, almost absent.

Polly went back to bed with a cup of tea: she had a script to learn for college. An hour or so later, she was padding around the upstairs landing, on her way to run a bath, when she heard her mother's voice, distinct, every word freighted. The kitchen door was ajar.

"And you can change the dedication while you're at it," she was saying. The coldness in her voice shocked Polly most. Alys was never cold. "It's not a tribute, it's an insult."

Polly didn't want to hear any more. She was used to thinking of her parents' relationship as harmonious. Her friends had parents who were divorced: mothers who were on their second or in some cases third husbands; fathers who lived in Geneva or New York with new wives and other, younger children, some of whom were still babies or at kindergarten. But Alys and Laurence were not like this. They were a partnership. They enjoyed each other's company. Of course they rowed from time to time, but they always laughed at each other's jokes.

When Polly still lived at home, she liked to lie in bed at night with the door open, listening to the sound of their conversation spiralling up through the house. It made her feel safe.

This was different. It was unwelcome. It frightened her.

She went down the landing to the bathroom and started to run the bath, and when she went back to her room to collect her shampoo, she whistled loudly just to let Alys and Laurence know she was around and within earshot. By the time she'd bathed and dried her hair, lunch was ready. A simple sort of lunch, the sort of thing Alys could always throw together without any fuss: a roast chicken, a pan of diced potatoes with rosemary, watercress salad. The atmosphere was still perhaps a little strained, but, as before there was nothing you could quite put your finger on. Laurence talked in passing about Nikolai Titov's forthcoming autobiography. Alys listened, as she always did. Perhaps she spoke less than usual.

Then after lunch, when Polly looked at her watch and realised she had only twenty-five minutes before the train went, Alys volunteered to drive her to the station. It was all a rush from that point: throwing stuff in the bag; Alys unable to lay hands on the car keys and Laurence finally finding them in his overcoat pocket; an anxiety, as they drove through the narrow lanes, about whether they'd make it in time. When the Audi pulled up in the station car park, the red warning lights were flashing, the alarm was sounding, the gates across the level crossing were coming down. Polly blew her mother a kiss as she ran through the ticket office onto the platform. "I'll call you!" she shouted, over the clatter and screech of the approaching train.

Alys waved back, smiling.

That was their good-bye.

Laurence rang Polly that evening, around eleven o'clock, and told her what had happened.

"Did you ever ask him what they had argued about?" I ask, when the room has fallen silent.

"No. How could I? Anyway, I only wanted to remember them together, happy. The disagreement, or whatever it was, only really came back to me when I heard about you. Then I let myself remember. And what you told us made me feel better—that she'd made her peace with whatever had happened. *Affliction* was published and of course it was dedicated to her. Most of them are, did you know? Apart from *The Ha-Ha*, which he dedicated to Teddy, and *Ampersand*, which he dedicated to me. Usually he just put her name, but for *Affliction* the dedication read, 'For Alys. Always.'"

I nod as if this is news to me.

"I think she wanted her name taken off that book," Polly says. "And I don't know why."

"Well," I say, sitting back; I've been leaning forward, listening and thinking hard. A siren wails louder and louder, then fades away as a police car speeds past the end of the street. "It was just one of those things, wasn't it? It doesn't sound very serious."

"It doesn't *sound* like it," agrees Polly, looking down into her empty glass. "But something had happened. Something which my mother was taking seriously. Still—I'm glad you heard her say what she did. I can't tell you how much it helps."

I look at my watch. It's nearly 1:00 a.m.

Together we take the throw and the cushions off the sofa and tug out the bed frame, then I help her to make up the mattress with some clean sheets. I give her a pillow and a blanket from my bedroom, and a T-shirt to sleep in, and I offer her a spare tooth-brush, but there's one in the interior pocket of her silver satchel. "It's nothing to do with being a dirty stop-out," she says, though I feel free to draw my own conclusions about that. "I'm a bit OCD about my teeth."

I say good-night and leave her to it, clicking off the light on the landing and starting to climb the stairs.

"Frances?" she calls. I go back and open the door wider, and she's sitting up in bed, the sheet pulled tight over her knees. "Can you leave the hall light on?" she asks. "I'm not very good in the dark."

I *sleep badly, disturbed by noises that are part of the usual nocturnal soundscape:* people arguing in the street, the double blip of car alarms being deactivated, the yowl of cats and, more distantly, foxes. My bedroom curtains slowly fill and empty with breaths of air. The harsh orange of the streetlamps gradually gives way to a softer, pearlier light.

Finally, my neighbours' days begin. I listen to the familiar sounds of sash windows being pushed open and the burble of radio phone-ins, the lunatic fanfare of Saturday cartoons.

When I go downstairs and peer into the sitting room, Polly is still asleep in the dimness. She is stretched out on her side, her long, pale legs kicked free of the sheet, one hand under her flushed cheek. On the table, a light pulses on her mobile.

I'm eating toast at the kitchen counter when she comes in, yawning, still pink and dishevelled, expressing amazement and satisfaction that she doesn't have more of a hangover. I push a cup of tea over to her as she checks her phone. It's a message from Laurence.

"He's asking me to come over for lunch," she says, rubbing sleep out of her eyes with her palm. "It's some sort of summit. Brilliant. Another bollocking." She sighs and slides onto the stool opposite me. Her bare toes—orange polish—grip the chrome bar like a chimp's.

"Well," I say. "Maybe this is an opportunity. Maybe you can use this to get a concession from him. Engineer things a little."

She looks at me blankly.

"Oh, come on," I say impatiently. "You want to skip college and go off with Sam for a bit. He wants you to stick at the course. Can't you meet in the middle somewhere?"

"How would that work?" she's asking, aggrieved. "He's made up his mind, and if I don't do what he wants, he'll stop my allowance."

"Right," I say. "But I've been thinking, what about if you managed to convince Tony Bamber, or whoever, that you needed a break from the course? Just temporarily—maybe for a year, or even just a term? I'm sure because of your circumstances they'd consider it. Compassionate leave, isn't that what they call it? So you'd have a sort of sabbatical, which would allow you and Sam to go off and do your tour . . . and then you'd be able to go back to the course once you'd got the other thing out of your system."

"I won't go back," says Polly stoutly, but I can tell the idea is starting to appeal to her. "Anyway, Dad won't buy it."

"You don't know until you try," I say.

"No, you're right," she says doubtfully. "It might be worth giving it a go. I just hope I can explain it as well as you did just now. You made it sound completely reasonable." She looks at me slyly. "I don't suppose you'd come, too?" she says, and there's suddenly a kittenish, imploring edge to her voice.

I umm and ah for a little, for form's sake; and then—as if I'm overwhelmed by the expert deployment of charm—I say okay, I'll do it, I'll come.

We walk up to Highgate together, turning off the steep road that leads past the hospital—the road where Dick Whittington heard the bells, now clogged with double-deckers—to enter the park. It is already hot. There is a purple haze in the borders where the bees are rolling and tumbling rapturously, and the small playground is full of babies in sunbonnets. Daisies sparkle in the grass.

We pass along narrow, inky corridors of shade and through scented clouds of lilac blossom. As the path curves round past the shrubbery at the top of the park, we pause and look back over the green slopes sprinkled with the first picnics of the year, over the placid, oily expanse of the ponds, and far in the distance I see the towers and domes and Ferris wheel of central London, winking and glittering with a hard mineral light.

Leaving the park by the tennis courts, we cross Pond Square, where people with pint glasses are playing pétanque under the plane trees, and work our way through the side streets towards Laurence's house. Polly has a key in her satchel. She opens the front door and we step inside. It's cool and dark after the brightness of the day.

"Hello," she calls. "Daddy? Where are you?"

There's no answer, so she leads me downstairs. The big white kitchen is in a bit of a state. There are carrier bags on the counter and more slumped on the floor. A dirty pan has been left out by the Aga. Coffee grounds are spilled around the kettle. By the open French window a newspaper lifts and falls, like something breathing.

Polly inspects one of the bags and takes out a shiny gold bar of French butter and a couple of cheeses wrapped in waxed paper, which she puts in the fridge. She says that Laurence has hired a housekeeper who comes in most mornings to clean and prepare meals, but Mrs. King doesn't work weekends. Polly rolls her eyes and crosses the room to the French windows, pushing them wide, leading me out onto the soft brick terrace.

"Dad!" she calls, and waves.

Laurence is halfway down the long garden, sitting—as I'd once imagined him sitting—on the bench outside the summerhouse. In the moment before Polly calls to him, he's entirely unaware of our arrival. It's all there, unguarded: the endlessly miserable business of loneliness. I see it in his posture and written on his face. Then he hears his daughter and turns and rises and comes to meet us.

"I understand you rescued Pol last night," he says to me while we are rather awkwardly shaking hands; and then, to her, "You are a little fool, losing your keys like this."

"I haven't lost them, I left them in the flat," she protests, taking his arm as we walk back up the garden, along the brick path. Of course, I haven't seen the house from this angle before. Between the dark, glossy windows, thick, pale hawsers of wisteria twist upwards, thinning like smoke. The blossom isn't quite out yet. Another week or two, I think.

"Serena is coming back this afternoon anyway," Polly is saying.

"Well, I'm glad you could both make it for lunch," he says,

holding the French windows open for us and following us inside. "Pol tells me you've been seeing quite a bit of each other," he adds, stooping for a carrier bag. Something in his voice is less formal now, as if he's surprised but pleased, for his daughter's sake, that the two of us have made a connection.

"I enjoy her company," I say directly to him. "She's so . . . young. It's rather energising. And flattering, too, I suppose."

Polly laughs, as if this is a silly thing to say, and Laurence looks at me, a thoughtful, assessing glance. Among other things, I know he's trying to work out how old I am. Thirty? Thirty-five? "I hear you gave her some good advice a few months ago when she was going through a rough patch at drama school," he says. "Talked some sense into her. She certainly wasn't interested in anything I was saying at that point, so thank God she listened to you."

"I wouldn't say I did anything," I say. "I just asked a few questions, that was all. She came to the decision by herself. Isn't that right, Polly?"

"Mmm," says Polly, who has been busy upending little paper bags. Purple and pale green lettuces, earth still clinging to their frills. A tub of queen olives leaking oil. Bagels spill out over the counter like deck quoits.

While Laurence is tipping the olives into a dish and wiping up the mess, she meets my eye, and I give her a tiny shake of the head: *Not yet, not quite yet, let's have a drink first.* "Have you got any white, Dad?" she's asking, and he's directing her to a frosted bottle in the fridge. There's not much else in there, I see. Some Greek yoghurt. A carton of semiskimmed milk. A couple of Pyrex dishes sealed with cling film, which I imagine have been left by Mrs. King. Lasagne, by the look of it. Some sort of chicken casserole.

I rinse the lettuces and Polly mixes a vinaigrette while Laurence gets glasses and unwraps the cheese. Then we take our plates and go out to the ironwork table. Around us at some remove, discreetly shielded by dense, dark hedges waxy with heat, the neighbours are living their comfortable lives: children on trampolines, the hiss of hoses. This time I guess it's okay to look as if I'm enjoying the wine.

Laurence asks all the questions Polly has failed to, and I answer them, without going into much detail. My modesty is real enough. Used to Polly's solipsism, I find his polite interest makes me uneasy. I don't like feeling exposed.

As if he has sensed this, he takes the conversation elsewhere: to Mary Pym, whom he remembers from the Sunderland prize panel; to Frynborough and Biddenbrooke and the seaside at Welbury. He went to Welbury as a child most summers: his parents took rooms in a boardinghouse there every August. Those childhood memories (swimming off the groynes; the annual crabbing contest) were the reason why he and Alys started looking for a holiday house in the area when they left America. We talk about the pier and the bandstand and the boating lake, the closure of the fishmonger's and the colonisation of the high street (he and I agree this is lamentable, Polly is rather pro) by cupcake merchants and boutiques selling patterned Wellingtons.

The bottle empties and he goes to get another one. Smoke from a barbecue drifts lazily through the hedge.

A window opens somewhere releasing the *Jazz Record Requests* signature tune.

"I was talking to Frances about Sam's Shakespeare project," begins Polly carefully.

He raises an eyebrow and slides deeper into his chair, steepling his fingers in front of him. "Ah," he says.

"I was wondering if we couldn't find a compromise," she says.

He sits there, waiting.

"Sam's plan—it's such an amazing opportunity," she says, then sees his expression. "Well, anyway, I thought that perhaps if we worked on Tony Bamber, he might let me take some time off the course. Special circumstances and all that. Compassionate leave. So I wouldn't be dropping out, I'd just be taking a break for a while. A term—or maybe a year at the most."

We watch him as he considers this for a moment, running his thumb absently over the bristle on his jaw. "And if I helped you lobby for this, you'd definitely rejoin the course?" he says.

"Absolutely," she says, her eyes shining with innocence. *Maybe she has got some talent after all,* I think.

He makes a contemplative sort of noise and shifts position, tapping his index fingers together.

"What do you think about this?" he asks me eventually.

"Well, if Mr. Bamber agrees, it appears to solve the problem," I say hesitantly.

"I take your point." He sighs. Then to Polly he says, "I think we'd better book in to see your Mr. Bamber sometime next week."

Soberly Polly nods, but when he has gone inside to answer the phone, she leans over the table to me, hissing, "Yes!"

"It's not a done deal yet," I caution, my voice low.

"No. But it will be," she whispers back. "Wait and see. No one ever refuses Dad anything."

Laurence comes back, picking his way over the grass. Like so many men, he looks at a disadvantage in bare feet. "Teddy's coming round," he calls. "And Honor."

"Not Honor," Polly groans.

I remember the Sargent postcard and suddenly feel anxious to be gone by the time they arrive. The afternoon has been a success, I feel, and it's good to leave on a high. "Oh, look at the time," I say, rising to my feet. "I really must go."

"Oh. Must you?" says Polly, unconcerned. "Thanks for last night."

"Anytime," I say, kissing her cheek in a sisterly fashion. "Let me know what happens at college. I'll see myself out."

But Laurence insists on accompanying me to the front door. There's a tiny, quick confusion at the French windows, as we both feint and hesitate, prepared for the other to go into the house first, and then he lightly touches the small of my back to encourage me to step ahead of him, and I note the gesture, and I save it.

"You seem to be a good influence," he says quietly as we pass through the white kitchen and up the pale stairs, into the hall. "I've been worried about Polly recently, but she seems to listen to you, and your advice seems to be very . . . sensible. Of course, I don't want to be too hard on her. She was very close to her mother. We're all still coming to terms with what happened. It's going to take some time."

I don't know exactly how to respond to this, so I stand still in the hall, on the Turkish rug, my hand resting on the cool, polished table. An insect knocks itself against the fanlight, trying to get out. In the silence of the empty house, I hear the rustle of the trees in the street.

"So, really, thank you," he says. "I'm grateful."

I say it's nothing, a pleasure, anything I can do to help, and I smile and look up at him, and as I do so, I feel a shock in the air, another tiny moment of possibility like the one I felt months ago, only this time I'm fairly sure he has felt it, too. And then it passes, and I'm walking away through the long shadows on the pavement, while behind me the front door closes quietly.

One afternoon I'm waiting by the printer when Tom comes over and says if I'm at a loose end on Saturday night, he and his flatmate are having a party.

I'm half-minded to text him at the last minute saying I'm a bit under the weather, but I find I keep thinking, quite idly, about the way he dislikes Oliver so very much. And also about his eyelashes.

Midevening I catch the bus to his part of town and turn down a street with a Paddy Power on the corner, passing—as he instructed—a curry house and a minicab firm. The little front garden is choked with bindweed and shepherd's purse, and as I press the bell, I notice the terra-cotta pots that no one has bothered with for years. I am buzzed into the shared hall: a bulb on a string, dirty carpet, a bike with a flat tyre, drifts of pizza flyers, and brown envelopes addressed to tenants who moved out months ago. Sometimes it seems we all live in the same places.

When I go up to the first floor and into the flat, pushing through the knot of people in the corridor, I find Sol from work in the kitchen, talking to a man in a checked shirt who turns out to be Tom's flatmate, Hamish. I put the blue plastic carrier bag on the kitchen table and take out the bottle of red wine, and then—because Hamish's attention is already elsewhere—I look around and find the corkscrew and a clean plastic cup among the shiny pillows of corn chips on the counter. Underfoot, the lino is already sticky with beer. The music is loud.

Oh, how I hate parties. I hate standing around on the edge of things, feeling awkward and conspicuous, having to pretend that life doesn't get sweeter than this: a crowded room full of strangers, a warm drink, and a handful of processed snacks.

As I take my wine and move through Tom's flat, smiling blankly, trying hard to look as if I know where I'm heading, I find myself thinking about my mother, wondering whether this is what life feels like to her: messy, noisy, unsympathetic. A little bit frightening, I suppose.

Just finish your drink, I tell myself. *You've made the effort to come, he won't have expected that. Then you can go.* The flat comes into view, behind the people who are leaning towards each other and telling jokes and showing off, and it looks like all the others, like Naomi's flat and, I suppose, like mine, too. White walls, varnished pine floorboards, a lumpy, blue sofa. The individual touches are similarly predictable: a phrenology head on the mantelpiece; bits of taxidermy; a NOW PANIC AND FREAK OUT poster; Amis, Auster, and—I look for him, and of course I find him—a recent Kyte in between the India and Guatemala *Lonely Planet*s on the shelves.

Then Tom comes out of nowhere. "Hey, nice one!" he is saying. "You made it, then."

"Yes, hello," I say, and looking at him now—the T-shirt with the ironic slogan, the Puma trainers with dirty laces—I can't remember why I came. What was I thinking?

He's very personable, very attentive. I allow him to refill my glass, and I put it to my lips and drink it down quite quickly while he introduces me to some people, Nick and Catriona, and I hear myself asking questions and talking, about films and work and where and how I live. I sound quite unlike myself, but of course nobody here knows the difference.

I listen to Catriona making a joke about the host of a reality TV show, the line of her asymmetric bob swinging against her jaw as she turns her head to monitor our responses, and I think, *We're all pretending*. The room is full of constructs and inventions. People are experimenting, trying out lines, seeing what goes down best and takes them furthest. I watch the ways they betray themselves and their intentions, the way they draw closer to and turn away from each other. I hear the things they say and the things they leave unsaid.

A girl with a green-glass necklace is in the doorway with Hamish, and they're arguing about something, and then they're kissing. Some people start to dance, and Tom is there with them, attempting a flashy, humorous little sequence of steps—jazz hands, his tongue poking out the corner of his mouth as he concentrates— and then he looks around to see whether people are watching. Whether I'm watching.

A little later, I go into the kitchen to get my bag and find Tom and Sol slicing up giant wheels of delivery pizza, then Sol takes the stack of flat, damp boxes into the next room and I'm alone with Tom, and it's suddenly quiet, despite the noise of the music and laughter from the corridor, and he comes up close and looks at me and says, "Frances," and I know what's going to happen next, and I don't want it to, I don't want him, the thought now fills me with a kind of horror, so I wait until there's absolutely no room left for doubt and then I step back. "No, sorry, that wouldn't be a good idea," I say, raising my palms, making another barrier between us. "Really, don't take this the wrong way, but . . ."

And I leave, in quite a hurry, anxious to get out of there: away from Tom, his flat, his drunk friends.

When I see him at work the following week, we are cordial and a little bit cool with each other, and that's as far as it goes.

A month or so later, I hear he's seeing the new work-experience girl on the magazine. People giggle about it at the tea trolley. He's quite an operator, they say.

The weather holds. For weeks, it seems, I've been sleeping under just a sheet. When I wake in the morning, just before my alarm goes off, I throw the sheet down over the bottom of the mattress, so it billows and pools over the floorboards. I lie there, hands at my side, and watch the light blooming and shifting on the ceiling, pitted with the interruption of leaves.

Mary gets ratty as August approaches. Her children start ringing her up as soon as she arrives at the office, asking her where the bicycle pump is, telling her one of the dogs ran off in the park or there's no loo paper in any of the loos.

Plus Oliver has booked a fortnight off (Sardinia: he's wangled a travel freebie), then I'm away for two weeks, and somehow the pages have still got to come out.

On top of all that, Ambrose Pritchett has gone AWOL owing twelve hundred words on a controversial new biography of Sturges Hardcastle.

From my desk, I can see the little men in the crane cockpits: remote, mysterious figures alone in the moving air, high over London. The city is white-hot, hard to look at. The pale, dusty skies seem to go on for ever.

When Mary asks whether I could do a rush job reviewing the Hardcastle, I say no problem.

She glances up at me. There's something in her expression which you might almost mistake for warmth. "What would I do without you," she says breezily.

Oliver sits silent at his terminal, head down, a mime of industry. He has cut back on the stagey phone calls and now slopes off for a smoke with Sasha from Fashion only twice a day.

I often see him edging anxiously into the knots of people puzzling over the latest memo from Human Resources. These emails are extremely long and involved, banging on about synergies and platforms and tasking and traction, but no one around the tea trolley really knows what any of these words mean. No one really knows anything at all. The one certainty is that the heads of departments are going through a "consultation process" during which "the strengths and weaknesses of their teams will be assessed."

Tiny little Robin McAllfree paces his glass office like a prisoner, waving his arms and shouting at the HuRe gorillas seated around his groovy Perspex desk. We know they've only been invited up so he can put on this floor show.

"All this for us?" murmurs the comment editor, passing on his way to the printer. "What a prick."

In low voices we talk about how ridiculous it is, then we go home and eat and sleep and eat and come in again, and the days roll on. Sometimes it feels as if nothing will ever change.

One afternoon Mary drops a card on my desk. It's an invite to the launch of a poetry magazine. She can't go herself—she has promised to take Leo to the new *X-Men* movie—but some quite big names are on the board and we might get a diary story out of it. "Only if you haven't got anything else on," she says.

From time to time, I'm thrown these so-called perks, like a bear at the zoo being chucked a stale bun. I don't have high hopes for this one—there's no money in poetry, so it'll be cheap bottled beer and Costco crisps rather than rationed fizz and canapés—but it's being held in Bloomsbury in a guild with an Arts and Crafts hall, and I've always wanted to see the interior.

No one is at the door and the room is already pretty full by the time I get there, so I sidle in and wander around the edge of the space, looking at the span of the beams, the stained glass, the way the light falls on the long, waxed floorboards. The speeches are just about to begin when there's a small stir of interest around the entrance and Laurence comes in, deep in conversation with beaky Audrey Callum, one of Mary's contributors. I turn away as if to examine the list of the Fallen, not wanting him to see me here, alone; and as I do so, I notice a young woman in a blue dress, a woman with a streak of white in her dark hair. I notice her particularly because of the way she notices him.

Without dropping a beat, somehow without really disconnecting from the conversation she is having with two older men, she transfers—and it's only for a moment, a fraction of a moment—all her energy to Laurence, over there on the other side of the room. I feel her anxiety and the pitch of her anticipation. It signals itself in the way she returns to her companions, applying herself fully to their discussion, laughing and nodding and raking a hand through the tangle of black curls. The white flashes like the beam of a light-house.

I remember her brushing past me in the Kytes' hall on the day of Alys's memorial service. I remember the pale, stunned look on her face.

I stay at the back of the room during the speeches. Afterwards the party relaxes again, given a new lease of life, and Laurence is claimed by a group next to the platform. I've lost track of the young woman in the blue dress. I'm on the point of leaving when Audrey Callum recognises me and comes over to find out more about the dreadful atmosphere at the *Questioner* as it goes down the tubes. "Well, they'd be mad to get rid of you," she says. "You're an asset to that desk. I've told Mary."

Eventually I extricate myself and leave my glass on a side table, stepping out into the hot evening. In the square, the light is just going out of the trees, but the pavements are still blood-warm underfoot. The cars parked along the railings are sticky with lime pollen.

I'm walking along the square towards the bus stop when I hear a low voice in the garden, and then another. One of the voices is Laurence's. I see a flash of white through the leaves as she turns on her heel and comes out of the garden, the iron gate clanging behind her.

Mary expects gossip, so I bring it to her. Thanks to Audrey Callum I have some decent stories, though they are all unprintable.

I tell her about the air-con scion who has sunk cash into the project as a tax dodge; I pass on a rumour about the editor's proclivities.

"Anyone there?" she asks.

"Laurence Kyte. I didn't get a chance to say hello," I say. "He was talking to an interesting-looking person, a girl with black hair, with a streak of white. Rather dramatic looking. Do you know who that is?"

Mary is tapping away at her keyboard. "Julia Price," she says. "Oh, she's quite the thing, Julia Price."

At lunchtime, when all the desks around me are empty, when everyone has hurried out to the concrete plaza in front of the office to eat sandwiches on the scratchy circle of grass, I google Julia Price.

What I read makes my heart sink, just a little.

I *haven't made any definite plans for my fortnight's holiday. I'm* intending, finally, to paint the sitting-room shelves, and the general understanding seems to be that I'll visit my parents for a night or two, but otherwise my diary is clear. So I text Polly to ask whether I can come and watch Lord Strange's Men performing. According to the email she sent me a while back, they might be in Worthing next week, or Eastbourne.

She rings me on the Thursday evening when I've come in from work and says it's all off: the play was a disaster, the whole thing has been shelved. Pandora started seeing a new boyfriend who invited her to the South of France at the last minute; Ben got glandular fever; and when the rest of them looked into it, they realised that they needed "permits and stuff."

"And so Sam said it was time to rethink," says Polly. "He felt his artistic vision was being kind of compromised? It's such a shame." She doesn't sound too bothered. I imagine Sam is consoling himself with his allowance.

"Anyway," she says, "I'm in Biddenbrooke. If you're around, why don't you come down for a bit next week? There's lots of room." Over the phone I can hear the acoustics of the space around her: expansiveness, high ceilings.

Why not, I say. I'd love to.

The village is under friendly occupation when I drive through it in the late afternoon. In the lengthening blue shadows cast by the flint church and the graveyard yews, holidaymakers and second-homers picnic and throw balls on the green. Beneath the teashop parasols, most tables are busy. The women in print sundresses with oilcloth shoppers at their feet; the men in long, baggy khaki shorts with lots of pockets. Every child wears a stripy T-shirt.

The Kytes' house, Nevers, is at the far end of the village, off the Welbury Road, a couple of miles from the sea. I drive past an old, red phone box almost entirely hidden by sprays of cow parsley, and a couple of cyclists sprawled on a grassy verge, draining their water bottles, and then I turn off and follow the pebbly track down through a fenced meadow full of sheep, the sun in my eyes. An olive-green gate, propped open with a rock. Gravel skirls under the wheels.

It's a small Edwardian country house, or maybe a large villa: part brick, part flint, gabled ends, entirely unpretentious. It's not a beautiful building but it has a solidity that makes it nearly handsome.

I park the car up against the knackered-looking outhouses, next to an old Saab and a white Mini that must surely belong to Polly, and just sit there for a moment, watching the hollyhocks nodding in the breeze. It's quiet, apart from the murmur of the wood pigeons. Croquet mallets are lying on the lawn, and here and there beneath the hydrangeas I can see the red, blue, green, and yellow of the wooden balls, planets frozen in orbit.

The front door is locked and has the look of something seldom used. I don't want to ring the bell so I sling my bag over my shoulder and walk around to the side of the house, through a brick arch, and onto another lawn, which is dominated, some distance from the terrace, by the spread of a copper beech. Three empty deck chairs are set out beneath it. A litter of books and teacups and sun creams and wineglasses fills the grass.

"It's Frances, isn't it?" says a voice behind me. I turn around and see Honor stepping out of the house's dim interior, twisting the rope of her hair in front of her, so the water runs out of it and drips onto the brick. She is wearing a pink vest and a short, stripy cotton skirt, tight on the hips and then flaring out in frivolous, little pleats. "Polly said you were coming down, but she didn't say you were arriving today."

She probably doesn't mean to sound unwelcoming, I think. "Well, that was always the plan," I say, smiling. "You must be Honor. Where is she?"

"At the pool, last time I saw her," says Honor, twisting the rope again. "I came in for a shower: it's my turn to do supper. I hope there's enough for four."

As if I am at a sufficient disadvantage, she now makes a few slim concessions. She says she'd show me my room, only Polly hasn't told her where I'm going. "Do you want a swim? It's down there, through the orchard," she says, pointing. "The gate's in the wall." If I want to change, there's a cloakroom and lots of spare swimming towels in the cupboard.

I follow her indoors, through a long, cool sitting room: a piano, books, copper bowls of alabaster eggs, a pair of sofas—their cushions dented with evidence of leisure—facing each other in front of a generous fireplace over which hangs an abstract oil in ochre and black. The cloakroom is off the hall, full of bootjacks and waxed coats with corduroy collars. When I've changed into my swimming costume and folded up my clothes and shoved them in my bag, Honor is nowhere to be seen, so I wrap the towel around my waist and retrace my steps into the slanting golden sunshine, then pick my way barefoot down the lawn.

Edged with smooth curves of silver foliage spiked with foamy flurries of white, the lawn gives way to the longer grass and lusher shade of the orchard: the apple trees, which Malcolm Azaria mentioned at the memorial service. They're venerable, stooping trees, probably older than the house.

A brick wall runs along the edge of the orchard, radiating the stored heat of the day, and in the middle of it, between two espaliered pears, there's a gate. I unlatch it.

No one is in the pool or around it. The sunloungers with their bold print cushions are empty. An orange towel lies in a tangle over the flagstones, which are splashed with water around the shallow end, proof that someone has emerged from it fairly recently; but the footprints lead into a bright patch of sunshine and vanish.

The rectangle of water stretches ahead of me, a calm, holy blue snagged with the smallest circle of wrinkles where an insect is floundering. I drop my towel over a chair and stand at the edge with the sun on my back, watching my shadow flying over the pale mosaic, the random neon geometry of sunlight far below. Then I take a breath and dive in.

It's cold, very cold, and the shock forces me to the surface, but already I'm becoming accustomed to it, and I start to swim, fiercely at first. I do a few fast lengths of crawl, pushing hard through the water, feeling my chest starting to tighten, then I slacken the pace and turn on my back and float, enjoying the cool suck and slide of the water as the activity leaves it.

At the edge of my vision I see the gate opening, and I flip over and swim to the side. Polly and Teddy are standing there in shorts and tennis shoes, looking down at me. Both of them seem slightly taken aback.

"Hello," I say, resting my arms on the edge of the pool. "I've been looking for you. Honor said you were having a swim, and when I got here—well, it just looked too good to resist."

"We were having a quick knockabout next door," says Polly. "We heard the splash and wondered who it was. Is it Monday already? Christ. I've totally lost track." She says they usually play at this time of day, when the sun goes off the court.

While she talks, Teddy patrols the perimeter of the pool, dragging the skimmer through the water. From the way he avoids my eye and doesn't address me directly, I am made aware that he's displeased to find me here; and not simply because I've caught him off guard.

I get the feeling that he would quite like to fish me out, too, along with the flies and leaves.

He has something on me, perhaps. I wonder what it is.

He keeps his gaze fixed on the task, ignoring me, and when he has finished, he slides the skimmer back behind the poolhouse, pulls off his T-shirt and shoes, and dives in: tidy, exact, not much of a splash. He comes to the surface with a gasp, throwing his head back so the pool is briefly marked with a flurry of tiny droplets, then he rotates in the water and says to me, quite coolly, "So, how's tricks?"

I don't enjoy this sort of question. Too open-ended. It could go anywhere. So I say work's grim at the moment. "It's a bit like 'Oranges and Lemons.' *Here comes a candle to light you to bed, and here comes a chopper to chop off your head.* There's no way of knowing if you're going to get a candle or the axe."

He smiles politely.

Polly is tugging off her T-shirt and shorts, revealing an even

tan and a faded red bikini. Cautiously she starts to inch down the
rickety metal ladder, making little showy screams about the temperature. Finally she pushes off, her breath coming in snatches. We
bob around in the water for a while, and once she has got used to
the temperature, Polly tells me about the neighbours, Colonel and
Mrs. Williams, who let them use the court whenever they want.
"We could play tomorrow," suggests Teddy. "Doubles, if you play,
Frances?"

"Oh, sorry," I say. "I'll play chess, if you like. That's the only
game I'm any good at. I'm useless at tennis, I'm afraid."

"Shame," says Teddy. But I don't get the feeling he minds all
that much.

Polly shows me to my bedroom. It's smallish, on the first floor over the
front porch, with a view of the croquet lawn and the sheep
field. Rather to my surprise, the double bed is a tangle of linen. A
pillow is on the floor. The cupboard is open, yawning hangers.

"Oh, shit, I forgot," says Polly from the doorway, as I put my
bag down, noting as I do so the apple cores and cotton-wool balls
blackened with kohl lying in the bin. "Jacob and Marie-Élise were
here at the weekend, and Mrs. Talbot doesn't come in until tomorrow. Just grab some clean sheets and pillowcases from the airing
cupboard." She wanders away in search of a drink, her plimsolls
sounding softly on the stair carpet and then, more distant but precisely, on the parquet in the hall below.

I put a copy of the *Spectator* in the bin and drag the sheets
from the bed, revealing an unpleasant wad of dried-up tissues
under one pillow, and then I set off to find the airing cupboard.
Polly hasn't told me where it is, so I use this as an excuse to glance
into all the rooms opening off the landing. Polly's room is under

one of the gables: it's papered with a rosebud print marked with dark Blu-Tack stains where her posters once hung. A doll's house is on the floor next to her suitcase, which has yet to be properly unpacked. Clothes and cosmetics spill out of it and drift across the floor. Designer deodorant. A tiny, little black bra. A pair of jeans, tugged inside out like a snakeskin.

There are two other unoccupied guest bedrooms: a cramped boxroom single with sailing boats on the blind, suitable for a child, and a large double with an unwrinkled linen coverlet and a view over the orchard towards the sea, a low blue haze on the horizon.

Teddy and Honor have chosen to stay in what is clearly his boyhood bedroom: they've dragged the mattresses off the twin beds and pushed them together on the carpet. Possibly they are amused by the nostalgic thrill of having sex in there, with the matchstick galleon on the dresser and the bookshelves full of *Asterix* and old *Beano* annuals.

Through the open window, I can hear Polly and Teddy talking on the terrace beneath, the clink of a glass or a bottle being put down on a hard surface, and then I smell cigarette smoke.

"She didn't realise it was anything special," Teddy is saying defensively. "She didn't do it on purpose."

"Okay, but she might have thought," Polly says. "I mean, you'd never know she was the guest here, would you? Sheesh."

The last room is Laurence and Alys's. I glance over the bannisters before I go in, listening for Honor, and when I hear the sound of running water from the kitchen, I know I'm safe and I place my hand on the doorknob, carved with a spiral to resemble a beehive.

Clearly he hasn't been down to the house for some time. The curtains are partly drawn to keep out the sun. The housekeeper has pulled the blue-and-white cover tightly over the high bank of pillows and left a satin-edged blanket neatly folded at the foot of the bed. I go around the room in the half-light, examining things: the gooseneck lamps on the bedside tables, both angled for reading; the inlaid box on the dresser, its worn velvet trays full of a mess of cuff links and kirby grips and buttons and an old silver thimble; the wedding photograph—outfits, confetti, the kiss on the step—in the mother-of-pearl frame; the curling snaps of Polly and Teddy stuck in around the edge of the looking glass. I open the wardrobe, and it's full of clothes, his on one side, hers on the other. Handfuls of sundresses in primary colours, guernseys, thick walking socks, polo shirts, white shorts for tennis.

A bottle of French scent is on the dresser, just a faint film of yellowish liquid left inside, and I take off the lid and sniff it, and then I spray a little into the air in front of me. It's a clean, fresh smell, a morning smell, energetic, lively. Not what I was expecting. I put the bottle back, beside its matching jar of body cream. A birthday present, I think. Alys wouldn't have bothered to buy a set herself.

In the bathroom, I pick out some linen and a bath towel, then I make up my bed and empty the bin into the carrier bag in which I packed my shoes, and I go downstairs, my arms full of Marie-Élise's detritus. I ask Honor, who is laboriously grating cheese, whether she wants any help with supper, and in a long-suffering sort of voice she says no, she's fine; so, when I've put the rubbish in the kitchen bin and left the laundry in a basket in the utility room, I head out to find the others on the terrace. I'm walking through the sitting room when I hear their voices. They're bickering over whose turn it is to do the next supermarket shop.

"But that's not fair, I did the last one," Polly is complaining.

"Yes, but Jacob and Marie-Élise are your friends—and so," says Teddy, lowering his voice significantly, "is Thingy. What on earth is she doing here, anyway? Even by your standards, Pol, she seems a bit random."

I pause for a moment in the shadows, absently picking up one of the alabaster eggs—cool and heavy in my hand—as I listen to his snicker of amusement, waiting for the inevitable betrayal.

But to my surprise, it doesn't come. "Oh, she's all right," Polly is saying, resisting the temptation to turn me into a joke. "I feel a bit sorry for her, I suppose."

"Well, exactly," says Teddy, and I can hear him stretching and starting to yawn.

"Look, Frances has been through something horrible, too, you know. And she has been kind to us. She didn't have to meet us, did she? And she has really been there for me the last few months.

"Anyway, she's good at fitting in," adds Polly crossly, in summary. "She's easy to have around. Whereas Honor . . ."

Ridiculously, my heart leaps as I listen to Polly's speech, though I know I've become a cheap shot, just another instalment in an ancient sibling argument. Her defence of me is certainly not proof of any real sort of loyalty.

Still, despite everything, I can't help finding her reaction endearing; touching, almost.

"Whereas Honor," Polly is saying, ". . . with her soya milk and organic shampoo and Peace Oils . . . Surely she must be running out of Peace Oil by now?" When Teddy starts to speak, she says, "It's definitely your turn. There are two of you. I don't see why I should have to do another."

"I think you're being very unfair. After all, it's not as if Honor actually *eats* anything," says Teddy, and they both laugh. Carefully, I put the egg back in the copper bowl and go out to join them.

I t is a rather bad supper. Green salad, inexpertly drained; a vegetable lasagne with large, hard coins of carrot and lumpy béchamel.

We sit at the kitchen table, surrounded by all of Honor's mess: mustard jars with the lids off, spoons in puddles of tomato juice, a packet of flour standing in its dusty white shadow.

"Is it okay?" she keeps asking, but I don't think she really cares too much either way.

She works for a TV production company. She's the baby of the family: the youngest of three, by quite a long way. Her father, it transpires, is an old friend of Laurence's, a Labour peer, an expert on industrial relations. Her mother is an interior designer. It slowly dawns on me that I've heard of her pioneering work with taupe.

"They must all be chuffed about you two getting together," I say, and Honor rests one elbow on the table, propping her chin on her knuckles, smiling complacently at Teddy while he says his father's response was *Oh, thank God. At last.*

But as the evening progresses, I start to wonder about Honor. She's rather distant with Polly, and sometimes when Teddy is talking about work—sinking all his energies into taking off an oligarch's girlfriend, or a superhumourless German video artist—I notice her attention slipping away from him, drawn to the window, or the pattern on a tea towel, or the patch of dry skin on her heel.

Hmm, I think, watching her fiddling with the candle in the silver candlestick, picking at the molten wax so it spills and hardens on the table. *You're getting bored, aren't you? And you can't quite bring yourself to admit it yet.*

I offer to do the washing up, and after Polly has been outside to have a cigarette, she brings her wineglass back to the kitchen and sits on the counter, swinging her smooth, brown legs and idly drying the same saucepan over and over. She has been staying at Nevers for the last fortnight: groups of friends have filtered down from London, though not Sam, with whom she is now on "non-speakers."

Her brother and Honor arrived last Wednesday. "And," adds Polly furtively, "she's driving me crazy. She keeps grumbling about staying in Teddy's old room—I think she'd like to move into Mum and Dad's, can you believe it? And don't start me on the topless sunbathing." She mimes sticking her fingers down her throat. "It's good you've come. I'd had it up to here with the pair of them."

"Poor old Polly," I say, grabbing the flour from the kitchen table and looking at her for directions. "You're having a rough time of it at the moment, aren't you?"

Polly puts her head in her hands. "Oh, I know you didn't mean it like that," she says, lifting her face and seeing my expression. "But I just have this constant sense that something, some*one*, is missing. I think about her—my mother—all the time. High summer when the garden was in its prime—or just on the turn, just beginning to fade so she could finally relax . . . well, it was her favourite time of year, really." Briefly she presses the heels of her hands over her eyes. Then she notices the packet of flour I'm holding. "Ummm, I think it goes in there."

I open the cupboard, which is full of serving dishes and cast-iron casseroles.

"Or maybe not. Try that one," she suggests, starting to giggle. The moment passes.

N*o one has asked me how long I'm planning to stay.*
I've taken possession of this room. My clothes are lying in modest piles in the chest of drawers, on top of crackly sheets of ancient wrapping paper; or hanging in the wardrobe, suspended between cedar balls and lavender bags from which all scent has long since departed. I know the names of the books—their old

covers bleached to palest greens or pinks by the endless cycle of summers—lined up on the shelf. I know that in the morning the sun lies across the bed in a big gold slice. I know there's a chip in the Blue Italian ewer that stands in its matching basin upon the windowsill, and if you angle it just so, no one would ever notice.

In the mornings I lie in bed and listen to the quietness outside: birdsong, wind easing through long grass.

I'm always the first to get up. I like the sensation of being alone downstairs, wandering through empty rooms while everyone else sleeps on. In the mornings I pass through the house and make it mine, pulling curtains, straightening cushions, collecting glasses, unlocking the doors onto the terrace and stepping outside with a mug of tea.

At this time of day, the house and the gardens are full of ghosts. The vanished children make themselves known indirectly: the torn shrimping nets at the back of the cloakroom cupboards, the lost planks in the abandoned treehouse, the scoured-out paint-boxes and brushes dried into hard little commas that I find in the cavity beneath the kitchen bench seat.

Alys is everywhere, too. At the back of drawers, under the stairs, in the greenhouse when I'm picking her tomatoes and inhaling their sharp sour scent. She's there as the Japanese anemones appear among the asters.

I'm browsing through her collection of cookbooks when I notice a tatty folder shrugged in at the end of the shelf. When I flick through it, the handwriting is dashing but not always terribly clear, and on the back of a recipe for almond biscuits I find a sketch of a sleeping child. Polly. Just a few economical lines of Biro, but it's absolutely her: the eyelashes resting on the curve of the cheek, a strand of hair falling across the mouth.

I think of Alys whenever I help myself to the hand cream which she kept in a bottle by the kitchen sink.

Some mornings, everything I look at seems to refer backwards, to the past, to her.

I spend some time going through the photograph albums, which are kept behind the piano. The story is incomplete—I imagine the rest of the archive is stored in London—but the plot is clear enough. Laurence and Alys sitting at tin café tables or goofing around Roman ruins or walking along coastal paths; with a newborn over a shoulder and shell-shocked, wondering expressions; with another newborn and a little blond boy, looking as if they know what they're in for with this one. There are shots of Laurence creased up with laughter or caught mid-anecdote, his hands blurring in front of him as he gesticulates. Looking at Alys's pictures of her husband, I see how old he has become.

The snaps of Alys peter out around now. It's mostly Teddy and Polly from here on—paddling, learning to ride bikes, ice-skating at the Rockefeller Center, on the front step in school uniform, dressed up in Hallowe'en outfits. Now and again Laurence edges into focus, supervising an Easter-egg hunt or having his legs buried in sand on a beach somewhere. Alys, who has stepped behind the camera, becomes more or less invisible.

I put the albums back on the shelf, ensuring they are arranged in the correct order.

One morning I find myself walking on the dewy lawn wrapped in a thin, grey shawl which I pulled off a hook in the hall without thinking about it. It's hers, of course; it belongs—belonged—to Alys. I glance anxiously back at the house, apprehensive about being caught. But no faces are at the windows. No one is watching me wearing her shawl, stepping where she stepped.

I try not to show Teddy and Honor that their company makes me uneasy, and I think I'm managing it pretty well. Neither of them takes much notice of me, in any case. Teddy is interested only in Honor, and Honor is interested mainly in herself. I hear them talking in other rooms or out on the terrace or under the copper beech, about people they know and places they have been to, but if I join them, their conversation often dwindles away or abruptly changes direction, as if I'm not entirely fit for it. When I speak, I feel their attention drifting elsewhere, not quite held by my delivery, and once or twice—when he yawns or wanders off—I find myself wondering whether Teddy might be making a point; but I tell myself I'm probably imagining it. Why would he bother to dislike me? I doubt he has the energy.

In general, I'm content for them to think I'm dull. It's safer that way.

If Polly is hot, Teddy is cool; watchful where she wants to be watched; guarded where she is exposed; assessing where she is all impulse. He talks knowledgeably about collectors and collections, about New York and Berlin, and his gossip is adept, circumspect, never spiteful. Money impresses him, I hear that in what he says, but otherwise he's good at disguising his weaknesses.

And then there are moments when he forgets himself and all his precious dignity.

When Polly cuts her foot on a piece of glass—a beer bottle which she dropped on the terrace and failed to clear up properly—he goes pale at the sight of all the blood. But while she panics, he fetches a clean tea towel and binds it around her foot to staunch the flow and somehow tricks her into telling me the story of how as a child she once crept up behind Sidney Poitier and, wanting to know what it would feel like, surreptitiously put out a hand to touch his hair. By the time the story is over she is laughing and the blood, forgotten, has clotted.

One evening, quite out of the blue, he starts to talk over dinner about Alys and how last summer she lost track of who was coming to stay when, so that the Crewes turned up just as Clive Dawson and his boyfriend were unloading their car, and how Laurence had come into the kitchen and leaned against the door, biting his knuckles and saying it was an absolute fucking disaster, they'd be throwing punches by six o'clock, and Alys had said rubbish and sent him back out with a jug of Bloody Marys, and within an hour or two both parties were all over each other, sharing gossip about advances and flinging around invites to the Lot willy-nilly. Halfway through the story I see his eyes are shining bright and I think he's about to lose control, it's about to overwhelm him; but he keeps going and the tears retreat. I'm not sure whether anyone else notices.

But for the most part, Teddy and Honor are one unit, and Polly and I are another. Polly shrinks away from Honor and cleaves to me. She's restless, self-absorbed, tiring, sometimes amusing, constantly needing an audience, as children do. As long as you pay her attention, I find, she's happy enough. She makes few demands otherwise. She doesn't want wit or insight or affinity or a glimpse of a different sort of life, the sort of thing that most friendships are built on; she just wants company, the reassurance of being looked at, the consolation of not being alone.

I adjust quickly to the rhythm of the days—the short, cool mornings, the scorched afternoons, the drawn-out evenings—and as they pass, I almost forget myself. I begin to feel as if I really am on holiday here, as if relaxation is appropriate rather than dangerous. I've never volunteered any information to any of the Kytes, but a few evenings after I arrive, I nearly make a mistake.

We'd just come back from an afternoon at Welbury. The beach was fairly crowded, but we'd walked to the far end of the shingle and set up camp against a groyne. The sky was full of seagulls and diamond kites: someone was selling them on the common. Along the curve of the shore, the distant dome of the power station's reactor gleamed like an ornament.

We all swam, wading out over the sharp points of the shingle, enduring the waves; and then, once clear of them, floating off out into the chilly, grey swell, the endless rise and fall of the sea.

When we came back to Nevers, I switched the kettle on to make a pot of tea, but before it had time to boil, Polly opened a bottle of wine and rolled a spliff. We forgot to eat.

Later, someone put on Lou Reed and I lay on the grass watching the light fading out of the copper beech while Polly danced on the terrace singing along to "Satellite of Love."

Dusk fell. The moon rose. Honor picked her way around the lawn and orchard, putting out brown paper bags weighted with handfuls of gravel, then dropping in tealights. As the house sank into darkness behind us, the orange glow from these little, winking beacons seemed to stretch on, intermittently, for ever. It seemed like the prettiest thing I'd ever seen.

My heart felt full of it, full of the sun, of the moon, of the garden, of these hopelessly spoilt creatures who asked so few questions of me and, as a consequence, were such easy company. I lay back and stared at the stars coming out. Then I twisted my head sideways and looked over at Polly, lying a little distance away with her legs crossed at the ankle, an unlit cigarette stuck to her lip.

"Pol," I said. "It's lovely to be here. With you, I mean. It means a lot."

"Mmm," said Polly, not very concerned.

I rolled over onto my elbows and watched her profile in the darkness: the tangle of hair, the straight nose, the definite sort of chin. I wanted to ask her a question about Laurence, and then maybe another one about Julia Price, and I was just about to put it into words when suddenly I saw what I was about to do, how close I was to showing my hand.

From that moment on I am careful not to forget myself. I keep an eye on what I'm drinking, and I don't smoke anything, and I make sure that the questions I ask are the usual ones. Shall I cook tonight? How much do I owe you for that? Red or white?

Don't mistake them for your friends, I tell myself, again and again. *Watch them. Watch yourself.*

Watch yourself, I tell myself, as I wander through Alys's garden, cutting roses for the bowl vases in the sitting room; *Watch yourself,* I tell myself, as I lie by the pool, my face tilted to the sun. *Stay on your guard.*

For three, four, five days, it's just our little group, and although I'm still conscious from time to time that Polly finds Honor hard work and that Honor is less keen on Teddy than he is on her, it's still a lazy, peaceful sort of coexistence. We wake late and go to bed late. We make sorties to the beach, the off-licence, the local farm shop, but otherwise stay close to the house. Mrs. Talbot comes quietly and tidies up after us.

Then on Friday evening, or maybe it's Saturday, the phone rings in the hall. No one ever rings the landline. Polly looks at Teddy and they both say together, "Dad."

"You get it," says Polly, but Teddy is playing Racing Demon with Honor and won't put down his cards.

When Polly comes back, she says, "He's coming down tomorrow. He says he can't work in London, it's too hot. He promises to keep out of our way."

"Is he writing again?" Honor asks. It's the first time I've heard her express curiosity about anyone else. "I didn't know he was writing."

"I guess he must be," says Polly. Then she goes off to put the garlic bread in the oven.

Laurence arrives the next day, in the late afternoon. I'm lying on my bed reading when I hear wheels on the gravel. I edge myself over the bed and peer through the window as he parks the Volvo next to my Fiat. Then he gets out and opens the boot and reaches in for his bags. One's a slim briefcase, a laptop probably. The other is a small canvas holdall, just big enough for a washbag and a few shirts. I remember the wardrobe in his room: of course, he doesn't need to bring much down, it's all here waiting for him.

He stands there on the gravel, stretching, looking around. I can see him feeling the sun on his face.

The others have gone next door to use Colonel Williams's tennis court. I'm alone in the house. As I hear him shutting the boot and moving off towards the brick arch, I slide off the bed and go to the mirror hanging over the chest of drawers, running a hand through my hair so it doesn't look too tidy. These last days of sun and sea salt and chlorine have shot it through with a few colourful streaks and my skin is flushed, sprinkled with freckles. My eyes look bright. I smile at myself experimentally. Then I wait, standing by my bedroom door, listening to his footsteps on the parquet, his preoccupied whistle.

"Oh, goodness, Laurence, it's you," I say as he walks into the hall. I've come out of my room and I'm leaning over the balustrade on the landing. He spins around, looks up at me, smiling. I place my hand flat above my heart, expressing relief.

"Hello," he says. "Did I frighten you? Did Polly forget to tell you I was coming?"

"No, she told us, I just forgot," I say.

He's coming up the stairs towards me now, step by step, still smiling; as if I'm the new arrival, rather than it being the other way around. The cool, airy expanse of the hall starts to reduce in scale as he approaches. I feel the walls sliding a little closer, the ceiling lowering, so we're enclosed in a more intimate, almost secret space. As he comes onto the landing, the air between us starts to shimmer faintly. I wonder whether he's experiencing this, too.

"They're all next door, playing tennis," I say. "Shall I go and fetch them?"

"Oh, no, let them play." Laurence stands in front of me, then puts down his bags. We kiss, formally. "You've caught the sun," he says.

"We've been so lucky with the weather." *Yes*, I think. *He does feel it. He's just starting to feel it.*

"You have family around here, don't you?" he says. "I suppose you must know Biddenbrooke quite well."

He picks up his bags and carries them into his room, looks out at the view. I follow him but halt in the doorway. Mrs. Talbot has removed the coverlet and set a small bowl of roses on the dressing table. "Would you like some tea?" I say, and he says he would, he'll be down in a minute.

In the kitchen I make a pot and put some almond biscuits on a plate, and then I carry the tray out to the terrace. Far away, drifting on the breeze, I can hear the *pock-pock* of the tennis game, the occasional shout of irritation. Then the wind changes direction and I can hear nothing but wood pigeons.

"I wanted to congratulate you on your plan," Laurence says, coming out of the house behind me.

I look at him. For one vertiginous moment, I'm not sure what he's talking about.

"Your plan. About Polly and the course," he says kindly. "The idea of the sabbatical."

"Oh, yes," I say. All that seems far away. We haven't talked about real life for the last few days. I meant to ask Polly lots of questions about her future, but somehow once I'd arrived at

Biddenbrooke the time never seemed quite right. And, just as important, I didn't want to bore her.

"She probably told you," he says. "About Mr. Bamber. He was very understanding, actually, when I spoke to him. And now that Sam's production has fallen apart, I rather suspect she'll be rejoining the course in the autumn. Not such a disaster after all."

"I hope you're right," I say doubtfully, because somehow I don't share his confidence.

He tilts his head. "You think she won't go back?"

"I'm not sure," I say.

He puts down his tea, reaches for a biscuit, and crunches it, staring out at the copper beech. "Oh, I thought we were over the worst," he says wearily. "I don't think I can cope with another of Polly's little . . . indecisions. Although of course *indecisions* is entirely the wrong word. The whole problem is her cast-iron will. And whatever I say seems to make her dig in just a bit deeper."

There's silence for a moment. The trees move almost imperceptibly. The sky is covered with tiny, distant herringbone clouds, so gauzy they're barely there.

"Could I enlist your support?" Laurence asks. "She does seem to listen to you. You have a knack. . . . Of course, I don't want to put you in a difficult position, but—"

"I could try," I say, and then there's the sound of a gate opening, and the other three come across the orchard, whey-faced and damp from the exercise, shouting out greetings when they see him.

"The Jacksons have a place off the coast in Maine," Honor is saying, "and of course it's better than staying in New York in August when it's so hot and no one's there—but they will keep ringing up and telling us to pack evening dresses and ties. The country club! Imagine it. I wish I hadn't agreed to go."

We are all sitting around the table on the terrace, but she's really only talking to Laurence. As she leans forward to take another of Polly's cigarettes (I note that Polly no longer feels the need to hide the habit from her father; perhaps it was Alys who always objected most forcefully), the little silver *H* and the tiny horseshoe strung on a chain around her neck spin and sparkle over her breastbone. She has been showing off all evening, parading her worldliness, her sophistication, in a manner that highlights the naivety just a scratch beneath it.

In a strange way, I find this display—the animation, the widened eyes, the fingers at her throat and lips—quite touching. It makes me feel rather differently about Honor. I'm always affected when I see people unable to gauge a situation. Occasionally I feel pity for them, more usually contempt; often I'm amused; but just sometimes, and this is one of those moments, I find their obtuseness almost endearing. I can't imagine how luxurious it feels, that sort of blithe unthinkingness.

Polly has the same adolescent quality, but I sense she'll grow out of it one day. With Honor, the way she looks and the way she has been brought up have fixed her like this. I doubt she'll ever change.

The moon sails up over the copper beech, bringing with it a soft aura of lighter, purer blue. As I put a strawberry in my mouth, I smell the taint of silver polish on my fingers. The air is so still that I've carried out the big candelabra from the dining room. The flames are burning as steadily as gas jets.

Teddy bends over to fill Honor's glass. "Let's face it, you were at a loose end, and then your parents said they'd stump up for a first-class ticket," he says. His voice has an edge, faint but distinct. I can tell he has only the vaguest sense of what's going on, but it's enough to make him bridle.

"You'll miss me, though, won't you?" she says, putting her hand on his forearm, reeling him in again. Then she leans back in her chair and stretches out her legs. I imagine she's looking at her toenails. She painted them this morning by the pool, first removing the old gold varnish with little, damp clots of cotton wool that smelt of pear drops, then stroking on the new colour—a hot, glossy pink—with absolute concentration, her knee beneath her chin.

Teddy is turning to his father. "So you're writing?" he asks. "Polly said you mentioned something about writing."

"It's early days." To me, to be polite, Laurence says, "It all . . . just stopped for a while."

"He couldn't see the point after Mum died," says Polly loyally. "That's right, isn't it?"

"Writing suddenly felt like a silly way to pass the time," he agrees lightly. "Sitting alone in a room, inventing things."

We wait.

"I lost faith in myself, I suppose," he goes on, almost as if he were talking to himself, trying out the words, seeing how they sound. "And I had no ideas. Life lost its texture. But maybe that has started to change. We'll see."

I get the feeling he wants to move the conversation on. Probably he feels superstitious about this new project. "Charlotte's on my back about it," he says to his children. "She might come down for a visit."

Later, when Honor, Teddy, and Polly have gone off for a swim in the dark, I'm left alone at the table with him. Because of the heat in the air, the candles were soft to the touch when I picked them out of the box at the start of the evening, and they've burned down fast. Now, as the wicks begin to dip, they sputter and hiss. One by one the flames are going out.

I start to stack the plates and bowls, but then Laurence says,

"Are they all right, do you think? Do you think they're doing okay?"

"You're worried about them," I say, halting, gradually easing back into my chair, sensing he needs something: a confessor, maybe.

He shrugs. "Of course," he says, a little exasperated.

I realise he wants some reassurance, not an opportunity to open up. So I say, "I don't really know about Teddy, but I think Polly's coming to terms with it."

"She has been very angry with me about something," he says. "I'm not sure what."

I remember the night when she turned up at my flat, the things she told me.

"She was always a funny little girl," he's saying wistfully. "She lived so much in the present, as most children do, it was amazing to watch. Teddy was always more careful somehow, more systematic, even when he was small. He trusted less to chance. But Pol—well, she never made plans. Things just happened to her. Good things, mostly. But now, this." He pours some water, drinks it.

"It's innocence, I suppose," he says eventually. "I hate the idea of her losing it." The words carry over the dark lawn. A sheen of moonlight is on the grass, a silver glitter in the leaves.

I want to say: that sort of innocence in an adult is a form of stupidity, really. It's proof of corruption: too much privilege and indulgence. But I don't say that, of course. I sit there beside him in the airless garden as the darkness envelops us, waiting for the last candle to go out.

It turns out Laurence is quite right: *Polly has indeed had a change of heart and now says she is really looking forward to going back to college in the autumn.*

"I'm going to knuckle down. No, I mean it," she says when I ask her about it. "Just going through that whole thing with Sam made me see what a waster he was, and how easy it is to fall for all that bullshit." She has ordered half of next year's reading list from Amazon and is "loving Euripides," she tells me (although the only thing I see her studying is a *Grazia* she picked up at the petrol station).

I pass this information on to Laurence as we stand together under the apple trees. I'm careful about how I phrase it. "I really think she talked herself around," I say modestly. "I can't take the credit for this."

I'd volunteered to make an apple tart for Charlotte, who is due to arrive any moment, and I was out in the orchard when Laurence came back from the pool, a towel slung over his shoulder, and offered to help. He's picking, being the right height, and I'm carrying the basket. "Watch out," he says as I step backwards. "Look, just there." The grass is treacherous with windfalls and wasps.

He squints up, reaches through the leaves. The tree flinches a little as he twists off the fruit.

"Well, whoever's responsible, I'm relieved," he says, inspecting the apple for flaws, polishing it against his sleeve, and putting it in the basket. "It's really quite a weight off my mind."

Not for the first time, I wonder at his ability to leave other people to sort out his family business. But then it's becoming increasingly clear that Alys always shielded him from this sort of thing: the tantrums, the sudden enthusiasms that petered out just as quickly, the running hot and cold. I'm only now sensing the extent of his emotional laziness. Of course he knows this stuff matters—after all, he engages with it endlessly in his books—and yet he's more than happy to let someone else deal with its petty and frequently tedious real-life intricacies.

We head indoors. He goes off to his study, I go to the kitchen. I cut cold butter into cubes and rub it into a basinful of flour with just a little bit of sugar. I try to keep my hands light, cool, full of air, and as I work the feel of the flour changes as it gains weight and texture. I stir in an egg yolk and some dribbles of cold water, and then I leave the ball of pastry in the fridge to chill.

The rinsed apples stand on the marble-topped table, drying on a striped tea towel.

Alone in the kitchen on this bright, quiet morning, I allow myself to imagine that it's mine. The china coffee-grinder bolted to the pantry wall, the deep cupboards piled with cake tins and glass jelly moulds, the snagging drawers full of old implements suggesting a more leisurely and satisfactory life: nutcrackers, cherrystoners, sugar tongs, grape scissors. The view of the herb garden, the pots of geraniums that Mr. Talbot waters during his gardening visits, the moss-speckled sundial near the tall hedge where Alys took Laurence's picture.

Just for a moment, as I stand by the sink peeling a long rosy spiral from the yellow flesh of an apple, I think about all of this and what it means to me.

Charlotte Black *arrives late morning with Selma Carmichael in tow.* They're expected at Bunny Nesbitt's house in Allwick, a little farther down the coast, but not until the following day. Bunny's house parties are famous: Charlotte never passes up on an invitation. "Wait till she hears you're around," she says to Laurence. "You won't get out alive."

Laurence tells us a story from a few summers ago involving a fashionable American writer, a bottle of Ricard, and the coastguard. Selma Carmichael's eyes are out on stalks.

I've seen Selma before, of course, but have never spoken to her.

"You're *that* Frances Thorpe, aren't you?" she says, when we are introduced. "Of course, I know your byline. I've started to look out for it, actually."

I can't help myself, I feel myself flushing with pleasure when she says this—though of course it's the sort of thing people tend to say in these circles, whether they mean it or not.

"How are things at the office?" she asks. "Don't tell me—ghastly, I imagine. We've just been through the same ordeal. Terrible for morale, isn't it?" Selma is literary editor at a rival paper, one with a rather richer proprietor. She's tall, bony, midfifties, full of a tremulous nervous energy. "Is it true what they're saying about Robin McAllfree and Gemma Coke?"

I give her a coolly apologetic smile and say I don't know, I really have no idea, and she lets the matter rest there.

To my secret amusement, she is allocated the tiny boxroom with the sailing boats on the blind. I picture her bending her long, thin limbs and lowering herself onto the bed, and the image that comes to mind is of an umbrella being folded up.

Charlotte gets the large double farther down the landing, the one with the sea view.

At lunchtime we drive to Welbury and buy fish and chips from the tar-painted shack a little way down the estuary. We eat them sitting along the jetty, dangling our legs, watching birds fastidiously picking their way over the shiny expanses of mud. Their boats confined to a narrow channel of water, people are swabbing decks and furling ropes and drinking tea while they wait for the tide to turn. The rigging chimes irregularly.

It's slightly overcast now: it's still warm, but the sky is that in-between shade of grey that could go either way.

After we've eaten, we walk around the headland to the beach. Teddy and Honor lag behind, and the sound of their argument rises up over the bickering of seagulls. Honor wants to go back to London, I gather, and Teddy wants her to stay.

"You're not flying until next week," I hear him say.

"But I've got a lot to sort out," she says. "And there's Jack's party."

"Oh, well, if *Jack's* having a party," he begins scornfully, but I can hear the anxiety in his voice. It's an undignified exchange. I feel almost sorry for him. *You won't hold on to her that way,* I think. *Have some self-respect.* But Teddy, usually so self-possessed, so composed, still has this lesson to learn.

Charlotte Black drops back to join me. She's one of those rare women who looks as pulled together off duty as she does in more formal circumstances. I have to admire her slim-fitting, dark cotton dress and flat, plain sandals and the few adroit bits of silver. "Are you having a good holiday?" she asks as we pause to let two teenagers drag a dinghy over the road, up towards a boatshed.

"Oh, yes. I didn't really have any plans, and then Polly asked me down, and I've never quite got around to leaving," I say, with a laugh.

"Yes, it seems you've really become part of the family." Something in her voice reminds me, as if I needed reminding, that I shouldn't underestimate Charlotte Black. "What an unusual way to get to know the Kytes."

"Oh. I suppose that's one way of looking at it," I say, letting the smile fade from my face. I think it's probably time to make Charlotte Black see she needs to take more care when speaking to me. I would like her to realise I'm offended by her remark; that I find it distasteful. "Naturally I wish it hadn't happened like this. It's an appalling thing they've all been through."

"Oh, that goes without saying," she says quickly. "God knows, it must have been dreadful for you, too. I can't imagine what an experience like that does to a person." We walk on for a bit without saying anything. At this point the harbour road turns hard left towards the town, running parallel to the beach, but we make our way off the tarmac and onto the boardwalk that leads down through the dunes towards the sea.

"I hear you've been a real friend to Polly," she says, and her tone is softer now, as if she has reassessed me, come to a slightly different opinion. "Laurence has told me how good you are with her."

"Really, it's not a matter of being *good*," I say, looking ahead at Polly, who is walking with her arm through her father's, Selma on his other side. "I'm very fond of her. Of course, I was nothing like her really, but somehow she reminds me of myself at that age." This is, of course, a lie; but I know it's also a fairly persuasive argument. It'll take me far. Even Polly might buy it, if she ever thought to query our relationship.

"All that hope, all that energy," I go on, warming to my theme. "You know, 'the unfailing sense of being young' . . . Of course, it's early days, but if I've been any sort of support to her . . . if I've helped her, in even the smallest way, during the last six months, well—that's good enough for me."

"Perhaps you've helped each other," she suggests as we step off the boardwalk onto the sand. The path, rutted with footprints, weaves between the dunes and around dry tangles of marram grass. I kick off my flip-flops, but even so it's a struggle. Whenever I walk along a beach, I'm taken back to those recurring childhood nightmares: the sand holding me back, spilling and drifting beneath my weight and making a mockery of my efforts, while all the time something nameless and intent approaches steadily from behind.

"Kate Wiggins, the police officer who arranged the first meeting between me and Laurence and Polly and Teddy, that time when you were there—she told me that witnesses who meet the bereaved families often find it helpful," I say as we trudge towards the sea, towards the three figures up ahead, who are now stopping and dropping their big cotton bags on the sand. The horizon is nothing more than a vague suggestion where an indeterminate sky meets an indeterminate sea. "I suppose I realised I had something to offer them when they had lost so much. Yes, getting to know Polly has helped me, I suppose."

Charlotte Black looks at me then and gives me an understanding smile: a quick burst of sympathy and warmth. "Alys was always good at taking people in," she says. "She was a very welcoming sort of person. It's lovely that her family has been so welcoming to you."

We reach the sea. The sand slopes down into a glittering band of shingle which is scattered with driftwood and dark, blistered ribbons of seaweed, and the waves are sluicing over it, greedily sucking and tugging on the pebbles, making them rattle.

Laurence has left his clothes in a heap by his sandals and is already wading out with Polly. I watch their spare figures bending and leaping as the waves crash into them and then they vanish into the wall of water, their sleek heads eventually appearing in the shifting surge of surf behind. I pull my dress over my head and drop it on the sand and run in after them—away from Charlotte Black and her sharp, alarming interest, her speculative gaze.

H*onor is on edge for the rest of the afternoon. She's short with* Teddy, whose efforts to appease her appear to be having quite the opposite effect. No, she doesn't want to walk into Biddenbrooke for a drink at the King's Arms; no, she doesn't want a game of tennis, a swim in the pool, or a cup of tea. I'm in my room getting dressed after my shower and my door is slightly ajar so I hear his voice from the other end of the corridor, low, imploring; and then hers rings out sharp as a whip: "Oh, can't you just give it a rest?" Then a door slams shut.

When I go downstairs someone is moving stealthily around the living room. As I push the door wider open there's a sudden movement, and I find Selma stagily examining the black-and-ochre abstract over the fireplace—leaning close, then backing away from it, head tilted to one side—in the self-conscious manner of a guest who knows she's not entirely welcome.

"Can I help with anything?" she asks when I say I'm just going to start on supper. I say there's nothing to do, it's all cold stuff which just needs to be plated up. Does she want a drink? She says she is happy to wait until the others come down. Then she sinks into one of the gold sofas, murmuring about feeling "terribly spoilt." I wonder what she was getting up to before I came in. Flicking through the postcards and invitations on the mantelpiece, perhaps? Nosing about in his collection of Pevsners? Of course, she'll really have her eye on the photograph albums, but I doubt she'll have the nerve.

In the kitchen I put glasses and cutlery on a large tray, ready to be taken outdoors, and find the clean napkins which Mrs. Talbot has ironed. I'm just making a salad when Honor appears in lots of eye makeup and a rather tight, pale green dress which I haven't seen before. Without saying anything she goes to the fridge and pulls out a lemon and a bottle of tonic. "Want a sharpener?" she asks, sloshing Gordon's into a tumbler and then reaching into the freezer for the ice cubes.

I say I'll pass for now.

She drinks down her first glass quickly, then makes another: again, almost as much gin as fizz.

"Oh. That's better," she says, leaning back against the counter, pressing the cold glass to her temple. "I need a bit of reinforcement tonight. Back to London tomorrow."

"Of course, you're off to the US soon," I say, pouring olive oil and vinegar into a cup.

"Well, I think my time here's probably up anyway. Me and Teddy—looks like it's run out of steam, really." She sighs pragmatically, pulls herself up onto the counter and sits there, ankles neatly crossed, looking down into her glass.

"Ah," I say neutrally. "Does Teddy feel the same?"

"Probably not," she says. The ice cubes chink as she lifts the glass again. "But *tant pis,* right? No sense flogging a dead horse."

Polly appears and Honor slopes off again, glass in hand. I hear her laughing rather wildly in the hall with Charlotte, and then there's a hush as they go through into the sitting room. "Silly cow," says Polly, ripping cling film off the lentil salad while I fetch the dish of cold roast chicken which Mrs. Talbot has left for us in the fridge. "Poor old Teddy. He may not have seen it coming, but the rest of us did."

Polly has been so bored this afternoon that she has spent ages decorating the table on the terrace. I've never known her to concentrate on anything for any length of time, so the spectacle takes me by surprise. She has put out a white damask tablecloth and the ancient gold-edged Spode which usually lives in the sideboard in the dining room. Jam jars crammed with lavender and blowsy roses are arranged between the candle lanterns at either end. When I follow her out with some salads, she stands back, arms complacently crossed, admiring it and, to a lesser degree, my reaction.

I don't say anything, but the weather isn't on our side. Because of the motionless, grey sky the daylight seems to be fading earlier and faster than usual; the flares which Polly has lit along the paths and set out on the terrace steps are burning with a smokey intensity, creating strange leaping shadows at the edges of the garden. It's still hot: sticky and airless.

"Oh—how pretty!" says Selma, when we call everyone out to eat.

Teddy, drawn and distant, sits next to Charlotte. Polly grabs the chair on her other side. I'm left to slide in between Selma and Honor. While the salads and the rolls are passed around, I see Honor nudging her empty glass towards Laurence, who is opening another bottle of white. "Do tell me how far you're getting with your new project," I hear her saying.

While Selma begins to steer us towards the subject of her recent divorce, I nod and look stricken on her behalf, but I'm concentrating on the conversation Laurence and Honor are having on my right, with all its false steps and misapprehensions and dead ends. Honor must be completely off her face already, I think, because Laurence's reluctance seems barely to register with her. She just keeps on at him, her fingers toying with the horseshoe on its silver chain, drawing attention to the length and shape of her neck.

"Where do you get your ideas from?" she's asking, and "What would you have done if you hadn't become a writer?" and "Do you use a word processor or do you prefer pens and stuff?" and "Do you have, like, a routine when you work?"

She's asking the questions you're never meant to ask, and now he's actually giving in, he's taking her seriously, he's starting to answer them. I hear him lowering his voice, and out of the corner of my eye I see him spreading his hands expansively, and I think, *Oh, no, he's confiding in her, he's enjoying it a little. She's actually making some headway.*

In the meantime, here I am, stuck with Selma and the dreary story of Steven Carmichael's midlife crisis and the charity motorbike rally around South America from which he never returned, instead falling in love with a girl from Chile and taking up a position in Santiago as a TEFL teacher. I could scream. But I don't. I just nod slowly and frown and nod slowly again, while doing my best to eavesdrop. I hate hearing Laurence talking like this, but I'm unable to tear myself away.

Honor is crunching through a stick of celery and asking, "And was Daniel Day-Lewis, you know, really *intense?*" when I hear Selma say, "So, Frances, are you happy where you are?"

For a moment I can't think what she means, and I sit there with a fork in my hand, gazing at her blankly, hoping for clues; then I realise that she's trying to find out how I feel about the *Questioner.* So I say that apart from the general air of uncertainty, I'm not exactly *un*happy there: Mary's a decent person to work for, I'm interested in books, I like most of our contributors.

She pops a piece of bread into her mouth and says, "Because I'm about to start looking for a new deputy, there's going to be an opening, and I was wondering whether you'd be interested in applying."

"Me? Really?" I say. "Because I'm not all that experienced, really. I mean, I've been subbing the pages for ages, and commissioning and editing the odd thing, working with writers quite closely, but I've only really been writing for Mary for a few months."

"Oh, I know all that," says Selma, spooning some cucumber salad onto her plate. "But you're a safe pair of hands, that's obvious enough. Only last week Audrey Callum was singing your praises. You know how it works, you've clearly got the contacts. Well, why don't you think about it."

"I will," I say. "Gosh. Thanks. I will." Then I accept the bowl of cucumber salad and help myself, then turn to pass it to Honor. But she's distracted; she's leaning away from me, resting her cheek on her hand, staring up at Laurence. I can't see the expression on her face but I don't really need to: this has been building for some days, like the break in the weather.

I wonder what Teddy makes of it. When I glance over at him,

I see he has a bright, artificial smile on his face as he pretends to enjoy a story Charlotte is telling about an Australian author she had lunch with last week, a story which makes Polly double up with laughter. All the drama on the other side of the table seems to be passing her by. No surprises there, then.

Poor Laurence, I think, as Honor, inviting a refill, tilts her glass, which flashes green-gold in the candlelight. He doesn't have a clue. For a clever man, he is rather stupid. He can't resist Honor's attention tonight; he's dazed by the velocity of her interest. And of course she's young and terribly pretty.

So he sits there, eating salad and cold chicken, talking in a rather sheepish voice about the habit he has of mapping out plots using different-coloured Post-its; about "the legwork" mostly getting done first thing and in the late afternoon; about his early superstitious devotion to American legal pads, which he stockpiled whenever he went to the United States, and how much easier things are now he's used to a Mac. "I never quite know how novels begin," he's saying now. "Sometimes you start with a sentence. Sometimes it's something you hear someone say. Or maybe you get stuck on an image, an image that holds your interest for some reason, and you can't work out why, and then you realise you have to write about it to find out what it means."

I don't want to hear this. There's no magic in what he's saying. It's as if someone has let the genie out of the bottle, only it's not a genie, it's just some stale, sour-smelling air.

I scrape my fork across my plate.

It's almost a relief when Honor, making some big encapsulating gesture, knocks over her water glass. The wet races steadily across the damask. "Whoops!" she says, giggling and pushing her chair backwards, sending her knife skittering onto the brick beneath. When she stands up, she weaves a little on her heels.

"Oh, for God's sake . . . ," says Teddy, unable not to.

"It's only a bit of water," she hisses at him. Polly's staring at her now, nose wrinkled in distaste.

"I really think you should try to eat something," I say in a low voice, trying to catch Honor's arm, and I see Laurence—the spell broken—swiftly glancing over at me, noticing my intervention and grateful for it; but she ignores me, she's giddy with relief at the public break with Teddy, and she's full of adrenaline because of all the attention from his father, the Great Man himself. She thinks she's flying. I'm fairly sure she's crashing, but I wouldn't stake my life on it.

Now Laurence is standing up, too, his sleeve dark with water. "If you'll excuse me," he says with a rather stiff smile, pulling his chair back and crossing the terrace.

It seems obvious that the first course is over. Selma and Charlotte and I start to collect the plates while Polly and Teddy walk off down the lawn between the flaming torches, their pale heads close together.

"Oh, dear," says Charlotte, pausing to watch them. "'Take Honor from me and my life is done.'"

"Do you think she's *on* something?" Selma is whispering excitedly. "She seems rather high."

Honor has vanished. The sky over the copper beech is darkening to lavender now, the colour of half mourning. Rain is on its way. I wonder whether there's any point in bringing out my apple tart, the neatly fanned slices glazed with apricot jam. It took me hours to make it look beautiful and now no one will notice it.

I pick up the stack of gold-deckled plates and go indoors.

All the lights are off in the hall, and I can't switch them on because my hands are full. But as I pass from the soft Oriental rugs of the sitting room onto the hallway parquet, I look up and see Laurence and Honor at the top of the stairs, lit by the little red-shaded lamp which stands on the table there. For a moment I can't work out exactly what's happening, I hear only the indistinct murmur of their voices. Then there's a flash of sudden movement. I see he's shrinking away from her, his hands raised in a gesture of apology, of helplessness, possibly of fear, while she tries angrily to catch his wrists. "You do, I know you do," she's saying, and then she's craning up towards him, reaching for his face, pulling it towards her, and he's pushing down her hands, breaking away, walking off towards his room, not saying anything.

I wait in the shadows, half-expecting her to follow him, but she doesn't. She stands there for a moment or two as if indecisive, then I hear her going into the room she shares with Teddy, and the door closes.

I'm in the kitchen, rinsing cutlery under the tap, when she puts her head around the door. "Do you know any taxi numbers?" she asks. Her cheeks are faintly flushed, but otherwise she looks quite normal.

I find the little cards which are kept in one of the dresser drawers, along with the string and candle stubs and plasters and the big box of cooks' matches, and then I hear her booking a cab "as soon as possible, please. I've got to catch the nine fifty."

When she hangs up, I say, "Are you feeling okay?"

"Fine, thanks." She goes to the sink and fills a glass with water and drinks it down.

"Let me make you a sandwich for the train," I say. "You hardly ate anything at supper. You're going to feel awful in the morning."

"Oh, don't bother," she says, but I've got nothing better to do, so I quickly cut some bread and wrap it, with some ham and cornichons, in cling film. I cut her a little triangle of apple tart, too, just in case; though (as Teddy said, all those days ago) she never eats anything, even at the best of times.

"Aren't you going to say good-bye to everyone?" I ask, as the lights of the taxi briefly flood the kitchen window and then sweep on, over the outhouses, the wall of hollyhocks.

"I don't think so," she says. "I think I've overstayed my welcome. Just say something came up. An emergency." Then she shoulders her bag and goes out into the hall, her shoes sounding assertively on the parquet, and a minute later there's the noise of the taxi moving off, scattering gravel.

The house is still for a moment, then suddenly there's a burst of wind, startlingly cold through the wide-open kitchen window, and after that I hear it: the rush and rattle of rain. Charlotte and Selma and Teddy and Polly come hurrying in from the garden, incredulous, already soaked; and there's laughter, as if the weather has given them something else to think about, and they're all rather relieved.

I tell them what she told me to say—*"Honor got a call and left in a hurry,* she said it was an emergency"—but to Polly I say, in an undertone, "I think she was embarrassed, I think that's why she went."

Polly says, "Honor doesn't do embarrassment, haven't you noticed?" She assumes the breakup with Teddy is the whole story: that Honor just took off because after that little scene at supper there was no reason to stay. I don't say anything to correct that impression.

Laurence comes down in a dry shirt and says, "I thought I heard a car," when told the news, and then there's a halfhearted attempt to extend the evening over apple tart and coffee in the kitchen, but it all feels flat, even though Teddy strives to crack some jokes, just to prove how fine he is.

The rain is ferocious, squally, beating against the house like something trying to get in.

When I go up to my room, I see that I've left both windows wide-open. The sills are soaked, sopping wet, and water has sprayed over the carpet and a corner of the bed. I shut one window and then I stand at the other one, feeling the roar of the weather, taking deep breaths of the mineral-scented air, staring out at the glittering darkness. Then I close that window and mop things up as best I can.

Later, the dream comes at me with force. I am hurrying over an endless stretch of hot sand, horribly exposed, too frightened to look over my shoulder at the thing that is chasing me, and I'm faltering, stumbling, and tripping, my feet forever losing purchase; all my efforts counting for nothing.

T*he storm moves off sometime in the night. As usual I'm the first* person downstairs in the morning, and when I step outside to drag the sodden, stone-heavy damask off the table, the sky is a bright, sharp blue and the air has a freshness to it, a suggestion of the year on the turn.

I wring most of the water from the cloth and have just put it in the washing machine when Laurence appears in the kitchen, saying he intends to spend the morning in his study. We have a brief conversation. I tell him I'm planning to leave before lunch, and he says, "Well, see you again soon, I hope," and then he goes off carrying a cup of coffee and an apple, a piece of buttered toast clamped between his teeth. I can't help feeling a little flat as I hear the study door closing behind him.

Selma and Charlotte are the next to appear. They're on their way to the swimming pool—"A last dip before we leave for Bunny's"—and they wonder whether I want to join them.

When Teddy comes down a little later, he's glassy-eyed, as if he, too, has slept badly. He sits in front of his cornflakes, moving the spoon in the bowl and hardly eating anything.

"Are you okay?" I ask, but he just makes a vague noise and turns a page of the newspaper.

I've tidied up the kitchen, and I'm about to go upstairs to pack my bag when Teddy pushes his bowl away and says, "Oh, and, Frances. I've been meaning to ask you something."

I wait with my hand on the door handle. I have no sense of what is coming next.

"I know you lied to us about the accident," he says. "I know what you told us wasn't exactly the truth."

I stare at him, looking blank, confused, but of course I know precisely what he means. Blood starts to sound in my ears.

"I'm sorry?" I say, and because I suddenly feel unsteady, I sit down opposite him at the table, though my instincts are telling me to get out of there and as quickly as possible.

"I know you lied. I saw your statement, the statement you gave to the police at the scene. I asked Kate Wiggins if I could see the police report, and she made it available to me." He sits there, leaning back in his chair, arms folded, regarding me with those cool, pale Kyte eyes—Alys's eyes. It all makes perfect sense: humiliated by last night's events, Teddy has chosen this moment to show his hand. His vulnerability has made him vicious. He doesn't want to be the only one suffering.

"I don't know what you're talking about," I say. "I didn't lie."

"Oh, no? You didn't invent my mother's last words? That little killer detail at the end? 'Tell them I love them'? Because as far as I can tell, you first came up with that when we met you. There's no record of it before that point. And I understand you'd been through events with two individual police officers before then."

I lower my gaze. I can't meet his eyes. I don't want him to look me in the face. I don't want him to see how angry I am.

Of course, most of the anger is directed at myself. I hate that I gave in to temptation all those months ago. I hate that I took the risk, even though at the time it was what I needed to say to forge a connection with Polly and with Laurence. And I hate that he has this to throw at me when he is at his most wretched.

"What I don't understand," he's saying slowly, carefully emphasising every word, "is why you felt you had to do it. Why would you lie about something like that, to perfect strangers?"

The ambient hum of the washing machine in the utility room next door changes pitch as it progresses through the cycle. The herb garden is bathed in sunshine. A blackbird flies down onto the sundial, and flies off again.

"It was a stupid thing to say," I say eventually. "I'm not sure if I can really explain it. It's unforgivable, of course."

He waits.

"Was it so harmful?" I say in a sudden rush, raising my head. "Was it so wrong to want to give you all a little scrap of comfort?"

He doesn't move, but his expression subtly changes. *He's not unreachable,* I think. *He wants to trust me. He wants me to make this okay.* The insight gives me courage.

"Yes," I say, "it was completely wrong of me. But, oh, Teddy—when I came to the house and met you all . . . well, I can't quite explain it. I felt it was what you were waiting for. I wanted to help, even in some tiny, insignificant way. I got carried away, I suppose. I am so very sorry if I've caused you more unhappiness."

We sit there in silence for a moment.

"Please believe me," I say.

He pulls his hands through his hair and sighs. "I do," he says.

The relief spills through me. I feel quite giddy with it. "Do you want me to tell Polly?" I ask. "Does she know? Have you talked about it with anyone else?"

He puts his head back and looks at the ceiling, considering.

"No, I haven't mentioned it to her, or anyone. I'm not sure what to do. What do you think? Should I tell her? Should you?" Then he gets up and carries his bowl over to the sink and stands there, gazing out over the gravel drive to the croquet lawn and the field beyond, drumming his fingers lightly on the kitchen counter.

"Look, let's keep it between ourselves," he says finally. "No point in causing anyone more distress. I don't think Polly would handle it very well. Dad neither. You did it for the best of reasons, I accept that."

"Oh, Teddy," I say. "Thank you for being so good about it. I feel like a total idiot."

He comes over to me and gives me a hug. "You *are* an idiot," he says, half-laughing, and when he puts his arms around me, I sense the relief in him, too: a sense that he is off the hook somehow and is grateful to me for that.

I *leave Nevers later that morning. Selma and Charlotte have already* departed, and both women's farewells to me were warm, considerably more than cordial. Selma is in the bag, and Charlotte is nearly there. Somehow I think Charlotte is not going to be a problem.

Laurence does not appear to see me off. His study door stays firmly shut. "Give my best to your father," I remark to Polly and Teddy as we say our good-byes outside the house. "Tell him how much I enjoyed being here."

As my car passes through the olive-green gate, I raise my fingers in a final acknowledgement, but I see in the rearview mirror that Teddy's and Polly's hands are falling to their sides and they're turning away, walking off towards the archway leading to the back lawn. I know they are already thinking about something else: a game of tennis, perhaps, or whether they can be bothered to walk to the village for a pub lunch.

I carry on driving down the rough track leading along the side of the meadow, and then I turn onto the road that heads through Biddenbrooke. A few listless children hang around the climbing frame on the green. A chalked board outside the King's Arms is drumming up interest for a hog roast.

My parents are expecting me for lunch. The roads are quiet, so I make good time. On the outskirts of my parents' village, just past my old primary school, I stop at a red light. While I'm waiting, I reach over into the passenger seat to unzip my bag. There it is, tucked in at the side: the grey shawl that belonged to Alys, the one that used to hang on a peg in the hall. It's such a pretty colour, and it's so soft: cashmere, of course. I hold it to my face, and I think I just catch a faint memory of her scent caught up in its fibres: the fresh, lively scent that made me think of morning.

I wrap it around my shoulders as the lights change, and then I drive on.

My parents have set up a picnic table in the garden. "Isn't this glorious?" my mother says, unpopping foldable chairs and disregarding the rather stiff breeze that is sending the paper napkins fluttering like giant yellow butterflies into the euphorbias. I imagine this alfresco lunch was sketched out in some detail a few days ago, and the improvisation needed to revise and relocate it proved too daunting. So here we sit, a little cold, under a jaunty striped parasol that lifts and strains in its moorings, offering each other coleslaw and cherry tomatoes and slices of baguette and triangles of quiche lorraine.

"Just some people I know," I say, when they ask about the

friends I've been visiting in Biddenbrooke. "It turned into a bit of a house party. We went to the beach a few times, but mostly we just stayed at the house. There was a pool," I add, despising myself for the boast.

"Lovely!" says my mother, who cannot swim.

Of course, they know Biddenbrooke quite well. I probably remember the Howards, don't I? Brian and Maggie? Their son, Mark? He's on the radio a fair bit nowadays, something to do with the Office of Fair Trading. Only last week he turned up on one of those consumer programmes, talking about extended warranties.

I sit there, holding my face perfectly still, waiting for her to get to the point.

"Mill House," my father says gently, spooning out Branston pickle. "Biddenbrooke."

That's right. Mill House. Biddenbrooke. Oh, it's such a shame about all that, my mother says, adopting a sorrowful expression. I can see her sails filling with a sort of gloomy superstitious triumph, as if other people's misfortune means there's likely to be less of it in general circulation. Less for her.

The Howards bought Mill House—when was it, Robert? Five, six years ago? Such a pretty spot. Anyway, they've just put it on the market. It's too much for them now. Gas bills are getting to be a real worry. Maggie says in winter the hot air just flows out through those old sash windows like a river. And though Brian has almost completely recovered from his stroke, the stairs weren't getting any easier. They're looking at something much smaller. Easier to manage. There's a new development outside Fulbury Norton which they're considering. It sounds rather swish, she concludes, and with that word all sorts of reservations are economically conveyed.

Handy for the golf club, my father says wistfully.

"Brie or Boursin, dear?" she asks, passing me the cheese plate with its fussy little knife, the knife that forks at the end like a serpent's tongue.

M*ary is away from her desk—I can see her from here, she has been* in Robin McAllfree's fish tank for the last forty-five minutes—but her extension is ringing. It's an internal call, so I pick up. "Mary's phone," I say.

It's Colin from the front desk. There's someone here to see Mary, he says. "Lady called Julia Price? She has an appointment."

I thank Colin and ask him to send her up.

God knows where Oliver has got to.

I stand by the elevators, checking myself in the stainless-steel doors. I still have my healthy summer colour, and my new haircut suits me: it's shorter, more definite-looking. I lean forward to inspect my eyes, my teeth.

The doors open and Julia Price is standing there, with a security pass clipped to her lapel.

"Julia, hello," I say as she steps out. "I'm afraid Mary's a bit tied up at the moment. She won't be a moment. I'm Frances."

We shake hands. Her palm is cool and dry. She's wearing a blue-and-white seersucker jacket and espadrilles which tie with a ribbon at the ankle. A thin cotton scarf is knotted over the strap of her bag, just in case she wants to pull it around her throat later. The white flash in her hair shows up the absolute freshness of her face. It's the perfect foil for her sort of attractiveness.

I walk back with her to the books desk and I sense people lifting their gazes from their terminals and noticing only one of us. There's something about her, I can see that.

"Would you like a drink? I can get you coffee or tea from the machine. Or some water," I say when I've found her a chair.

She says she's fine. "Don't let me hold you up," she says, giving me her huge white smile, and reaching for her phone. "I'm sure you've got things to do—really, Frances, I'm happy to wait."

"If you're sure," I say. She starts inspecting her emails while I go back to Berenice's review, but while I'm doing this, I'm aware of her presence behind me, her scent. Her tiny frustrated sighs and half laughs as she works through her in-box. The sound of her swallowing.

A few moments later, Mary sails out of Robin's office. "Julia," she calls as she approaches, and she actually does sound rather stricken. "I am so sorry to have kept you waiting. Crisis meeting," she adds, in a quieter tone. "You know the mess we're in."

They embrace, and then Julia is delving into her bag, producing two books, saying this is just a taster, there are more to come. Mary pulls her spectacles low on her nose and flicks through one of them, making complimentary noises: nice jacket design, where are they printed, who wrote the forewords. "Oh, I'm sure we can do something with these," she says, lingering for a moment or two on a page, then closing the book with a decisive snap. She glances down at her watch. "Right, I've made us a reservation at Salvatore's. Let's take these and have a proper brainstorm over lunch."

As she walks past my desk, Julia Price catches my eye and gives me a little jolly salute. "See you, Frances," she says, and I suspect it's a technique she's picked up somewhere: *Remember people's names. Use them to death. You never know who may come in useful in the future.* "Take care," she adds, moving after Mary.

"And you," I say, watching her go, and watching TV and Travel watching her go, too.

The eyes, the smile, the air of assurance. *The whole package,* I think. I imagine Julia Price never doubts herself. Probably she's right not to.

A little while later, waiting for the lift, I look myself over again in the stainless-steel elevator doors, and this time I'm not quite so pleased with what I see.

S elma Carmichael *rings me about ten days later. We meet for a drink* in a quiet little pub around the corner from her office, and she makes me an offer. When she mentions a figure, I am careful not to react. She adds she thinks she can probably arrange a few extra grand, but that would really be it.

I say I'd like to think it over, if that's okay, and she says of course, take a few days to let it sink in.

"By the way, how was Bunny Nesbitt's?" I ask as we're on the way out. She says it was fun, if rather exhausting. Ambrose Pritchett was there, full of doom and gloom about the *Questioner*. He had some tales to tell about Oliver Culpeper, related to a fight with Jez Shelf after the *Spectator*'s summer party. Oliver came off the loser, apparently.

Laurence drove over to Allwick one evening for dinner after Teddy and Polly had left for London. Selma said she didn't like to think of him going back to Nevers afterwards: all alone in that huge house. Charlotte was quite bothered about him. But reading between the lines, he's making progress with the book.

"Do you think he's okay?" Selma asks me, softening her voice as if hoping for a revelation. I say I'm not sure, but I think so.

"It's so sad. Alys was such a wonderful woman," she sighs, and I feel a flash of annoyance.

"Mmm," I say. "Of course, I never really met her. Well, only the once." She looks at me then, a quick sideways glance, as if I've shocked her, and I lower my eyes. Briefly she lays a hand on my sleeve. And then we say good-bye and walk off, heading in opposite directions.

I take Mary aside and tell her I've been offered a job by Selma Carmichael and I think I'm going to accept it.

"I feel that would be a mistake," she says, inspecting me over her spectacles. "I know Selma, and frankly I think you can do considerably better."

"Really?" I say, not sure what she means.

"Really." She spins around on her chair, picks up her turquoise diary, and flicks through it. "I'm clear for lunch today. Do you have plans?"

And that's how I find myself sitting in the window at Salvatore's, ordering the *linguine alle vongole* and being offered a promotion. Deputy books editor. Mary's deputy. Oliver's job.

"But it's Oliver's job," I say.

Mary snaps a *grissino* in two. "Don't be dim, darling," she says breezily. "Oliver's on the way out. He doesn't know it yet, and I'd be grateful if you could keep it quiet for the time being, but as you're aware, we're under pressure to make cutbacks. I've been talking to Robin about restructuring, and we're in agreement. I need a deputy who can write, edit, commission, and sub across all platforms, plus all that dreadful blogging and tweeting he's so keen on. On top of that, I do need someone who can behave in public. The whole kit and caboodle. I think you'll be perfect. How do you feel?"

"What about the money?" I say.

Mary says she can match Selma's offer. Maybe slightly improve on it.

Salvatore carries over our plates. While he fusses around with the pepper grinder, I look out at the street: cycle couriers, black cabs, a girl with white cords trailing out of her ears waiting listlessly for the lights to change.

"Do you know, I'm not feeling very patient," says Mary, twiddling a fork through her pasta. "I need your answer straightaway."

"Yes," I say. "Thanks. I accept."

M*ary says I have to wait until Oliver is told the news before I can* turn down Selma's offer. Otherwise she might let the cat out of the bag.

They were going to announce the editorial redundancies on Friday, but after Mary has spoken with Robin and HuRe, it's all brought forward a day or two.

I feel just a bit sick, sitting at my desk, waiting for the news to break.

Oliver is in good and early, as is usual these days. He offers me an apple Danish, which I refuse, and perches on the edge of my desk drinking his coffee and telling me about the party he went to last night, marking the publication of some new biography or other. He has become quite confiding in recent months; keeping his enemies close, I suppose.

"Julia Price was there," he says. "She said Mary's interested in her new publishing venture. We might be doing something, apparently."

"Oh?" I say, looking encouraging. I'll never pass up an opportunity to hear news of Julia Price. "Was she with anyone?"

"Julia Price is always on her own," says Oliver. "I used to think she was involved with someone unsuitable—she seems the type, if you know what I mean—but I see her around more now, I think it must be over. Oh, here's Mary." And he scoots off to his desk, dusting flakes of Danish from his shirtfront.

Just after ten thirty, Oliver's extension rings. He picks up and says, "Yup?" and then suddenly he's still, entirely focused on what he's hearing, like a stag catching the sound of a foot on a twig. "Right," he says. "Sure. I'll come through now." Then he replaces the handset and stands up and walks down the aisle between the banks of desks, into Robin McAllfree's fish tank, where Robin is waiting, seated at the Perspex table along with Mary and the managing editor and the top brass from HuRe.

He's not in there for long, and as soon as they're opening the door for him and letting him go, Robin McAllfree's PA is picking up the phone and calling in the next poor sod.

Oliver comes back down the carpeted aisle. He has got himself together, I see: he's pale, but he's sauntering. Sasha from Fashion is rising to her feet, mouthing, *What the fuck?* and in answer he makes a pistol out of his fingers and fires it at his head.

"Well, that's me, then," Oliver says, coming back to Books and dropping into his swivel chair. "I've got the chop."

"Oh!" I say. "I don't believe it. You're joking, right?"

He looks at me. For a brief moment I see something cold and contemptuous bright in his eyes and I think, *He knows, he knows the whole story.* Then his expression changes and he's shrugging, managing to laugh a little as Sasha comes rushing over, her hands pressed to her mouth, while he says, "Fuck's sake, people, it's a sinking ship anyway, losing a few rats isn't going to change that."

The day after Oliver's departure, two silent men come up from the basement and unplug his phone and computer terminal, then remove his desk and chair, too. It's rather Soviet, as if he has never existed.

People keep asking me whether I know what's going to happen on Books, but because nothing official has yet been said, I just shake my head and say, "Search me."

A few days later Robin McAllfree sends round an inter-office email, announcing—among other structural changes—that I'm to be Mary's new deputy, a role I'll combine with many of my current production responsibilities. With so much kerfuffle over the slew of redundancies and the redistribution of workload and the snazzy new contract handed out to Gemma Coke, my small elevation creates little interest.

News gets around, though: Charlotte Black sends me a nice card, and so does Audrey Callum. Even Ambrose Pritchett, when I make my weekly call chasing up copy, says, "Oh, Frances, you are a dark horse."

When I tell my parents on the phone, my father says, "Well done," and "The only surprise is that it took this long," which just shows how much he knows. I ring Hester, who sounds more impressed; but then Rufus knocks a lamp off a table, so she never gets a chance to congratulate me properly.

I'm walking down my street on my way to the tube one morning when I see a man in overalls carrying paint tins into number 18. A few days later I see the woman who lives there—Tina, I think her name is—buying cat food and courgettes at the corner shop. She says he's doing a good job, and he's not that expensive either. So I ring him and book him to tackle the bookcases, and while he's at it, I'd like the sitting room and the bedroom repainted, too.

The sales are on, so I spend a Saturday morning wandering around furniture shops, and in one of the grander stores I place an order for a new sofa bed. I pay a bit extra to have it covered with a dull gold linen. The colour's not dissimilar, I think, to that of the sofas in the living room at Nevers. The assistant taking my order commends my taste. "Good choice," she says, tapping away on her computer, organising a delivery date. "A little bit unusual."

I leave the store and cross the road, and I'm heading for the bus stop when I see a familiar figure approaching, flip-flops snick-snick-snicking along the pavement, a big jute bag hoiked over her shoulder. For a moment, I wonder whether we're going to pretend we haven't seen each other, whether we're going to be too dazzled by the sunshine, and then it's simply too late for the alternatives and we're embracing, making astonished, delighted noises. "I wasn't sure if it was you," Honor says, pushing her sunglasses on top of her head. "You look different: I like your hair. I'm going to get breakfast—do you have time for a coffee?"

At the organic grocery around the corner, lit to arctic brightness and air-conditioned accordingly, a girl in a penitential-looking grey apron finds us a space at the huge communal table in the in-house café. Honor orders granola and a soya latte. She lives nearby, in a mansion block in Marylebone. We talk a little about this and that—the holiday in Maine, work, a terrific French film she saw last night—and then I'm overcome with impatience and I say, "How's Teddy?"

"I was going to ask you," she says, lifting a crackle-glazed cup between brown fingers. "I haven't seen him for weeks—not since Biddenbrooke."

"So that really was it? That scene at dinner? I can't even remember what you argued about," I say, and it's true: of course, it had been brewing for days, but the crisis itself came out of nowhere.

"Oh, that was just the last straw. It hadn't been working for a while."

"It's a shame. I think Teddy was really into you."

"He's a sweet boy," she says rather remotely, as if talking of someone much younger than herself. "Too sweet, maybe that was the problem."

"How have your parents taken it?" I ask. "Is it going to make things awkward between them and Laurence?"

"Oh—I don't think *that's* going to be the problem," she says, glancing around the room as if she's casing the joint, working out whether she's under observation. "There are *other* complications, if you know what I mean."

I look at her blankly, wondering what on earth she has cooked up now. She pulls off her sunglasses, runs a hand through her hair, leans towards me. "It's kind of embarrassing," she says confidentially. "But you probably won't be surprised. He was a bit all over me the whole time I was down there, you must have noticed."

"Who?" I say. "Teddy?"

"Laurence," Honor sighs. "Trying it on, here and there. Pretty subtle, but enough to make me feel uncomfortable."

"Really?" Half of me feels cross, fired up with loyalty and indignation on the Kytes' behalf; and the other half is amused, struck yet again by her endless self-regard and wondering whether I can't make use of it somehow. "Really, Honor? I had absolutely no idea."

She must have heard the incredulity in my voice because she puts down her cup and says, "No, really, he's not what you think. The whole thing is quite shocking."

I don't say anything, I just wait.

"It all came to a head on the last night. I had to sit next to him at dinner, and then he monopolised me all the way through, droning on about work, his new book. And then there was that scene with Teddy—I can't even remember what sparked that off, actually, can you?—and when I got upset and went inside, he followed me, Laurence did, I mean. Laurence followed me and—oh, it was disgusting, he kind of grabbed me and tried to kiss me."

"Unbelievable," I say, and I make myself shake my head, and then I put my hand on hers and give it a comforting squeeze. "How awful for you."

"Yes, it was," she says gratefully. "It was horrid: it was such a shock, I've known him all my life, he's my parents' friend, and he's Teddy's *dad,* you know, and in any case he's so *old,* and I thought he was still in mourning—and then *this.* Yuck! Anyway, I pushed him off, and obviously after that I had to get out of there."

"Does Teddy know?"

"Oh, God, no. I thought I should keep it to myself. You won't tell Polly, will you? I don't want to cause either of them more upset." When she says this, I know she knows it's a lie, it's a story she has invented to save face, and somehow I'm relieved by this insight. I'm relieved to know that there's a limit to her capacity for self-delusion.

"I think that's very thoughtful of you," I say. "Maybe he'd had too much to drink. I'm sure it was a one-off."

But, no, Honor has more to tell. I can see the excitement shining in her eyes. The glee of being in possession of valuable information. "Oh, Frances, that's where you're wrong," she breathes. "It turns out this is what he's *like.* Affairs. Loads of them. All the way through his marriage."

I raise my eyebrows and drink some of my coffee, and she goes on, "No, honestly—Miriam told me."

Miriam, I remember distantly, is her mother. The taupe pioneer.

"I came back to London and quite naturally I was in a bit of a state, and, well, I told my mother the whole story. It all came out. And then she told me that Laurence is kind of famous for going after younger women. He cheated on Alys. Lots of women. Most of them much younger than him. Mum even saw him out with one of them a few months before Alys died, at Malcolm Azaria's.

I don't think they'd turned up together, but it was obviously prearranged. Mum said she saw them leaving in the same cab."

This all sounds thoroughly inconclusive, and I'm about to dismiss it as worthless, when she says, "Maybe you know her through work. The woman he was with. Julia Price. She works in publishing."

"Rings a bell," I say. "Gosh. Really? What else did your mother say about her?" I try not to sound too eager.

"Well, Miriam thinks that he put a stop to it after, you know, the accident. Overcome with guilt. Jo Azaria told her so. And—God, this is top secret, I can't believe I'm telling you, promise you won't tell anyone—Jo heard it from Laurence himself: he just fell to pieces after Alys died and confessed a load of stuff. He didn't talk about the other affairs, my mother assumes they were just small fry, but Julia Price—well, that one was the biggie, apparently. He admitted as much. After poor Alys died, he felt so dreadful about the whole thing that he knocked it on the head. He said the relationship was worthless. It was *tainted*."

I remember Julia white-faced in the hall after the memorial service, the scene I half-witnessed in the square garden; and now everything is fitting together.

On reflection I feel fairly sure that Julia wasn't the first betrayal. I imagine there were other girls over the years, girls who wrote poetry or did academic research and as a consequence were in thrall to the ruthlessness of the creative impulse; or maybe girls who worked in publicity and understood the need for discretion. Girls with bright eyes and dark flats, girls who asked nothing of him. People haven't mentioned them but I expect they exist. The lack of any vaporous trail of speculation merely underlines Laurence's position in this world, his ability to run rings around the gossips who spend their evenings moving between the tables where the books are arranged and the tables where the bar staff set out the glasses.

But Julia Price: well, that no one talked about *her* makes absolute sense.

"You must feel you got off quite lightly," I say, and Honor says she does, she had no idea, it's funny the stuff you don't know about the people who have always been in your life. Her hand goes, as if for security, to the delicate chain around her neck. There, alongside the silver *H*, the other pendant spins and catches the light: the tiny horseshoe for good luck. "Teddy gave it to me ages ago," she says, noticing my interest. "It used to belong to his mother. Do you think I should give it back?"

"Do you suppose Alys knew—about this Price person?"

"Oh, God, we hope not. She was lovely, wasn't she? So kind. So *good*. But if you're wondering whether Miriam said anything to her about seeing him go off with Julia Price after the party, no—she didn't."

I think back to what Polly told me about the last argument.

"And you can change the dedication while you're at it," Alys had said. "It's not a tribute, it's an insult."

In the end, the dedication read, *For Alys. Always.*

Somehow, Alys found out about Julia. Maybe Jo Azaria told her after all.

Did he do what she wanted? Or did the dedication stand as originally written? I wonder whether I'll ever know. I wonder why it matters to me.

Honor finishes her breakfast and flags down the waitress. We settle the bill, then she says she has to buy some household essentials, so I walk around the shop with her, curious to see what qualifies. Vegan cheese. "Detox" herbal tea. Washing-up liquid made with essential oils from organic Corsican lemons. We kiss goodbye on the pavement outside the shop, in the shade of a striped awning, and then she walks off, her jute bag over her arm, her flip-flops snick-snick-snicking over the pavement. Sunlight glitters off the line of traffic. The air smells of petrol. The sky is scored with the dissolving plumes of contrails.

Later I visit Naomi and her new baby, and we spend the afternoon aimlessly waving things at it and then aimlessly pushing it around the hot, dusty streets of Shepherd's Bush. After that I go alone to an early-evening screening of the French movie Honor was so taken with: a movie about a good-looking Parisian couple with lovely clothes, great jobs, and a dark secret. I enjoy it very much.

I catch the bus home and walk back skirting the locked park, passing thickets of shadowy, parched vegetation held in check by iron railings. As I walk, I think I catch an airborne hint of something decaying in there.

I send Polly a few texts wondering how she is doing; and she replies, saying it's not so bad being back at college, and she has been given a decent part in the autumn term play. She is meant to be coming over for dinner one Thursday, but she blows me out at the last minute, texting at five thirty to say she's not feeling well and can we do it another time. Later that evening, after a solitary supper, I switch on my laptop and see she has tweeted from a bar in Westbourne Grove where she is celebrating Louisa's birthday. Alexa Chung's on the next table, apparently.

I try not to feel too irritated. I remind myself that I know what to expect from Polly, and it's not much. But what she offers, I will take.

I have a few things to work out but I try not to overthink them. If I overthink, events will feel rehearsed, and that would be no good at all. So I run through the possibilities, trying not to get snagged down by details. It's a bit like making pastry. Light, cool hands, no hurry, lots of air. Wait for the moment when the texture changes.

Work is going well. Gemma Coke does the interview with Julia Price, pegged to the new publishing venture, and it looks good in the paper: a photograph of Julia standing by the window in her office, the white flash in her hair drawing attention to her skin. There's a breezy quote about her single/child-free status— "I probably wouldn't have had the energy to do all this if I had gone down another route"—as well as a reference to her popular reputation as "the most proposed-to woman in London." She has entirely seduced Gemma, and as a result it's rather a bland, forgettable piece.

Afterwards, Julia sends Mary an orchid in a glass bowl to say thank-you.

When I stand in for Mary at morning conference, I find my voice stays steady when I make my contributions. Tiny little Robin McAllfree says, "That's a good point," when I comment, and he takes to popping over to Books occasionally, perching on the edge of my desk, swearing energetically and polishing his spectacles while talking about "you bloody bluestockings." I assume it's a sort of default flirting—he can't help himself—and I laugh at his jokes politely, and soon he goes off to bother someone else.

When Malcolm Azaria writes a memoir for a literary magazine about being contacted by a love child he'd known nothing about, McAllfree springs something on me the day the embargoed issue lands on his desk.

"You're muckers with old Azaria, aren't you? Give him a ring and see if he'll meet Gemma before the end of the week? Tell him we'd use it as the arts front. Nice big plug for whatever."

"Absolutely," I say, and when I get back to my desk, I put in a call to the magazine's publicist, who tells me he's already done an interview with the *Sunday Times* to run this weekend, so it's a no-go.

I email McAllfree to tell him Malcolm's awfully sorry but he's already committed elsewhere, and that's the end of that. But now I know beyond doubt how Mary sold my promotion, and it reminds me—as if I were ever in danger of forgetting—to tread carefully.

The Indian summer is ending. It slopes off quite suddenly, without much fanfare, like a cad making a run for it. One morning I find myself grabbing my red-and-purple scarf as I leave the flat. One evening I walk out of the office and it's almost dark.

When I stop off at the high-end deli to buy my lunch, I notice they've made an arrangement of pumpkins and gourds and paper leaves in the window, placed among flounces and twirls of orange and brown tissue.

I wait. Sometimes I'm patient, content to wait; and sometimes I wonder—fretfully or desperately, depending on my mood— whether it will ever happen. It's out of my hands now, though. I've done what I can, and one day the opportunity will present itself. I'm almost certain it will.

A *mbrose Pritchett has contributed to* The Road Less Travelled, *a* book in which literary types celebrate the hidden charms of their favourite British counties. Pritchett's essay is on Worcestershire.

"Oh, I had no idea that's where you're from," I say when he comes into the office to pick up his post.

"Gracious, Frances, I'm from Egham. Worcestershire was the only one left." He'd never been there before accepting the commission and, he tells me, he has no plans to go back in a hurry. Most of his information came from the Internet and an old AA guide.

The launch party is being held upstairs at the Meat Safe, a Soho restaurant specialising in the sort of British food—pigs' cheeks, brawn, chard, whelks, posset—that manages to sound utterly horrid on the menu. I accept the invitation because you never quite know who's going to turn up to these things; you never can tell. But when I arrive, I see it's just another party, like all the others.

I've had one damson cocktail (more than enough) and am on the point of waving my fingers at Ambrose to say, "See you, I'm off," when the atmosphere of the room changes, as if someone has dimmed the lighting or turned it up slightly.

"Oh, look who's here," murmurs a voice behind me.

I turn to the door to see whom they're talking about. It's Laurence. The girl from the publishing house is trying to take his coat but he's resisting, smilingly pressing past her, saying, "I can't stay, I won't be a minute," and then he's entering the room, embracing Nikolai Titov, here to support his wife, Peggy, who has written the chapter on Somerset. A man with a camera steps forward to take their picture. Obligingly Laurence pauses, his arm around Peggy, showing his teeth, until the photographer backs off, thanking him.

"I was passing—I can't stay—but I wanted to say hello," I hear him say as he stoops to kiss her on both cheeks.

I stand at the side of the room, waiting, waiting, willing him to turn and notice me.

When he does, I meet his gaze, and I feel the satisfaction of seeing his expression alter.

I hold myself still, in the unnerving sharpness of his scrutiny. I let him look. It's only for a tiny moment, a second, less than a second, but in that time I feel that many things change. Then he nods at me, quite casually, not quite smiling, and glances away.

He has a few more words with the Titovs and then excuses himself and makes his way through the crowd towards me, murmuring apologies to people who step aside to let him pass, people who can't help peering after him to see whether they know me.

This is the third kiss and it's a quick, familiar, easy one. Briefly

I feel the warmth of his cheek against mine and his hand on my sleeve, the light pressure of his palm through the fabric.

"How are you?" he's saying, and I say, "Fine . . . Oh, it's been a long time since Biddenbrooke," and then he says, "I've only got a few moments, the cab's outside; Polly's cooking me supper—she's staying the night."

"I don't suppose you could drop me home on the way?" I ask.

He says that would be fine, he'll just go and say good-bye to the Titovs and he'll see me outside.

It's no big deal. I shake hands with a few people and collect my coat from the rack in the corridor, and then, carefully, I descend the stairs. There's a mirror at the bottom of the staircase, and as I pass, I catch my eye. I look quite unlike myself, I think, almost shocked by the sight. The woman in the glass, with her bright eyes and flushed cheeks, looks like someone to whom things might happen: interesting things, exciting things, even dangerous things.

The cab is idling outside, its windows glittering with raindrops. Laurence leans forward from its depths to open the door, and I step over a puddle slick with neon and slide in next to him.

"Highgate," he says. "But via—where exactly do you live, Frances?"

I give the address to the driver, and the cab moves off into the sparkling night.

He asks me about the party, and I tell him what Ambrose Pritchett said to me, and he laughs, which makes me feel good.

Then I raise the subject of his work and he says, cautiously, that he thinks it's going well. He seems to be making progress. "It's a very different experience this time," he adds, as the cab stops and starts through Camden Town. "My wife, Alys, was always my first reader. She had a very good eye." I think it's the first time he's spoken to me about her.

The roads clear as we head north. We whip through Kentish

Town and Tufnell Park, past the animation of gastropubs and fried-chicken joints, past the dimmed windows of pound shops and organic-food halls, and he tells me a little about Polly, who has a new boyfriend and seems to be much happier now at college, and again he refers to my role earlier in the year. "She gave me a scare back then. I really think she was on the brink of walking away from the course," he says. "Thank God you managed to make her see sense. I certainly wasn't having any luck."

"I really don't think I had much to do with it," I say.

"Oh, I'm not so sure about that," he says. "Sometimes we get so snarled up in the business of being a family, it takes an outsider to see through the muddle."

I like that remark very much, so I let it hang there in the air between us; then he refers to my job, offers congratulations. I wonder who told him about it. I wonder who thought he might be curious to hear about me.

Then we stop talking.

We're not far away from my neighbourhood now. The taxi-driver is listening to a talk-radio show, but the partition is closed so the noise is indistinct. It's quiet in the back of the cab. I lean my head against the window and look out at pavements glossed with rain. People are clustering outside a kebab shop, smoking under the awning. Someone pulls his jacket over his head and jogs away from the tube station. In the darkness, I turn my face towards Laurence. He's watching me. He does not look away.

"I'd ask you to come on and join us for supper, but I'm not sure whether Polly . . . ," he says into the silence.

"Oh, no, of course," I say.

"Perhaps"—and yes, I can hear the clear reverberative note of fear in his voice, the chime of a fork on a glass—"perhaps we could do it another time?"

"That would be—," I begin lightly, and then he interrupts, in a hurry, "I'm sorry, I haven't made myself clear. I'd like to take you out to dinner. No Polly. Just you."

I don't say anything but I smile at him, and he smiles back, relieved—and embarrassed, too; a little awkward—and then the taxi stops outside my flat. I see him inspecting it, glancing out at the unruly hedge, the jumble of bins, the darkened line of windows on the first floor.

"I'll be in touch," he says as I reach for the handle.

"I'd like that," I say, and I gather up my bag and step out of the cab, and then I slam the door and the taxi moves off, and I see him turn a little to watch me and the flash as he raises his hand in farewell.

C*oming out of the lift, I am drawn to the plate-glass windows on* one side of the stairwell. The flat is in a modern block with a porter, an underground car park, communal gardens, and—even from this, the third floor—commanding views. I look out, over the hill, with the spill of gardens and parkland around the houses. A few faint scorch marks of autumn are still left in the trees.

The Kytes' street is only just out of sight. It can't have taken her more than seven or eight minutes to walk here.

Mrs. Brewer opens the door. She's probably in her late seventies, a fragile, scented creature with pearls in her ears, wearing a cashmere jersey the same colour as her Labrador, whom she introduces as Greta. In the dimness of the little hall, they're both pale shadows, barely there at all.

"How nice to meet you, Miss Thorpe," Mrs. Brewer says, putting out her hand. Her gaze is light and glassy, sliding over my face and then coming to rest at a point over my shoulder. The brightness from the atrium must register, I think. I've been told what to expect, but it's still discomfiting.

"Please do call me Frances," I say, but Mrs. Brewer laughs, establishing a boundary.

"Not yet," she says. "Maybe when I know you a little better. Won't you go through?" She moves sideways out of the hall into the little galley kitchen. There's the sound of a kettle being switched on and the fridge opening and shutting. When I offer, she says she does not need any help.

In the sitting room, comfortable but decorated in dispiritingly institutional magnolias and peaches, I see that everything is ready for us: the pair of armchairs at an angle by the window, a few pieces of paper on the table, a thick book.

"Is it light enough for you? Shall I turn on the lamps?" Mrs. Brewer asks, coming through with a small tray. I watch uneasily as she moves towards me, but she sets it down on the table without faltering, crisp in her movements, confident that everything is in its place.

"No, it's fine like this. It's quite a sunny afternoon."

Mrs. Brewer slips into one of the chairs. "Please," she says, gesturing towards the tray. "Help yourself to milk and sugar." Patiently Greta sits, then sighs and drops her jaw onto her paws.

"Mrs. Polter said you haven't done this sort of thing before," Mrs. Brewer says, leaning back with her cup and crossing her ankles.

"That's right. I just thought I'd see what it's like. If I can be of some use. That's the idea, anyway."

"How wonderful." She smiles towards me. "I'm very grateful. I haven't had a reader for quite some time now. I've missed it. Shall we make a start? I'm sure you've got your eye on the clock."

"Oh, of course," I say. "What would you like me to begin with?"

So I pick up the letters and read them to her. Nothing interesting, just mailshots from the council about recycling, and a photocopied sheet from the residents' committee asking for feedback on a proposed new planting scheme. Her son usually comes in regularly to help with this sort of thing, but she says he's away for a fortnight. Then I come to the paperback. It's a biography, several years old, of Rudolf Nureyev. The reviews were good, I remember. A fifth of the way through is a bookmark, a powder-blue strip of matt card printed with the Welbury Bookshop logo. I take it out and turn it over. *Her hands.*

On the flyleaf of the book, she has written, *To Nancy, "Hope is the thing with feathers . . ." With love, Alys.* I wonder why she bothered.

"You've made some progress with the Nureyev," I say, turning the pages and pausing on the black-and-white photograph of the infant Rudolf, a baby peasant in countless stiff woollen layers, sitting on his mother's lap. She appears amused, relaxed, on the point of speaking, but the child holds his hands formally at his side and his eyes are fixed levelly on the camera. It is a look I recognise.

"Oh, it's really exceptional," she says. "My late husband was on the board at Covent Garden, we used to see a lot of ballet, obviously before—and this is so marvellously written, it brings it all back. But I can't remember where we got to. It has been a few months . . . Longer than that, actually."

I leave the silence, trusting she'll fill it.

"I don't know what Mrs. Polter told you," she says, lifting her cup, her face turned again to the window. "I had a reader, a very good one, someone who became a friend. She died last winter."

"Oh, how sad," I say, watching her, the tremor on the surface of the tea. "Was it unexpected?"

"A car accident," she says. "She chose the book for me. It was a birthday present." I see her face working as she confronts something, maybe for the first time. "Do you know, perhaps it's not such a good idea after all. I think I'd prefer it if you started something new."

"Of course, this must bring it all back. It must be very painful for you, I do see that." A tiny involuntary flinch, an expression of distaste so fleeting I almost miss it; but just enough to irritate. "I like the inscription," I add. "*Hope is the thing with feathers . . .*'"

"Emily Dickinson," she says shortly. "That was a poem that always meant a great deal to her." Now she's placing her hands on the arms of her chair, preparing to get up. "There's an Elizabeth Taylor I put aside, a collection of short stories my son recommended," she's saying, but I'm suddenly getting tired of all this, so I open the book again and turn back to the page marked by the slip of blue paper.

"Oh, but this looks fascinating," I say. "I've heard such good things about it. And you've reached the part in Paris, when he defects. How exciting! Just listen to this:

"'The room, they told me, had two doors. Should I decide to go back to Russia, one door would lead me discreetly back into the hall from where I could board the Tupolev. Should I decide to stay in France, the other door led into their own private office. . . . By now I was locked in, safely alone, inside that small room. . . . Four white walls and two doors. Two exits to two different lives.'"

I see Mrs. Brewer open her mouth, trying to say something, but I carry on anyway, running my finger along the text, and soon I forget to monitor her reaction, I'm just in thrall to the story, carried along by the dancer's will, the fierceness of his desire to become something else.

L aurence rings me a few days later and I meet him at a brasserie not far from his house. It's pretty busy but we sit at a quiet table towards the back, and because it's a cold, wet evening we both order steak frites and he picks a good bottle of red. The waiters dance around us, adjusting our glasses, bringing new knives, pouring the wine and then standing back, waiting for his approval.

He's quite different tonight: open, reflective. With a little encouragement he talks about his early life, his father who died young from TB, and his mother, who raised him while holding down a job in the brewery down the road. Books were always a way out, he says. He worked hard for his places at grammar school and Oxford. Of course, things could easily have been very different.

I listen to him talking about his life, and it seems to me I'm an expert and subtle prompt, suggesting the themes that I've picked up from his novels and the interviews he has given to journalists over the years. I can see him puffing up a little with pleasure as, like someone shining a pocket mirror at the sun, I show him his own legend: the self-made man, creative, autonomous, significant. People never tire of their stories. Laurence is no exception.

I ask him whether success has interfered with his freedom, whether he finds it obscures the world sometimes. "Oh, hardly," he says. "My sort of fame, if you can call it that—it's a very small thing. Well, it hardly ever happens, but just occasionally, if I'm in a departure lounge or in a restaurant, someone might approach me, and if you could see the way they sidle up, convulsed with shame, desperate not to intrude . . . just to tell me they've been affected by something I wrote . . . Well, that sort of thing is not hard to bear. I can live with that.

"After all," he says, "it's not as if they want anything from me. No one wants the shirt off my back."

He used to think he led a charmed life, but—he glances down at his hands on the tablecloth—things don't look quite that simple anymore.

Then he changes the subject, asks me about my childhood near Frynborough, a little about my parents. Of course, he's closer in age to them than he is to me. When that becomes apparent, he smiles.

But before I can change the subject, he sees something in my expression, something that betrays me, and he's opening his mouth, about to ask a question, when I remember an anecdote Audrey Callum told me about Sean Templeman, and somehow I distract him with this. His laugh, when it comes, is both a blessing and a disappointment to me.

After the meal, we are helped into our coats and then we go outside, into the rain. "Let me walk you home," he says, and I say, "No, really, it's fine, it's not far away," and then quite shyly, quite tentatively, he puts his hand out and touches my cheek, and next he's bending down towards me, and I'm kissing him back, I'm kissing him, and it's everything I knew it would be.

Some cars go past. The rain falls on us.

Then he says softly, "Come back with me," and I say I will.

It rains all night. I'm aware of it from time to time, the steady ceaselessness of it and the occasional gusts of wind which make the sash windows rattle a little in their frames.

In the morning I inch away from the warmth of his body and the tangle of bedding and step across the room. I open the door carefully, not wanting him to hear, not wanting him to wake.

The distant sound of rain on the rooflight outside Polly's bedroom comes down the staircase. I think of her little bedroom up there, the walls painted the colour of a robin's egg, the string of chilli-pepper lights.

I wonder what she will do when she finds out.

In the bathroom I wash my face with hot water, using a white flannel which I take from the pile in the airing cupboard. I find a new boxed toothbrush in the mirrored cabinet and unwrap it and clean my teeth. Two robes hang on the hook behind the door: I take down the one which belonged to Alys, a slippery length of oyster silk, and I pull it on and knot the belt, and look at myself in the mirror. Then I take it off and pull on the navy waffled-cotton one, which is much too big for me, so I have to fold back the sleeves. Then I go downstairs. The oatmeal-coloured carpet is soft under my bare feet.

On the half landing below I pause on the threshhold of Laurence's study. Curiosity makes me push open the door. It swings back a little to show me the computer on the trestle table, the ugly office chair, the white blinds pulled up to reveal the racing sky and the solemn aspect of the house opposite set back behind thinning trees.

I move into the room, drawn to the wall to the left of the desk. At first glance I think it's covered with hundreds of tiny, bright fluttering wings: yellow and pink and orange, lifting and falling slightly in the draught from the window or the draught created by the open door.

When I go closer I see that they're Post-its, covered with Laurence's tight black writing. The words are clear enough, but the meanings are cryptic, mysterious. *N and R,* they say, and *Bach cantata,* and *D's running* and *R knows about D's episode—but how.*

It's his new novel, I realise. He's plotting it out, marshalling his characters, experimenting with them. Deciding fates.

I imagine him here, lolling back in his chair, frowning and biting his lip, glancing up from the screen to check the fluttering wings on the wall. I imagine him peeling a fresh note from the pad when a new detail comes to mind, and rearranging the coloured sheets, plucking them off and placing them elsewhere, smoothing a finger over the adhesive strips.

He's shaping the narrative, making it twist and fragment and re-form. He's working his way towards a resolution.

It's a pleasing thought. Poignant, too. Here in his study I confront his own sense of himself, and it makes the same impression that I get when I see him with Charlotte or the Titovs or in a public place. Here, as in the wider world, he's in charge, at the helm, the shaper of destinies.

I leave the room, closing the door softly behind me, and go on downstairs to make some tea. Mrs. Polter from the volunteer reading scheme has left a voice mail on my mobile, but I delete it without listening to the rest of the message.

F*or all my planning, I never thought beyond this point. Some* instinct—could it be superstition? A disinclination to tempt fate?—had always prevented me from imagining anything after the actual moment of achievement. This makes the things that happen now all the more exciting, of course—all the more strange and vivid and new—but the sense of danger is also strong. I'm used to being a few paces ahead, but suddenly Laurence and I are walking in step, neither of us knowing what is coming next.

This is the critical moment, I tell myself, trying to regain control. *This is where it could all go wrong.*

But it's difficult to remain levelheaded. Laurence has knocked me off-balance. Somehow, I hadn't fully anticipated this. Over the preceding months, he'd come to represent so many things, and as a consequence the man himself had somehow lost definition, become easy to overlook.

He may be old, he may be given to pomposity and self-regard;

but all the same, I can't help it: I love the way he makes me feel. I love it when he says, "What have I done, to deserve someone so *good*?" And I love the way he starts to need me.

Quite gradually, I find myself falling for him. It feels like falling, too: as if I've lost my footing, with all the potential for indignity that implies. As if there's a chance of being hurt at some point in the future.

But for now I'm simply suspended between states. Am I falling, or flying? I can't be sure.

I find my thoughts colonised by him, the things he tells me, the way he holds me.

Of course, I worry that this will work against me. I worry that I will lose my advantage, the clarity of my perspective. But at the same time, I find I can't do much about it. I have to trust him. After a while, I stop worrying.

We don't talk about the future. Not yet. We meet only in secret: at his house, or my flat. The day before he comes to my flat for the first time, I remember to inspect it with critical eyes, searching out the things he mustn't see here. Alys's cashmere shawl. The old silver thimble I took from the inlaid box in his bedroom at Nevers. An alabaster egg.

Polly's umbrella I decide can stay: it's anonymous enough, he won't notice that. But I fold the egg into the shawl and put the thimble in an envelope, and drop them off at a charity shop that I pass on the way to the office. I no longer need these talismans. Perhaps they'll bring luck to someone else.

When he rings the bell that evening, I let him in and he comes up the stairs and I'm waiting for him, feeling a little shy and nervous, as I usually do at the moment of meeting, and he holds out his arms and the anxieties melt away.

After a while he lets me go and moves around, examining things, much as Polly had done that evening in the spring, although the sitting room looks different now. The bookshelves are an even white, the cushions on the new wheat-coloured sofa are luxuriously plump and firm. I've thrown out the clip-frame art. The flat smells of ironed bed linen and furniture polish and the expensive tuberose-scented candle which is burning on the side table.

He glances through my books, and I see his attention going to the line of Laurence Kytes, my project for the year.

"You see, I'm your greatest fan," I say lightly.

He pulls out the hardback of *Affliction* and flicks through it, pausing for a moment on the dedication page. *For Alys. Always.* Then he shuts it and slides it back in between the others, and his eyes move on to the mantelpiece, over the stack of invitations, the fossil from Golden Cap. Then he comes over to me. "Oh, that's just as well," he says, and he sounds almost serious, more serious than I could have hoped.

We do not talk about Alys yet, though I imagine we may sometime soon.

One Saturday morning I tell him about running into Honor, and the claim she made, and how easily I discounted it. I don't tell him that I know he's innocent because I was watching the scene from the shadows at the bottom of the stairs. I let him believe I simply believe in him.

But he's too exasperated to notice my trust, my faith. Perhaps he will remember it later.

He pulls himself up against the pillows and tugs his hands through his hair, reminded of something tiresome from long ago. "Oh, dear," he says. "How ridiculous. What if she tells the children? What if they fall for her story?"

"They won't," I say. "If I know she's lying, they will, too. Anyway, she says she doesn't want to hurt them." But of course I have my doubts.

I've lost touch with Polly since the summer. She doesn't need me now; my occasional texts mostly go unanswered. It certainly makes my life a lot easier, but part of me misses her and the drama that trails around after her like scent or cigarette smoke.

Laurence sees her from time to time and tells me the latest: he's met the new boyfriend, a fellow student, a bright boy from Stoke-on-Trent. She looks well, happy. She's sticking at the course. Bamber's pleased with her.

Teddy I know less about. He works hard and meets his father for dinner in town. Laurence suspects he's still moping after Honor.

Our affair—carefully protected from both the past and the future as well as from the other people in our lives—settles into a pattern. Naturally it's not like real life; and though in some ways it's better than that, I'm aware, as the weeks pass, of a gradual restlessness, a sort of vague dissatisfaction creeping up on me. Little things begin to annoy me: if he's listening to music or the radio, the volume is usually turned too high; and sometimes, talking to him on the phone, I have to repeat myself.

When I wake before him, I find myself inspecting him quite dispassionately in the half-light: the thinning, faded hair falling away from his temples, the creases around his mouth and eyes, the liver spots on his hands. The murky stains of age.

His skin, I think sometimes, is too soft.

But these are just little details, and I try not to dwell on them.

One evening we are sitting over supper in the white kitchen in Highgate when Laurence mentions Christmas. He's planning to go to Biddenbrooke with the children, he says, quite casually. Then he sees the expression on my face and puts down his fork.

"Why, Frances—surely you didn't think we were going to spend it together?" he says, with a little steely edge of reprimand. "It's our first Christmas without Alys. Their first Christmas without their mother."

Of course, I say, I don't know what I imagined.

He sees the hurt on my face and reaches across the table. "Don't be a goose," he says more gently. "No need to rush. We've got lots of time."

This comment gives me hope, but otherwise I have to take a lot on trust. I'm careful not to put any pressure on him. I hold back, even as I want to push forward.

Gradually he lets down his guard, just a fraction every so often. The Laurence I begin to glimpse in these moments has little in common with the public figure, assured and self-contained and maybe faintly stuffy; he's someone else, someone less certain, still confused by grief but starting to see beyond it, beginning to have a sense of new possibilities.

From time to time I see myself through his eyes, and I appear to have plenty to offer: youth, independence, freedom. I understand people, their ambitions and desires, their fears and weaknesses. It's a talent that he finds both amusing and useful. And I'm new, too, free from associations with his old compromised life, the life he shared out meanly between Alys and those discreet obliging girls. Perhaps it's not so strange, after all, that we're together. I try not to think about his affairs; and he certainly does not mention them to me, though I have hope that he will one day make a confession of sorts involving Julia Price, at least.

This time it's different, I tell myself. Soon, circumstances will force his hand; soon we will go public. It won't be an affair at that point, it'll be a relationship. The girls without names never got that far. Neither did Julia Price.

But for now, we lie low.

There are a few scares. We are talking in his kitchen late one evening when his mobile rings, upstairs on the hall table. He leaves it. Not long after we are on our way to bed when we hear the doorbell.

He is not expecting anyone.

We stand motionless in the hall, staring at each other like characters in a farce, and then there's the sound of a key going into the lock. Without thinking I grab my coat and bag off the peg and back swiftly into the sage-green drawing room, a room which is rarely used, pulling the door to after me, while he goes forward to greet Polly.

I stand in the darkness, my heart hammering, listening to their conversation. She rang earlier; why didn't he pick up? She's had another row with Serena.

Their voices fade into murmurs as they go along the corridor, as he leads her down into the kitchen, switching on lights, the kettle.

Silently, furtively, I creep out of the drawing room, holding my bag against my stomach so nothing rattles, placing my feet carefully on the red rug to muffle my steps. As I let myself out into the cold night, I remember—with a faint guilty qualm of regret—that there's no evidence of me left for her to notice: the dishwasher set off, with its pairs of plates and forks and wineglasses; the toothbrush at the back of the cabinet.

M*ary Pym is the only person who senses something has happened.* One morning in late November I catch her watching me over her spectacles. I raise my eyebrows in interrogation, and she says, "You look different."

"Do I?"

"Oh, yes. You're up to something, aren't you?" She sounds almost affectionate, pleased for me.

I laugh, trying to sound offhand, and say I don't know what she means.

I hear from Polly in early December when she sends a text asking me whether I'm able to come to the end-of-term performance of *Footsteps on the Ceiling*. I ring Laurence and we agree I should go. Teddy isn't free that night, which is a relief, but Charlotte Black has also been invited, and I am both daunted and excited about subjecting myself—us—to her scrutiny. I can't believe we'll get away with it.

The auditorium is overheated, and as I find my seat, I'm already feeling flushed, ill at ease. All around me, groups of parents and friends are bent over programmes, pointing out names.

Charlotte Black and Laurence arrive together, deep in conversation: my mouth is dry with anxiety as they spot me and make their way sideways along the row towards the seats I've saved for them, coats over their arms. I kiss Charlotte and then I kiss Laurence, and suddenly our joint deceit seems awfully conspicuous and foolish. Laurence sits in the middle, and the three of us make small talk for a short while, and then the lights go down.

Polly has a sizeable part and she's not bad: she looks lovely and she gets a few big laughs.

During the curtain call, she shields her eyes from the lights, squinting out into the audience, and when she finds us, she waves and blows us kisses.

"You must come and eat with us after this," says Laurence in my ear. "It'll be fine, really it will."

"I can't," I say, not looking at him. "Not like this. Don't make me."

In the foyer, I wait with him and Charlotte, surrounded by happy, excited groups of people, and eventually Polly comes out and joins us. Someone's with her, a tall boy with dark red hair.

"Oh, Frances," she says, hugging me. "I'm so glad you could come."

"You were really good," I say, meaning it. "Congratulations."

"Martin," she says, tugging on his hand, dragging him out of the conversation he is having with her father, "Martin, come and meet Frances."

Martin shakes my hand and says he's pleased to meet me. He's striking, with his hazel eyes and pale skin. "How do you know each other?" he asks.

There's a tiny weighted pause while Polly and I are reminded of things we'd rather not think about.

"Through my mother," Polly says. "I'll tell you the story another time."

Christmas comes, and we convene at my parents' house. "'Tis the season to be jolly!" sings Toby as my mother circulates yet again with a long-suffering expression and a rubbish sack. The house is full of tiny wastepaper baskets and she empties them constantly, as if having a middling-sized bin with anything in it is a sign of extreme slovenliness.

The suspicion is always that without the wastepaper baskets my mother would have little purpose in life.

When I am sent out to the garage to get more green beans from the chest freezer, I see she has taped a piece of A4 to the lid, an index of all contents, with lines neatly scored through *cauliflower cheese* and *puff pastry*. Later additions are in green Biro:

half sliced granary loaf, Mrs. Craven's apple pie (WI), back bacon (3 rashers).

Hester and Charlie are in the room which used to be hers; the boys are sharing my old one; and I'm on a put-me-up in the study. When it all gets too much, there's nowhere to escape to. I spend quite a bit of time walking around the village with my hands deep in my pockets, thinking about Laurence not so very far away, wondering whether he will call me (he doesn't, though he leaves me a message on Christmas Eve to say he hopes I'm "having fun"); but I am careful not to advertise these excursions for fear of having the boys foisted on me, which would defeat the object.

Hester, as usual, vacillates between ostentatious maternal self-satisfaction ("Lovely sharing, Toby!") and a desire to spend as much time as possible away from her sons. "Probably it's the overexcitement," she confides tipsily on the sofa one afternoon—following a few parched Christmases, Charlie now travels with his own booze—when the boys have been removed to the playground at the end of the village. "But they've been pushing all my buttons." She has just read a book which has made her see that "I've got into this habit of intervening in every squabble. Boys fight, there's not much I can do about that, and they need to learn to sort things out without my involvement. So we've decided we have to step back, to empower them to find a solution by themselves."

After tea, while Rufus and Toby quarrel over the last chocolate Santa in the dish, she takes herself off for a bath. Charlie is slumped behind the *Telegraph's* festive quiz, oblivious.

The noise goes on and on until at last my mother switches on the television.

Every year at this time I'm forced to face my shortcomings, the many things I lack. And though this year is different, though I have my promotion (which everyone is dutifully pleased about), as well as my secret (which I turn over in my mind when I am alone, consoling myself with its exotic heat), I remain, as far as my family is concerned, the same funny old Frances. Uptight. Increasingly set in her ways. A little bit stuck, perhaps.

O*n his return from Biddenbrooke, Laurence gives me a small,* framed pen-and-ink drawing of the Heath as a late present. He seems low after the holiday. The children had agreed it would be good to do things differently this year, so they'd kept themselves busy and spent the day itself elsewhere, with friends. But as expected, he says, it was a rather wretched sort of Christmas.

Things appear to be fine at the office: the pages are working well and Mary seems pleased with me. When I am introduced to Malcolm Azaria at the Sunderland prize ceremony, I do not mention the Kytes. Instead I ask whether he'd be interested in contributing to the *Questioner,* and so he starts to write the occasional piece for us. Strangers approach me at literary events: PRs, publishers, other hacks. I'm building up my contacts, putting out my feelers. I begin to feel as if I belong in this world, as if I deserve to be a part of it; as if it accepts me. Respects me, even.

I know how fickle it is, though, and I'm careful not to attach too much importance to its whims.

From time to time I find myself next to Sasha in the tea-trolley queue or the lift and she tells me about Oliver: he's contributing to a late-night arts show on a satellite TV channel, he's blogging, he might have a book deal. "Give him my best wishes," I say, and she says she will, but I know if she does mention me, it will be a joke they share over a drink in some bar or other.

Well, let them.

The anniversary of Alys's death is approaching. Laurence has not asked me again about that day. It's as if he'd like to believe we dealt with it fully when I first met the family all those months ago. But then I've found out that he won't speak to me about Alys at all. When I mention her, asking questions about their shared history or her likes and dislikes, his answers are brief and bland, evasive.

Although his rebuff is always polite, he makes me feel ill-mannered for inviting it, as if I'm testing his loyalty.

Maybe that's exactly what I'm doing.

"Do you mind me wearing this?" I ask one morning, when his glance snags on the long wool cardigan I've pulled on. It's an amazing colour: an inky-dark purple. "I found it in a cupboard, I wasn't sure if you'd mind."

"I don't mind," he says shortly. The next time I look for it, I see he's finally cleared her possessions from the chest of drawers and the wardrobe and the hooks in the hallway. All those shoes—the heels with the bright red soles, the walking boots, the ballet flats in silver and bronze and black, the tall Hunters marked with old pale mud—have been removed. The bathroom cabinet has been emptied of its interior skyline of face creams and bath oils. The mascaras and bottles of foundation and the little blunt stubs of candy-coloured lipsticks in their chrome tubes: all gone.

The wisp of oyster silk is no longer hanging on the back of the bathroom door.

I'm confused by the way this makes me feel: should I be gratified to see her go, or should I be offended that I'm unfit to use her things? It's hard to know what to think.

"I see you've had a clear-out," I say at supper. He tells me Mrs. King organised it at his request. Many items were thrown out or given to charity, and the jewellery has been put in a bank vault for

Polly, but some of the clothes have been bagged up and put away in the loft. He supposes Polly may want to go through them at some point.

I want to ask how this has affected him but I know, looking at his face, that I can't. It's not something he wants to talk about, and I daren't push things. Maybe later. Not yet.

The date comes and goes, and I do not have the nerve to refer to it directly. We make no arrangements to see each other on the day itself, or indeed during the days on either side. I wonder what he and Polly and Teddy have planned, if anything.

I suspect Teddy takes a day's holiday and Polly is excused from college and the three of them spend it together. Maybe they visit the grave in Highgate cemetery first thing, followed by a blowy walk on the Heath and a low-key lunch at the Spaniards Inn. I imagine Polly crying all day, off and on. Laurence not saying much but putting his arm around her. Teddy wavering between melancholy and a desire to cheer everyone up.

On the Friday, as agreed, Laurence comes round to see me. He's spending more time at mine now; I sense I'm less welcome at the house. Polly's unplanned visit rattled us both, and at some point after that—around the time of the cardigan episode, come to think of it—the flat became the default meeting place.

He says it's less complicated this way: "It's easier to be anonymous in a flat. Look—you don't know anyone on your street."

And he's right: I know the girl who lives downstairs but only to say hello to, and otherwise—apart from the woman at number 18 who recommended her decorator—the road is full of strangers. "You've no idea how interested my neighbours are in my life," Laurence adds wearily. "It really would be much simpler if we didn't involve them."

So he rings the bell, and I let him in.

"I thought of you all on Monday," I say.

"That was good of you," he says politely. Then he leans towards me and all my intentions, all my questions, blow away like smoke.

Later that night I lie beside him, listening to his slow and easy breathing, wondering whether things will ever change. I'm starting to be unable to imagine why they would. It strikes me that Laurence is quite content with things as they are: the widower with his discreet little secret. Perhaps he is having his cake and eating it, as he always has.

I see Oliver as soon as I go in. *He's standing in the corner, nose to nose* with S. P. Nicholl. His rather wild laugh travels and unravels across the room.

He's wearing skinny jeans and pointed, lace-up shoes and his absurd hair is looking particularly toiled-over. He's plainly drunk but I still feel daunted by his presence. Maybe I'll get away without having to speak to him.

The party—held in an upstairs room at a Soho members' club—is crowded and noisy. Anne Abbott Smith, the reason we're all here, is holding court by the window, near the table stacked with copies of her memoir. I'm only showing up to say thank-you to Erica, the publicist who gave us the first interview, so I work my way round to her, nodding and smiling at people as I inch past them.

"Hope you were pleased with the coverage," I say when I finally reach Erica, and she says she thought Gemma Coke was a little unkind, but, oh, well, never mind, you can't look twelve hundred words in the mouth.

At the edge of my vision Oliver is being abandoned by S. P. Nicholl, who detaches himself with almost forensic elegance and floats away in search of more congenial company. Looking around for fresh blood, Oliver lurches off in the direction of the group surrounding Anne Abbott Smith, weaving towards her, a little unsteady on his feet. He pushes past the girl from the *Times* and into the semicircle and I can see him introducing himself. Oh, my, he's actually *bending over her hand* and *kissing it*. Anne Abbott Smith stares at him stonily, implacable. I can hear him saying, "The quality of your prose . . . ," and that's enough, I don't have to stay any longer, I've done what I needed to do.

I'm just at the door when I hear his voice, and he's calling, "Wait up. Frances! Wait up!"

I turn around, adjusting my expression. I want to look cordial but not too inviting. A little cool. But I soon realise any subtleties are going to be wasted on him tonight.

"Thought it was you!" he's saying, clapping his hands on my shoulders and coming in close for a kiss. "Good old Frances. Out fishing for diary stories, are you?"

"Something like that, mm," I say. "How are you doing, anyway? Where are you working now?"

"Bits of radio, bits of telly. 'S terrific fun. Probably going to do a book. Best thing is, no more Mary. How is the bloodless old witch?"

"Oh, missing you," I say evenly.

He cocks his head. "You're taking the piss, aren't you, Frances. Oh, you are bad."

I start to protest, but there's not really any point, so I shrug and pull my coat tighter and start walking down the stairs, towards the street. Oliver's right behind me, though his glass is still in his hand.

"Do stay, Frances," he says, losing his footing on the last three steps, spilling some wine and then giggling and righting himself. "I want to hear how it's all going without me."

"Oh, you know. It's going," I say as the door is opened for me and I step into the cold night air. Some taxis go by, and then there's one with a yellow light. As Oliver follows me out, I put my hand up to hail it, but I'm just too late. "We're managing somehow."

"I bet you are." A strange note of admiration is in his voice. "You're a survivor, aren't you. I knew it. You and your connections—"

"Connections?" I say, walking faster now, and suddenly furious. "Whereas you, of course, with your father . . ."

"I've heard some interesting stories about you recently," he's saying as he hurries after me. "You're getting quite a reputation, you know. Oh, it's a good one. Hard worker. Sharp mind. Leaves nothing to chance. But everyone wonders where you've come *from.*"

"How ridiculous," I say, spinning around and coming back to confront him. "I was on that desk with Mary for years before I got my break. I *earned* it."

"No, no, of course you did," says Oliver, and I can see he's taken aback by my reaction; he's a little excited by it. "But people are talking. About your friendship with the Kytes."

"So what? Yes, I'm friends with the family. What of it? Is it any of your business?" I wonder what he's got on me. Has someone seen me with Laurence?

"Well, there are these rumours . . . ," says Oliver, leaning in confidentially so I catch the wine and garlic on his breath. "You know what people are like. Only happy when they're sinking their teeth in! I've been defending you, I should tell you that. You know, when people use this phrase *ambulance chaser,* I tell them where to get off."

I stare at him, and I feel awful treacherous heat flooding my face. "Ambulance chaser? Who's saying that? What on earth do they mean?" But of course I'm thinking, *Charlotte Black and Selma*

Carmichael. It's Selma's doing. I should have been more careful about turning down that job.

"Isn't it true, then? That you only got to know Kyte and his daughter because you'd witnessed the wife's car accident?"

And in Oliver's voice, I hear an echo of several conversations he has had over the last few weeks: conversations about me, my ambitions, and my intentions. The thought of it, the thought of my vulnerability, fills me with a sort of horror. Oliver, running around town in his pointed shoes, shooting his mouth off, buying his way into the right parties with the right information.

But, I tell myself quickly, maybe that's the wrong way to look at it. Though I hate the idea of Oliver cracking jokes at my expense in the corners of noisy rooms, I have to admit that the idea is not entirely unpleasant. Here is confirmation of my new status. I have become someone whose actions now serve as currency for the little people.

I could give you something to gossip about, I think.

"I didn't witness the accident," I say patiently. "But I was the first person on the scene afterwards. I've never said otherwise." And I haven't. "How odd people are! I've never misled anyone. Why do they care, anyway?"

"Oh, you know what people are like," Oliver says, but now that I've regained my composure he's losing interest and glancing back over his shoulder at the door. "They love to talk."

"I suppose they do," I say, and I start to walk away, pulling up my collar. "I've got to go."

"Nice seeing you!" he calls after me, then I hear the door slam as he goes back to rejoin the fun.

I hide my anxieties from Laurence. I let him believe all this is enough for me.

My life shifts to accommodate him, though I cannot tell—and do not miss—what he has displaced.

Towards the end of the week, if I go to the supermarket, I might find myself buying croissants, a vacuum-sealed packet of the brand of coffee I know he has at home, an expensive wine I wouldn't think of for myself. And sometimes—usually—he rings; and sometimes he doesn't.

When I see him, I am careful not to articulate my feelings. I hold them tight to myself, as I held my bag with its telltale jangle of keys that evening when Polly nearly caught us in Highgate. I am fearful about putting pressure on him.

And then one Saturday in the spring the moment comes when I think it might be time to take a risk.

He calls on Wednesday, and we make a loose arrangement to see each other at the weekend. Does this mean Friday night? Or Saturday? I am not sure and feel unable to press him, so I spend the Friday, my day off, hanging around the flat, half-expecting him to arrive without warning.

Eventually, he rings on the Saturday afternoon. The lowered voice on the phone. "Are you free? Can I see you?"

I've been vacuuming the stairs and cleaning the bath. My hands are dry and chapped with detergent. I wedge the phone under my chin and squeeze out a little hand cream into my palm, and as I work it into my knuckles, my cuticles, I say, "Oh. Fine. If you like," wondering whether he'll hear the timbre of my voice, the sound of dissatisfaction.

This time when he comes round, I do not hide my resentment. I'm a little cold with him. I pull back early from his kisses. When he runs a finger down the side of my cheek, I catch his hand and move it aside.

"It's nothing," I say when he asks me what is wrong. And then I look away, towards the street. A few of the windows in the block opposite are open, making the most of the milder weather. Someone throws a bucket of water over a soapy car. The sky is an undecided colour.

"Would you like to go out? A walk? The cinema? Can I take you to dinner afterwards?" he says, a helpless note in his voice. This is unusual: he's normally cautious, in case we meet someone he knows, in case he is recognised.

I agree to a walk and we catch a cab to Regent's Park, striking out from Camden Town and skirting the edge of the zoo, turning south towards Baker Street as the minaret and copper dome of the mosque come into view. There is a suggestion of green in the trees. The boating lake ripples with ducks.

I seem to have his attention now. He's gentle with me, courteous and conciliatory. We talk a little about the office, a book I am reviewing, and then he tells me briefly about his progress with the novel. He says he is finally happy with the direction it's taking; he thinks it's coming together at last.

Some runners speed past us, tight in a pack, breath like pistons. The playing fields are scattered with five-a-sides, the goals marked out with piles of waterproofs and jerseys. Laurence takes my hand.

"You must tell me," he says, "when I do something wrong."

I allow my hand to rest in his. For a moment, I wonder whether I should just let this slide, wait for a few weeks, then try again. But I'm feeling impatient. Of course, it's a gamble. I can't be sure that he will do what I need him to do.

"It's awkward," I begin. "I'm not really sure how to explain it."

He's looking at me. I'm sure he's thinking, *Oh, Christ, what does she want?* But maybe he's not. Maybe he's thinking, *I don't want to lose her.* I can't be sure. I won't know until I've said it out loud.

"I don't want to be taken for granted," I say, in a burst. "I don't like feeling as if I'm your . . . dirty little secret."

"Is that really how you feel?" A stricken look is on his face.

I nod. He lifts my hand to his mouth and kisses it. "Oh, sweetheart, I had no idea. I'm sorry." We walk on, our steps synchronised. Cries of triumph and despair erupt from a game to our left.

"Of course I know it's not easy for you," I say. "You still have a lot of . . ."

"Baggage," he says, with a wry laugh. "Well, that's true. But it doesn't excuse the fact that I've made you miserable. You don't deserve that, my darling. Not least because you've made me so happy—just when I'd almost lost faith in happiness. What would make you feel better? How can I make it up to you?"

This is unfair, I think, with a quick blaze of indignation. If he bothered to think, if he bothered to put himself in my shoes, he'd know exactly how to improve things. But—as I'm already aware—he's emotionally lazy. He prefers other people to do the work.

"It might help," I say, the anger carrying me along a little, "if you treated me with more respect."

"That's not—," he's protesting, but I keep talking.

"I know you don't want to tell Teddy and Polly about us, and of course you don't want us to be seen together, and who knows, maybe we'll never even get to that stage. But right now I'm starting to feel as if we only ever meet on your terms, when it suits you. My flat—at your convenience."

He's nodding, frowning, the epitome of reason. A football rolls across the path and he moves towards it and kicks it back into the game, raising his hand to acknowledge the shouts of thanks.

"How can I make it up to you?" he asks again as we walk on. "What would make you feel better?"

I sigh and pull my hand away from his, rubbing my eyes.

"No, you're right," he says, as if he suddenly understands my frustration. "Perhaps it's time."

I wait. Time for what? Time to tell his children? Time to give me a key for the house in Highgate?

"Let's work out how we're going to do this," he says. "I'm sure you'll understand that I don't want to rush it. We're going to have to handle it carefully for the children's sakes."

"Of course," I say, not sure what he is suggesting.

"Well, let's begin by going out to supper," he says. "Somewhere in town. Somewhere nice."

"Oh, that would be lovely," I say, hating the way I have to sound grateful for such a tiny concession. "Are you sure?" and he says absolutely.

"Go on. You decide. Where do you want to go?"

So I pick a smart, new Italian restaurant I've read about, off Marylebone High Street, and I get the number and pass my phone over to him, and there's a little problem about getting a table until he gives his name, and then there's no difficulty at all.

We are shown to a round table covered with a stiff white cloth as the evening sets in. The waiters dart around us, in spots of bright light, coaxing our coats from us, distributing and collecting menus, providing us with bread and water and wine, and then they retreat to the dimmer edges of the room, waiting until they are required. Across the street, lamps are lit in an upstairs flat. A shadowy figure moves to and fro within: the mysterious, appealing choreography of a stranger's life.

I unfold my hard, starched napkin and put it on my lap. "You never talk about Alys," I say once they have brought our plates.

He says he'll tell me anything I want to know.

She was a good woman. It's important I understand this. He's not stretching the truth when he says she was far too good for him, he adds, bowing his head as if to suggest, *Maybe it's the same with you.* He was not always an attentive husband. He has regrets about the things he did, the things he did not do. Work distracted him from their life together, he accepts that. She bore the brunt of reality for him, more or less uncomplainingly. She was a wonderful mother. The children loved her. His friends, their friends, loved her.

I say I remember how affectionately Malcolm Azaria spoke about her, and he stops buttering his roll and looks at me, surprised, momentarily baffled. "Oh, of course—you were there," he says. "I'd forgotten. You seemed so different back then."

"Did I?"

He puts down his knife, frowning with the effort of remembering. "Yes, you seemed so . . . shy isn't quite right. Retiring, I suppose. Hmm. I can't quite put my finger on it." I know the words he's too tactful to use: colourless. Unimportant. Forgettable.

The memory makes him reassess me. I can see him puzzling over it. Perhaps he has never thought so hard about me before. "Where did you come from?" he murmurs, sliding his hand over mine.

I smile and take my hand away, lifting my glass to my mouth. "Tell me more about Alys," I say.

So he tells me about her kindness, her patience, her tolerance. He makes her sound, to be frank, a little dull and wholesome. All the time he is describing her, he's inadvertently describing himself: his unkindness, his impatience, his intolerance.

For the first time, I feel a little sorry for Alys. *She let you get away with everything,* I think. *She lost control of you.* I think of his study, the fluttering coloured Post-its, the way he marshalls his fictional creatures, the way he runs his little universes. The nameless girls. The Julia Prices.

I promise myself that I must never forget. I must marshall him in the same way.

As the evening unwinds, with its candles and heavy cutlery and rich, shiny sauces, I wait for him to broach the subject of Julia Price, but her name never comes up. I could ask about her, I suppose; I could say that Honor told me about the affair. But I have an instinct that might be a step too far tonight. It's one thing to be a careless husband; quite another to be a faithless one. So I listen to his invented version of their marriage, and I wonder, idly, where the truth lies.

One thing comes of the evening, at any rate. Laurence decides—he believes the decision is all his—that he needs to tell his children.

"I don't think you should say anything to them," I say. "I really don't, unless you are completely sure about it. It would be awful for them if you weren't absolutely sure."

He nods, in full agreement, but not before I see a tremor of unease.

"I mean," I say, "look at it from their point of view. Teddy and Polly won't want to know that you have a . . . a girlfriend. Something casual. Imagine how that would feel to them. It would be a betrayal of their mother—your marriage."

"Go on," he says, and then there's a pause as the waiter puts an espresso cup before him.

"Oh, God, this is embarrassing," I say, fiddling with my coffee spoon.

He looks at me, smiling, but the unease is still there. "Go on."

"I think you have to be sure"—I take a deep breath, and then I say it, as if it's being dragged out of me, but as if it has to be said sometime—"about *us*. And do you know what, Laurence? I don't think you are."

The words hang there in the air over the table, twisting and re-forming.

This is it, I think. *Crunch time.* I've staked everything on this.

I'm pretty sure what he'll say in response—I'd never have said the words, were I not—but of course there's a chance I've miscalculated.

I watch him sitting there: the colour of his shirt, the shape of his hands, the fingers curled daintily, ludicrously, around the doll's cup. The moment stretches on and on. I wait for the snap.

And then he's saying, "Oh, but you're wrong; I am, I am absolutely sure. Don't you know? Can't you tell?"

And I'm laughing, too, with happiness, relief, and satisfaction also, and I'm asking him how, why, when: all the questions I've held back for all these months, for fear I'd scare him off.

He says, catching my hand, "Oh, I've known for ages—since Biddenbrooke, since that day when I arrived, I came into the hall and you were at the top of the stairs, do you remember? I'd startled you. You'd been asleep, I think . . . you looked as if you'd been sleeping. Do you remember? I saw you and I came up the stairs, and something happened, a sort of electricity. . . . It was the strangest experience. Do you know what I'm talking about?"

"Of course," I say hesitantly, smiling, but frowning faintly as well, narrowing my eyes as if I'm trying to remember.

"Oh—Frances," he says, flooded with amusement and indulgence, but stung just a little. "You're such a bad liar. Your face. It's a picture. You don't know what I'm talking about, do you?"

I protest that of course I do, while leaving him in no doubt that I don't. Why do I dissemble on this point? I think it's good for Laurence to remember that he put the chain of events in motion. It's good for him to believe he had a moment of revelation and acted upon it decisively, authoritatively.

And, yes, possibly this is a little less than kind; but I also find I want him to believe that when he first noticed me—properly became aware of me, during that strange vivid moment on the stairs—I was almost oblivious of him.

"So, yes, we must tell the children," he goes on.

I notice he doesn't bother to ask me how certain I am of him. He just assumes I'm in accordance. Why wouldn't I be?

"Unless . . . ," he adds, struck by an afterthought. "I don't suppose you'd do it, would you? What about *you* telling Polly? Maybe it would be better, coming from you."

I think this is a bad idea, for many reasons, and the ones I put to him seem to be persuasive. "Of course you're right," he says, with some regret. "I suppose it's the sort of thing I should really deal with myself."

I wonder aloud what will be the greater shock: that he's in a relationship, or the identity of the person with whom he's having it.

"Oh, I'm sure once they've got used to the idea, they'll come round quite quickly," he says. "Polly's terribly fond of you, she has been from the moment she met you, and I can't believe Teddy will be a problem. They'll be glad, won't they, to think of me being happy?"

I say I'm sure they will be, but I know otherwise. It's the old problem: he's self-centred, optimistically deluded, unable to analyse the situation with the necessary clarity. It's not his way to scan family life for potential pratfalls or catastrophes. Not for the first time, I find myself pitying him his limited imagination, contemplating the gaps that patient, stoical, apprehensive Alys must have bridged for him for all these years.

"I tell you what," he's saying. "Come round next Thursday, after you finish work, and we'll drive up to Biddenbrooke for a long weekend." He says Polly is due to have dinner with him on Tuesday or Wednesday, and he'll invite Teddy, too, and tell them both at the same time, and then it'll all be out in the open.

I'm aware of a tension building up as the week passes. At work, my thoughts are clouded with scenes of Laurence, of Polly, of Teddy; of appalled astonishment and crying and, more distantly—so distantly, in fact, that it seems close to fantastical—of reconciliations and expressions of goodwill. Will he tell them as soon as they arrive, as he embraces them and takes their coats? "Oh, and by the way, I have a bit of news . . ." No. Surely he'll be nervous, he'll feel his way, build up to it.

I keep my mobile close: I'm half-expecting Polly to call. I daren't expect her to be pleased, but perhaps she'll be in tears, angry, horrified, and maybe I'll be able to reassure her or talk her down.

But Polly does not ring.

Laurence phones, as he promised he would, on Thursday morning. He does not offer me any clues. He sounds as he always does. Mary is at her desk, so I'm careful not to say, or ask, anything compromising.

He says he'd happily pick me up from the office, but it might make more sense if I could find my own way to Highgate: it's an easier drive out from there.

"Okay, I should be there by seven," I say. "Great. Yes. I'll look forward to it."

Putting the receiver down, I look at Mary's shiny head bent over her desk and it seems safe to assume she wasn't listening to the conversation, but a little later she walks past my desk and kicks—with the pointy toe of her chocolate suede shoe—my overnight bag, half-hidden under my desk. Then she says, with a deathly sort of innocence, "Doing anything nice this weekend?"

"Just visiting some friends," I say, returning her gaze. "No one you know."

We finish the pages in good time, and at six fifteen I tidy my desk and leave the office to catch the tube north, pulling my red-and-purple scarf around my neck because the day has been quite cool. It's a fifteen-minute walk to Laurence's house, initially along steep avenues lined with cherry trees and blameless redbrick villas, and then down some quiet streets where the houses require more space, more greenery, more privacy; the short drives, behind their high electronic gates, clogged by day with gardeners' vans and by night with Priuses and Range Rovers.

The houses are lighting up. There are glimpses of shiny kitchens, brightness lying in glossy bars across slabs of white marble, and living rooms arranged with modular sofas and sticks in tall vases. A dog rushes barking at the railings, his paws scattering the gravel.

I walk up Laurence's street, listening to the sudden drone of a jet circling round to Heathrow.

As the light dwindles, the air sharpens. I fold my scarf inside my collar, tucking it down.

The bag handle rubs a little on my fingers. I adjust my grip and think about the weekend ahead: three days alone with Laurence, at Biddenbrooke. It seems significant that he wants to take me there. It's another step in the right direction.

Left foot, right foot.

I'm nearly there, I think. Just a few more moves, and it's finished, complete, secured. But this stage is the stage I have least control over. Because of that, I'm eager to get it started. I want to see how it plays.

I remember Laurence as I once glimpsed him long ago, when Polly took me round to Highgate for lunch. I remember looking down the garden from the French windows and seeing him alone on a bench, nursing his grief, picked out by its dark, isolating lustre. He's happier now, I tell myself. He wouldn't risk going back to that.

I've distracted him from that vast and absorbing despair, but he knows it's still out there, unpredictable, fatal, a thin layer of ice in a dip in the road. He will do anything to avoid it again. Once you've experienced it, you know how dogged it is, how compelling. In his heart of hearts he believes I've seen it off, like a talisman, a lucky charm.

No, I think. He won't risk it. Of course it would be preferable if Teddy and Polly could come to accept the situation; but if they don't, he will still cleave to me. I'm his happiness now. He will not let me go. Will he?

When I reach the house, the front door is half-open, light from the hall spilling down the steps. Hesitantly, I wait on the gravel drive, listening, trying to work out whether he is alone. I hear nothing, and then the sound of feet on floorboards. I shrink back away from the steps, easing into the shadow at the edge of the house. The door opens wide. Laurence comes out, carrying something, his teeth set with the effort. I move forward.

"Oh, good, there you are," he says, coming down the steps towards me. He's carrying a case of wine. He glances towards the street and, balancing the box on the balustrade, risks a quick kiss. "All set? Can you get the boot for me?"

I open it and put my bag in, next to a carrier of groceries and his small holdall, and he lowers in the wine. "Shall we go? I'm quite keen to make a quick getaway."

"I thought the roads should be pretty clear on a Thursday," I say.

"Oh, the roads should be fine," he agrees, placing his hands on the boot and closing it. "Well. Thing is, Polly rang earlier, she's planning to stay here tonight with Martin. They're going to a party somewhere nearby. They may drop in beforehand, I suppose, to leave their things."

I stare at him. I can't quite see the expression on his face. A broken yellow pattern moves over the drive: the light from the streetlamps filtering through the trees.

"I take it you didn't . . . ," I say.

"Long story," he says briskly. "The timing wasn't right."

He looks away, adjusting the wing mirror. "Right," he says again, popping the driver's door. "Shall we . . . ?"

"I'm thirsty," I say. "I'll just run in for a drink of water. I won't be a minute."

"Oh, of course," he says, nice and expansive now he's over the hump of the bad news. "Just pull the front door shut behind you when you're finished."

I go up the steps and into the house. The tawny floorboards with their ancient whorled knots, the scarlet rug, the wall of coats, the pot of umbrellas, the hall table shining clear of post. I walk down the corridor and put my hand out for the switch and there's a faint charged hum as the lights over the stairs illuminate, flooding the oatmeal carpet, showing up the tiny loops in the pile. I follow the spiral of the stair down into the kitchen, turning on the lights as I go. It's tidy, the table free of crumbs, nothing out on the counters: a Mrs. King day.

While I let the cold tap run to get rid of the residual heat from the Aga, I reach up over the sink to get a glass from the cupboard. The stream of water is a crystal rope, fraying as it hits the white ceramic. I fill the glass, turn off the tap, and lift the brim to my lips. As I drink, I look around the room: so plain, so complete, so utterly impervious.

I take the water away from my lips and pour the rest of it into the sink and pull open the door of the dishwasher and insert the glass. Then I walk to the foot of the stairs and click off the overhead kitchen lights.

In the dimness of the room, I take a few steps back into it. I walk around the refectory table with its neat, self-satisfied arrangement of chairs, and I pull off my red-and-purple scarf, feeling the rasp, the burn of it against my throat, and I let it fall on the flagstones, halfway between the sink and the stairs. It lies there, a vivid shot of colour even in the half-light.

I go back through the silent, expectant house, touching switches as I pass, leaving first the stairs and then the hallway in darkness. When I come out onto the front steps, Laurence is in the car, waiting for me. I pull the door shut, hearing the heavy, reassuring click of the lock, and then I run down the steps and get into the passenger seat, and we pull off into the evening, the two of us.

During the long, flat drive towards the coast, he tells me about his week, the lunch with a screenwriter friend, an overture from a BBC documentary producer, progress on the book. The children came over on Wednesday, he explains, but Teddy seemed downcast: he'd seen Honor the night before, and for whatever reason it hadn't been an easy encounter. "There'll be a better moment to tell them," he assures me, beating his fingers on the steering wheel: a tic of anxiety. "We just have to wait."

"No rush," I say calmly, but that's not how I feel. *I've been patient*, I think, *I've been patient for months and months, and now my patience is running out.* I visualise it: sand sliding through a hourglass, the inexorable trickle. Only a few grains left.

I think of the red-and-purple scarf, lying on the kitchen floor, and the thought calms me a little.

It's nearly ten by the time we reach Nevers. The looming hedgerows, the phone box with its melancholy illumination, the pebbly track, the meadow full of silver in the moonlight. All the time we are carrying our bags in from the car and turning on lights, I'm thinking of the scarf, wondering whether Polly will even see it tonight. Tomorrow, I think, tomorrow, maybe then she'll notice it, when she goes down to make some tea in the morning. She'll pick it up and look at it and hang it over the back of a chair, or the bannister; maybe she'll recognise it. And maybe she won't.

Laurence is in the kitchen. Mrs. Talbot has left him a pork pie and salad and some cheese, and he's looking for a jar of Alys's gooseberry chutney, banging cupboard doors and moving things around in the larder, clattering cutlery on the marble-topped table. I stand by my bag in the hall, smelling woodsmoke from the fire Mrs. Talbot lit for him in the sitting room hours earlier, which has died down to a dim red rubble.

The house smells quite different now. The last time, in high summer, the doors and windows were always open and the rooms seemed full of air, air and sun-baked upholstery, the tang of chlorine and the suggestion that somewhere not far off Polly was having yet another cigarette. Now, there's a sense of the house being locked up with itself. There's a staleness hanging in the huge space of the hall, despite Mrs. Talbot's best efforts with polish and detergent.

Laurence's things lie in a tangle on the hall table. His coat has been slung over his bag, and his coat pocket yawns open a little, revealing his mobile. The face is illuminated and I can see that he hasn't locked the keypad. There are some figures—331*—on the screen. He must have knocked the phone as he came in and put everything down.

Without stopping to think I pick up the phone and scroll quickly through the address book. It's not very full: I'm in it, surname and initial, and there's someone called Price J, and then there are the names I recognise from work: the shorthand of the cultural elite, the direct lines and private numbers to which few ordinary people have access. I find the entry I need and press the button with the little green telephone on it, and then I slip the phone back into the coat and go through into the kitchen, leaving the door wide-open.

Laurence is there, standing by the sink, a bottle of red and two glasses on the table in front of him.

"Mrs. Talbot's left plenty of food," he's saying, "but I can't get the bloody lid off this pickle."

I go over to him and take the jar away from him and put it aside, then I turn my face up to him while I slide my hands under his shirt, and I say, "Do you know what, sweetheart, I would suggest going to bed, but I'm not sure I can manage the stairs." He bends his head to kiss me, and in between kisses he gives a shout of laughter and says, "Well, how about we see how far we get . . . ?" and it's not very far, as it happens, but it's close enough for the phone to be able to pick up pretty much everything. And partly because of that, I suppose, it's especially good. Particularly enjoyable.

W*aking up in that room feels like the long-awaited answer to a question.* I rest there, feeling the rightness of it at last, as tangible as the smooth satin edge of the blanket under my fingers. The spring morning dances on the curtains: a thin wash of light stippled with the movement of leaves.

It's all here: the little reading lamps, bent towards us like snowdrops. The dresser, with its scattering of silver and wooden boxes. The window seat with its ticking cushion. The grate full of pinecones. The snaps stuck around the looking glass. I remember the scent bottle and the body cream: these, I see, have been removed.

The wedding photo is at the more tactful angle I found for it when Laurence was brushing his teeth, after we'd finally made it upstairs.

Laurence is still asleep, turned away from me, his breath low and even. Curiously, carefully, I lean over and pull open the drawer in my bedside table to see what evidence remains. A pair of nail scissors. A cherry-flavoured lip balm. An old slim Penguin, *The Pumpkin Eater*, with a strip of newspaper marking page 58. I look at the paper, wondering whether it'll be significant, but it's nothing: a few lines from the sports pages with an advert for Greek villa rentals on the other side.

I put it back and shut the drawer and lie where she lay, between the ironed Egyptian-cotton sheets she picked out, my head upon her feather pillows, with her husband next to me, and I feel very close to her—perhaps as close as I've ever been, apart from that moment in the woods, when I briefly heard her voice and knew it, knew almost everything about her that mattered. The ease and comfort and significance of her life.

Somehow, I have a stronger sense of her here, in Biddenbrooke, than at the house in London. I expect she was happier here.

Where are they? Will Polly come alone, or will she have Teddy in tow? Martin? The excitement surges up in me: a sense that only this one hurdle remains.

Later, I hum while I cook us both a brunch of bacon and eggs. Laurence looks up over the newspaper he collected from the village shop. "You're very cheerful this morning," he says.

"Oh, I love being here," I say, cutting bread and buttering it. "I love being back. This is my kind of bolt-hole."

"Mm," he says, inspecting the paper, turning over pages, drifting away from me, into its world.

It strikes me that I am almost entirely happy. Out of the kitchen window, time moves slowly on the sundial. All along the terrace, in terra-cotta pots and stone urns, green shoots—daffodils, grape hyacinths—are pushing their way into the light. Birdsong. The tick of the kitchen clock. The gradual panicky scream of the kettle.

I remove it from the hot plate and fill the teapot, and then I listen. I listen. Soon, I know, I'll hear something. There's no hurry now.

They arrive midafternoon. We have been for a long circular walk through the woods, a route Laurence suggested. I'm sure he picked it because he knew we would be unlikely to meet anyone going that way. A small rain shower blew over us while we were crossing the stream at the bottom of the meadow, and so we're in the hall taking off our wet coats and talking about lighting another fire when we hear the sound of wheels, the hiss of gravel.

Laurence hangs his coat hurriedly on the hook. "I'll get rid of them. Whoever it is," he says. "Just stay here." Out of sight, he means he wants me to stay out of sight, but he doesn't have to say it; it's understood.

So I shrink back into the shadows of the hall while he goes to the front door, the door which was always kept locked and bolted in the summer. I hear him saying their names, loud enough to send me an urgent message. I hear the scrunch of gravel underfoot and car doors being slammed, and over these I hear Polly's voice, high, excited, and dramatic, full of vocabulary she must have picked up from the texts she studies at college: words such as *betrayal* and *sly* and *deceit* and *humiliation*. I do not hear Teddy speak at all.

I listen to the scene, standing there holding a wet coat which is dripping onto the parquet, and I say good-bye to the old life without any regret. Like my patience, that life has run out, ended. Everything will be different from this moment. My relationship with Laurence, Laurence's relationship with his children. And—I imagine the consequences radiating outward like ripples—Laurence's relationship with the people around him, the people who knew him and Alys.

My life, the life I lead apparently independently of the Kytes, will be different, too. Colleagues and acquaintances will find out, and then there will be subtle adjustments in the way they think about and treat me. I will appear in the landscape of their thoughts more often. I may seem more of a puzzle, or possibly less of one. People will stop talking when I approach; they may also be more keen to find out what I have to say, the direction of my opinion.

I'll have accumulated some light and shade. Some mystery.

I had none of these attributes when this enterprise began, over a year ago; I gathered a little over the months that followed; and now I will accumulate more.

Some people will say, "What does he see in her?" but others will be able to glimpse it, even as they narrow their eyes and express themselves baffled. Some of his glamour will rub off on me. It's starting already. I can feel it settling on me like dust or pollen. I look at myself in the hall mirror, angling my head, wondering whether it has started to show.

"Where is she?" Polly is saying, and I retreat a little, as Laurence will expect me to, so I'm standing in the doorway of the cloakroom when she pushes past him and storms into the hall. Her eyes find me immediately.

"I knew it," she says, almost triumphant. "You. Unbelievable. I knew it." She stares at me but I guess she's not really seeing me at all: it's Laurence she's confronting, a new Laurence, a father she never imagined existed: a man violating the memory of his late wife, betraying the family. "How long has this been going on?"

Laurence is coming into the hall behind her, in front of Teddy, who holds himself back, his eyes taking me in. His gaze is as pale and chilly as hoarfrost.

Polly turns to Laurence. "I said, how long—"

"A few months," he says, coming towards her, his palms open, asking for calm.

She backs away. "Since when? When did it start? At the play?"

"No . . . before then," he says, and she looks from him to me and then back again. "Jesus! How could you?"

For heaven's sake, I urge him silently, my hands still on the damp collar of my coat, *take control. Stop answering her questions, and just tell her what she needs to know before she has to ask it. Disarm her, you fool.* But Laurence is still on the back foot, trying to catch up. To be fair, I suppose he's the only one of the four of us who hasn't had time to prepare for this encounter. His disadvantage is also mine, but I can do nothing about that. It's not my place to speak. No one wants to hear what I have to say. Not yet, at any rate.

Polly has turned away from me. All her attention is directed towards her father. She has dropped her voice quite low, as if she can hardly bear to say these things aloud. "It's just like you, isn't it?" she says. "We've been hearing things, or rather Teddy has. People are talking about you. Your habits." She looks at her brother. "Tell him," she says.

Teddy murmurs, "There are some stories . . ."

Laurence glances between his children. I can see his mind whirring through various disastrous scenarios. *Exactly how bad is this?* he's wondering.

"Honor says you made a pass at her," Polly shouts at him, unable to wait any longer. "Here, that last evening in the summer—and that's why she left in such a hurry. How *could* you?" She spins on her heel to involve me, a vivid artificial grin on her face. "Did you know that?"

I nod. "Yes, I met Honor a little while afterwards, and she told me. I don't believe it, I'm afraid. I saw how she was behaving that night—"

"I'm sure you did," Polly is saying bitterly, but I keep going. "I saw what happened that night, and Honor was the one making all the running." I look over at Teddy. "I'm sorry to have to spell it out, but that's what I saw. I think she's something of a fantasist."

"Bullshit," Polly says. "That's bullshit. Why would she make it up? It doesn't make sense."

I shrug and look away, leaving the pause, hoping it'll foster the germ of doubt. Laurence is still just standing there, wild-eyed, unsure of his strategy, but sensing perhaps that it's not all that bad, that we might get out of this eventually. I wish I could go over and slip my hand into his, show some solidarity, but it's too soon.

"Well, and anyway . . . ," says Polly, a tiny bit thrown, returning to her mental checklist, stoking the fury again. "There's something else. Someone you were involved with—before Mummy died. Oh, yeah, we know all about her. Julia, Julia . . ." She looks at Teddy, who supplies it, a queasy expression on his face: Price. *Honor again,* I think.

"Yes, Julia Price—whoever the fuck she is," Polly says. "Oh, God, the thought of it makes me feel completely *sick.*"

Quickly, Laurence's eyes dart to me, checking my reaction, and she notices, sensing another victim in all this. "Oh, no, I see, Frances didn't know about Julia Price, did she? You didn't tell her about that one. But Mum knew. She'd found out, hadn't she? That was why she wanted you to change the dedication on your bloody book, wasn't it? That last night? I heard what she said to you: 'It's not a tribute, it's an insult.' I heard her say it!"

"Hey," says Laurence, shaping his face into a ghastly sort of smile. "Let's all calm down. Let's go through to the kitchen. I was going to make some tea—"

"Tea?" Polly throws back her head, laughing scornfully—channelling the young Judi Dench, I think. "Don't be ridiculous, Dad. You can't just pretend this isn't *happening.*"

I find I'm getting slightly bored with this already. No one's saying anything that's a surprise to me. The only danger is that somehow the debate will work its way round to me, and that Teddy will tell everyone that I exaggerated—or lied about—what Alys told me in the woods, not that in itself that's terribly incriminating. But my hunch is that they're too focused on each other to turn on me right now. Laurence is bearing the brunt. I'm rather invisible in all this. I might as well extricate myself for the time being.

"Look," I say quietly, humbly, appealing to them all. "I think you three have things to sort out. I'm going to clear off for a bit." I throw Laurence a quick, muted smile of sympathy, then I shrug myself back into my coat and start to move towards the front door. Teddy ignores me, but Polly's eyes fasten on me, almost in wonder, as if she hasn't properly noticed me until this moment. "You," she says again, almost whispering it. "Where did you come from, anyway?"

I look down modestly, discreetly—*this is really none of my business, I don't want to make this more awkward than it already is*—and I walk away from the three of them, leaving them to it.

The brief shower has passed and as I come out the front door the sun is shining, a million raindrops sparkling in the drenched lawn, and the sky is opening up, a perfect china blue. The wind is still fresh but the sun feels suddenly hot on my shoulders as I pass through the arch and walk round onto the back lawn, past the copper beech, which is just coming into leaf. I don't look back at the house, but I feel it behind me, the correctness of its proportions, its pragmatic expanses of flint and brick, its dark windows reflecting back the rippling, new foliage and the movement of the clouds.

I walk on as I walked in the early mornings in the summer, down the lawn, skirting the humped disorder of Alys's borders, and crossing into the orchard where the trees are knotted with buds. My feet leave a ruffled trail in the long, sopping grass. I go to the door in the wall and open it and look in. The sun terrace is empty—the loungers and chairs have been taken away—and the pool has been drained: a grubby turquoise box in the ground. Where the tiles slope down beneath the metal ladder there's a long, brackish puddle, too congested with leaves and twigs to capture the sky.

There's something so sad and sordid about an empty pool out of season, I think. No magic, no illusion. I remember floating in there between the heavens and the earth, part of neither; and then I close the door and walk on.

At the end of the orchard a gate leads into a narrow, green lane that hems the garden belonging to the house next door, the house owned by Colonel and Mrs. Williams. I push the gate open and walk along the lane, and distantly I hear the murmur of Radio 4 coming through the hedge, and then I see a woman in a headscarf and dirty corduroy trousers, tethering plants to stakes. This must be Mrs. Williams.

She notices me and calls out a greeting. As she speaks, I recognise her: the woman who did a reading at the memorial service. "Are you staying at Nevers?" she asks, coming down the bank towards me, dusting the soil off her hands, and when I say yes, she says, "Oh, lovely. How are Polly and Teddy?"

"I'm not sure," I say, "I'm a friend of Laurence's." And I introduce myself.

The look she gives me then—curious, frankly appraising—allows me a twist of satisfaction.

We exchange a few pleasantries about the garden and the weather, then I say good-bye and walk on along the shady green lane, thinking of the news beginning to filter out through the neighbourhood.

When I come to the road, I turn in the direction of Bidden-brooke. In the village shop I select some postcards and the local paper, then I sit at an outdoor table at the King's Arms in the fits and starts of sunshine, writing to Hester and Naomi. *Down here for the weekend,* I write. *Started seeing someone who has a place nearby. Happy! All love, Frances.* I sip my lemonade and flick through the paper, which is full of WI tabletop sales and RNLI fund-raisers, and when I look at my watch, I see enough time has passed, so I cross the green to the postbox and then I start to walk home, towards Nevers.

Polly's Mini has gone when I come down the drive. I go into the cold hall, calling his name. He's in the sitting room, hunched on the edge of one of the gold sofas, looking into the remains of a small fire. The table in front of him is a jumble of cups, tea-spoons. Some cigarette stubs have been ground out into a saucer. Quickly I go to him and put my arms around him. "What happened?" I ask.

At first he doesn't respond to me, then I feel him adjust his position, stiffly submitting to my embrace. "Oh—it's a bit of a mess." Next there's a moment when he relaxes, almost reluctantly, as if accepting there's no point in holding back. "It's a nightmare."

"Are they very angry?" I say.

"I wish they hadn't found out in the way they did," he says. "You were right. I should have told them ages ago. The shock of it, on top of everything else . . . well, let's say it hasn't done me any favours."

"How did they . . . ?"

"Too absurd," he says. "I didn't lock my phone, I must have knocked it, it dialled Polly's number, she overheard us. And then she found a scarf of yours in London."

"Oh, Christ. I am sorry," I say, putting my hand over my mouth.

"Polly's so disappointed." His voice sounds as if it's on the point of defeat. "She thinks—she's having to revise her view of me; she says I'm not the father she thought I was, and evidently I wasn't the husband she thought I was either."

I lean my head against his shoulder, waiting. We sit like this for a few moments, in silence. I feel the sigh come and go.

"Polly was right. I was unfaithful," he says, moving so he can look into my face. "I've got to tell you, I want you to know everything now. I've had enough of keeping secrets from the people who matter. There's this woman, Julia Price—you probably know her. I . . . We just fell into it. We saw each other every so often. It wasn't going anywhere, I was never going to leave Alys for her. That's no excuse, I know. Then Alys found out, just before the accident; Jo Azaria told her we'd been seen together. She'd had her suspicions anyway. Naturally, she was furious—so furious she wanted her name taken off the book which I'd dedicated to her, as I had most of the others—though in the end of course I didn't change the dedication, I kept Alys's name on it. I think that was right, don't you? I'm sure it was. In any case I'd said I'd end things with her, with Julia Price, and that's what I did, it was the last thing I promised Alys just before she died. It was the correct decision, I've never doubted that."

"Go on," I say.

"Anyway—when Teddy saw Honor earlier this week, all this came out, and then Polly put the whole thing together, and that's why they both came up here, to confront me. I really can't imagine them forgiving me, you know. Polly was boiling over with it, of course you know what she's like, and Teddy was so withdrawn, very cold. . . . I think he's even angrier than she is."

"Sweetheart . . ." I say.

"I don't know how to handle it," he says. "What a mess." He pulls away from me, running his hands through his hair. We sit side by side as the fire crumples into itself a little more, dislodging a few dusty trickles of ash.

I choose this moment to make my own confession. "I've lied to you as well. I need to be frank with you. I expect you'll be very angry with me."

After an introduction like this, and in the context of this afternoon, the story of how I twisted (though naturally I'm careful not to use that term) Alys's final words seems like a little thing, barely even a mischief. Laurence hears me out with a distracted look on his face. When I ask him whether he can forgive me, he pats my wrist absently. "I see why you did it," he says. "You were being kind. You thought it would help us. You were probably right." Then he lifts my hand to his lips and kisses it, and lets it go.

I stay with him for a few more moments, then I put some more wood on the fire and start to collect up the things on the table in front of us: the cups, the saucer, the spoons, and the milk carton. I carry them into the kitchen and stack the china in the dishwasher. It is starting to get dark now and a scattering of rain strikes the window. A big jar of bouillabaisse in the larder will do for supper, with some bread and salad.

We eat quietly in the kitchen and afterwards I hear him on the phone, leaving messages for both children, asking them to call him. Later when the phone rings, he answers it eagerly, but I see him shrink a little once he puts the receiver to his ear; and then he says, "Ah, Malcolm," and moves into the study and closes the door so I can't hear anything more.

When he comes out twenty minutes later, he says Polly has telephoned the Azarias in a state, and Jo has gone round to collect her and will take her to their house in Kentish Town for the night. Malcolm has promised to call with an update in the morning.

"I've told him I'm serious about you," he says, almost as an afterthought. "He sounded pleased for me."

Oh, good, it's out, I think. *I can handle it from here.*

Three months later. *A Sunday in Highgate. Just after noon. I sit at* the kitchen table, the newspapers—marked here and there with the faint overlapping rings left by my cup of tea—spread out in front of me. I've just looked through the *Questioner*'s books pages with a certain amount of satisfaction. I couldn't resist commissioning Oliver to review a new book on the history of nepotism, and to be fair to him he made a decent fist of it. I wonder whether he saw the joke.

Tiny little Robin McAllfree took me out to lunch last week. When he emailed to suggest it, he wrote, "Let's keep this between ourselves," and when I was shown to the table, he explained he didn't want "to upset Mary unnecessarily."

She's been spending quite a bit of time in the managing editor's office recently: there's some issue over her expenses, though I gather there might be more to it than that. In this climate, sadly, no one is invulnerable. She has had a good run. It's probably time someone else had a go.

Anyway, I talked Robin through my suggestions for the pages: a column I thought had run out of puff, a few contributors worth poaching from elsewhere, and some literary names due on the promotional treadmill with whom Gemma Coke might profitably wrangle. "Great stuff," he said. "Keep the ideas coming. Just ping them to me as you have them. And sit tight for now."

So, I'm sitting tight for now. There's no hurry.

As he settled the bill, he coughed into his fist, so I knew he was building up to something, and then he said, as if the thought had only just occurred to him, "So, this is all true, what I hear about you and Laurence Kyte?"

I said it was, and he gave me one of those funny sideways looks and said there had been stories, of course, and then he'd seen us last week at the Almeida during the interval, and he hoped it was all going well, and I smiled as if to say, *None of yours, thanks,* and that was how we left it.

Mary rumbled me ages ago. One morning she sidled up while I was editing an Ambrose Pritchett review and dropped that morning's *Daily Mail* on my desk, folded back to the relevant page. The small diary item, headlined "Kiss me Kyte: second shot at happiness for tragic brainbox," boiled the story of our relationship down to five or six sentences in which an impression of impropriety was skilfully conveyed, despite a woeful lack of evidence. The small picture of us had been taken as we exited an Amnesty fund-raiser: Laurence's mouth twisting as if he was saying something to me (I think we were discussing where to go for dinner), and his arm hovering protectively around my shoulders.

I looked at myself: the lowered eyes, the demure suggestion of a smile, the photographer's flash bouncing off my smooth hair. The general impression of freshness and discretion. Not a bad picture, I thought.

"Well, well, well," said Mary, tapping the page with a finger. "I've had my suspicions for a while now, but this seems to be conclusive proof."

"Oh, you can't believe everything you read in the papers," I said lightly, then I ran the cursor along the first line of Ambrose Pritchett's review and cut it out, so that we got straight to the central argument.

Mary shot me a look in which curiosity, irritation, and a sort of wary admiration were all represented, then she picked up the paper and moved away, back to her desk.

Fortunately by this point I'd already told my parents about Laurence.

"I'm not sure if Hester mentioned it," I said during my next visit, as we sat sawing away at leathery pork chops, "but I've started seeing someone. You might have heard of him, possibly."

They had heard of him. They remembered the BBC serialisation of the first Sidney Bark with Tom Conti and Lisa Harrow; and the Crofts always said *The Ha-Ha* (they saw it before the Gala shut down) was powerful, although it was a pity about all the swearing.

"How did you meet?" they asked, and "Isn't he much older than you?" and I decided to address that second issue initially and leave the first for another day.

As I talked, I could see they were daunted by the age gap, his comparatively recent bereavement, and by his success, too; but I took him to meet them one weekend when we were down at Biddenbrooke, and somehow he knew exactly what to say to them, how to put them at their ease. My mother, glazed with fright and hairspray, was so anxious that she asked us three or four times about the drive over, but after Laurence had warmly commented on the garden, she seemed as close to effervescent as I've ever seen her.

"Biddenbrooke's such a pretty village," she said, passing him a paper napkin. "And the butcher is meant to be wonderful, if a little dear."

He acknowledged that this was the case. There was some talk of Maggie and Brian Howard, whom he had met once at a neighbours' drinks party, and then he said, "I do admire your lawn. We have awful problems with molehills, don't we, Frances?"

As Polly once said, all those months ago, no one ever refuses her father anything, and certainly my parents gave him their approval after that.

"What very nice people," Laurence said as we drove away,

full of bite-sized cheese scones and pastel squares of Battenberg. "But—do you mind me saying this?—I can hardly believe you're related to them."

"I don't mind," I said, sitting back in the car, watching the hedgerows rush past in a multitude of greens. "I think I know what you mean."

Hester's reaction to my news, like that of Naomi and my other friends, has been rather more complicated. In part she is glad for me, glad I'm off the shelf, glad I've finally followed her example and have started to settle down (a phrase which always makes me think of a fat person on a sofa). My behaviour makes her and Naomi and the others feel better about their own choices, I know.

Yet I can hear in their approval and relief and advice a hint of something else: a suggestion of wonder and, yes, almost of resentment that *I* should have ended up with such a person. Who would have thought it? What's so special about me?

My sister and her husband came over to Highgate for supper a few weeks ago, and while Laurence humoured Charlie, asking him about sport and life in chambers, I could see Hester carefully evaluating everything from the food which Mrs. King had prepared (sea bass, panna cotta) to the china, the flowers, and the paintings on the walls. As I showed Hester and Charlie out at the end of the evening, as I stood in the hall with them, handing them jackets and offering them kisses, Hester hugged me with feeling, and then she stepped back, scrutinising my face, her fingers sharp for a moment on my wrists.

"It all seems to have happened very quickly," she said, an edge to her voice, a note of concern.

I bent to stroke the cat, who was purring and arching her back against me, and as I straightened up, I said, quite truthfully, that it didn't feel at all rushed to me.

"Laurence seems lovely," she said. "But, well—he is a lot older than you."

I said how funny it was to hear such a thing. After all, many people would consider me bordering on middle age. "It's hardly cradle snatching," I added, raising an eyebrow.

"Well, no." Then Hester had the grace to laugh. "Of course not. But he has only recently lost his wife. I suppose I have to ask, are you sure? Are you sure it's what you want?"

I told her I was, yes. "It is absolutely what I want," I said, and though she is only aware of a fraction of my ambition, I could see that she believed me, then she hugged me again and said, "I'm so pleased you've found someone who makes you happy. They do say, don't they, that if you've had one very successful marriage, you're more likely to find another relationship quickly." Then she asked me how his children had taken it.

After that weekend in Biddenbrooke, we mainly heard about Polly and Teddy—who would not return any of their father's calls— through the Azarias. Jo felt responsible for the situation. When she and Malcolm came round to tell us the latest, she cried and asked for our forgiveness, turning a Kleenex over in her hands as we all sat in the rarely used sitting room, the sage-coloured room that I'd first seen filled with white blooms all those months ago. "I should never have said what I did to Miriam," she said, pressing the tissue over her eyes. "I betrayed your confidence, and now this has happened, the children are so upset. . . . I can't tell you how sorry I am."

Laurence was generous. These things happen, he said. No point dwelling on it. The only thing that mattered now was to reestablish contact with Teddy and Polly. "Are they both very angry with us?" he asked.

Jo didn't speak, but Malcolm said yes, they were. "Less so with

Frances, I think," he added, as an afterthought. "That must be a good sign, don't you feel?"

Reading between the lines, Polly and Teddy were clearly most wounded—on their mother's behalf—by the Julia Price episode. It seemed to suggest all sorts of hidden horrors, a long history of betrayal. Later, Laurence would sigh and put his head in his hands, saying the whole thing had been a dreadful mistake: "One slip," he said. "One slip, that's all it took." I thought of the girls without names skulking in the darkness behind the fast-fading ghost of Julia Price, and I felt a prickle of contempt: both for Laurence, who imagines I do not know about them, and for Alys, who grasped only a fragment of the truth. The thought made me steely. Never again, I thought.

But as the days passed, as the Azarias had nothing new to report, Laurence became angry, too. As he fretted over what he began to see as his daughter's intransigence and his son's priggishness, he started to lose patience with them. I heard him on the phone to Malcolm a few weeks after the initial confrontation, and I was struck by his exasperation. "Oh, well, if they've made up their minds . . . ," he was saying. "No, Malcolm, I can quite see how bloody difficult this is for you, but frankly I can't see either of them backing down over this."

He stood there in the white kitchen, the receiver to his ear, staring out at the garden. It was early evening, and the French windows were open, as they had been for most of the day. I could smell the wisteria—a heavy, clinging, almost narcotic scent—drifting through the house on indistinct currents of air. I went to him and put my arms around him as he listened to Malcolm and drummed his fingers on the window frame and let out little despairing exhalations, as if only just holding back from saying something which really mustn't be said. "No," he said eventually, as if in reluctant agreement. "No. I take your point."

"I'm losing them," he said, when the call was ended. "It's hopeless."

"Well, you mustn't let them go," I said. "They're your family. You need each other."

"Do we?" he murmured, reaching for me. "Do we really?"

"Of course you do. You must try to speak to them yourself."

"But they won't take my calls," he said.

"Well—maybe you should doorstep them. Outside their flats. Outside Polly's college. Teddy's gallery. Show them you really mean it."

The suggestion was not, I could tell, appealing, but he agreed it was worth a shot, and that Polly was probably the softer target. The next afternoon he was standing across the street from the drama college when classes finished. She came out in the middle of a group, laughing and joking, but saw him and stopped on the kerb as he crossed the road towards her. Martin hung back, waiting for her, but she waved him on. "I'll catch you up. I won't be long," she said.

She told Laurence she wasn't ready to talk to him yet. She wasn't sure whether she ever would be. She and Teddy had "a lot to think about." Then, as he started to reason with her, she simply walked away, her silver satchel bumping against her hip.

He came home and told me about it, and he slammed his hand down on the kitchen table so the water slopped out of the glasses and the cutlery rattled. "Oh, what's the point. She's being ridiculous. I'll never be able to make this right."

I let him say it all. I let him talk about how Alys and he had overindulged both children; how they'd been encouraged, almost, to drift through life with no sense of how it really works. "We spoiled them both. We made things too bloody easy for them," he said angrily, "and now I'm going to have to live with the consequences."

I listened to him as we sat there at the table, my head bent sor-
rowfully over my clasped hands, thumb resting on thumb, fingers
knitted. Oh, it would be so easy, I thought idly. So easy to allow
his resentment to build. To harbour it, stoke it, foster it through
various subtle inflections.

To say things, or not say things.

But I didn't have the heart for it. Better, I knew, to be the one
to bring them back together again. Like Alys: always ready with
the right words; so good at finding common ground, drawing out
the best in people.

The thought of their eventual gratitude amused me.

So I listened to Laurence and made comforting remarks when
I felt he wanted to hear them; and then, without telling him, I
wrote a letter and posted it.

I met them both in my lunch break in a coffee shop near the British
Museum. At first neither would make eye contact. They sat
sullenly side by side on a worn black vinyl banquette and said little.
So I talked. I said the right things, as I've found I can, waiting
for the tiny signals—the sighs, the quick consultative glances, the
almost imperceptible beginnings of smiles—that herald a thaw.
But the signs didn't come.

When the minute hand hit twenty past, I said how sorry I was
to have deceived them both. I said I understood that they might
never be able to forgive me, but for their mother's sake I wondered
whether they could find it in their hearts to forgive Laurence, who
was lost without them in his life. "He misses you," I said. "You've
no idea how much he misses you."

Suddenly, a fragment of poetry came to mind: a piece of Emily
Dickinson. Worth a pop, I thought.

"He won't give up on you," I said. "And neither will I. There's this line from a poem, one particular poem which has always meant a great deal to me, and I can't stop thinking about it: *Hope is the thing with feathers*... Thing is, without that hope, he's finished. He's clinging to it. So we'll wait. Take your time. Please, just take your time."

I stood up and went to the counter and paid for three coffees, then I pushed the door open and stepped out into the street.

I heard her footsteps behind me, and when I turned around, I knew it was going to be all right.

S*o now I leave the papers and my cup on the refectory table and go* out into the garden. I step beyond the cool shade that falls away from the house and I look up. It's going to be another hot day: above the shimmering wall of trees, the sky is the thin blue-white of skimmed milk. At some point, I'll have to think about what to give the Azarias, who are coming for supper. But not just yet.

Laurence has been in his study since midmorning, consulting his fluttering wall of colours: planning, plotting, piecing the story together. He's coming to the end of his first draft. Last week he asked whether I'd be interested in taking a look at it, once he has knocked it into shape.

I wonder whether this novel will have my name printed at the front upon an otherwise blank page. Well, if not this one, the next one will.

I'm sitting on the bench stroking the cat, my bare feet in the grass, when he comes out to join me, walking along the brick path that winds between the fruit trees. Without saying anything, he sits down next to me and puts his hand out for mine; and after a moment I place his palm on my belly, even though there's nothing to feel quite yet, and rest mine on top. We sit there in silence as the sun moves over us.

It's tranquil. A dog barks. Someone turns on a hose. Distantly, a child shouts, "Coming, ready or not!"

I'm listening for it, not quite expecting it yet, but they are early. I do not hear the key in the lock or the feet on the stairs, and neither does Laurence. When they come out of the French windows, we are both sitting there side by side in the sun, the cat twisting around our ankles, enjoying the peace.

While they make their reconciliations, I stand back. Smilingly, I stand back, my eyes lowered, and I wait for their eventual gratitude.

Acknowledgements

My wonderful editors, *Anna deVries at Scribner and Arzu Tahsin* at W&N.

The early readers: Rachel Thomas; my parents, David and Sara Lane; and my sister, Victoria.

For various kindnesses, Sophie Buchan, Morag Preston and Damian Whitworth, Jane Dwelly, Lucy Darwin, Juliet Knight, Lynne Riley, Daisy Cook, Anna Mazzega, Jane Goldthorpe, Bethany Wren, and Natalie Roe.

Dr. Gordon Plant and his colleagues at Queen Square, particularly Merle Galton.

Clare Johnson, Penny Faith, and the Thursday group at Lauderdale House.

Poppy and Barnaby, who suggested buns for tea, "because that's what they have in *The Railway Children.*"

Two people seemed to believe in this book long before I did: my agent, Cat Ledger, and my husband, Stafford Critchlow. For that and other things, many thanks.